LONGING FOR YOU

Praise for Jenny Frame

Wooing the Farmer

"This book, like all of Jenny Frame's, is just one major swoon."
—*Les Rêveur*

"The chemistry between the two MCs had us hooked right away. We also absolutely loved the seemingly ditzy femme with an ambition of steel but really a vulnerable girl. The sex scenes are great. Definitely recommended."—*Reviewer@large*

"This is the book we Axedale fanatics have been waiting for…Jenny Frame writes the most amazing characters and this whole series is a masterpiece. But where she excels is in writing butch lesbians. Every time I read a Jenny Frame book I think it's the best ever, but time and again she surprises me. She has surpassed herself with *Wooing the Farmer*."—*Kitty Kat's Book Review Blog*

Royal Court

"The author creates two very relatable characters…Quincy's quietude and mental torture are offset by Holly's openness and lust for life. Holly's determination and tenacity in trying to reach Quincy are total wish-fulfilment of a person like that. The chemistry and attraction is excellently built."—*Best Lesbian Erotica*

"[A] butch/femme romance that packs a punch."—*Les Rêveur*

Royal Court "was a fun, light-hearted book with a very endearing romance."—*Leanne Chew, Librarian, Parnell Library (Auckland, NZ)*

"There were unbelievably hot sex scenes as I have come to expect and look forward to in Jenny Frame's books. Passions slowly rise until you feel the characters may burst!…Royal Court is wonderful and I highly recommend it."—*Kitty Kat's Book Review Blog*

Hunger for You

"I loved this book. Paranormal stuff like vampires and werewolves are my go-to sins. This book had literally everything I needed:

chemistry between the leads, hot love scenes (phew), drama, angst, romance (oh my, the romance) and strong supporting characters."
—*The Reading Doc*

Byron and Amelia "are guaranteed to get the reader all hot and bothered. Jenny Frame writes brilliant love scenes in all of her books and makes me believe the characters crave each other."
—*Kitty Kat's Book Review Blog*

Charming the Vicar

"Chances are, you've never read or become captivated by a romance like *Charming the Vicar*. While books featuring people of the cloth aren't unusual, Bridget is no ordinary vicar—a lesbian with a history of kink…Surrounded by mostly supportive villagers, Bridget and Finn balance love and faith in a story that affirms both can exist for anyone, regardless of sexual identity."—*RT Book Reviews*

"The sex scenes were some of the sexiest, most intimate and quite frankly, sensual I have read in a while. Jenny Frame had me hooked and I reread a few scenes because I felt like I needed to experience the intense intimacy between Finn and Bridget again. The devotion they showed to one another during these sex scenes but also in the intimate moments was gripping and for lack of a better word, carnal."—*Les Rêveur*

"The sexual chemistry between [Finn and Bridge] is unbelievably hot. It is sexy, lustful and with more than a hint of kink. The scenes between them are highly erotic—and not just the sex scenes. The tension is ramped up so well that I felt the characters would explode if they did not get relief!…An excellent book set in the most wonderful village—a place I hope to return to very soon!"—*Kitty Kat's Book Reviews*

"This is Frame's best character work to date. They are layered and flawed and yet relatable…Frame really pushed herself with *Charming the Vicar* and it totally paid off…I also appreciate that even though she regularly writes butch/femme characters, no two pairings are the same."—*The Lesbian Review*

Unexpected

Jenny Frame "has this beautiful way of writing a phenomenally hot scene while incorporating the love and tenderness between the couple."—*Les Rêveur*

"If you enjoy contemporary romances, *Unexpected* is a great choice. The character work is excellent, the plotting and pacing are well done, and it's a just a sweet, warm read...Definitely pick this book up when you're looking for your next comfort read, because it's sure to put a smile on your face by the time you get to that happy ending."—*Curve*

"*Unexpected* by Jenny Frame is a charming butch/femme romance that is perfect for anyone who wants to feel the magic of overcoming adversity and finding true love. I love the way Jenny Frame writes. I have yet to discover an author who writes like her. Her voice is strong and unique and gives a freshness to the lesbian fiction sector."—*The Lesbian Review*

Royal Rebel

"Frame's stories are easy to follow and really engaging. She stands head and shoulders above a number of the romance authors and it's easy to see why she is quickly making a name for herself in lesfic romance."—*The Lesbian Review*

Courting the Countess

"I love Frame's romances. They are well paced, filled with beautiful character moments and a wonderful set of side characters who ultimately end up winning your heart...I love Jenny Frame's butch/femme dynamic; she gets it so right for a romance."
—*The Lesbian Review*

"I loved, loved, loved this book. I didn't expect to get so involved in the story but I couldn't help but fall in love with Annie and Harry... The love scenes were beautifully written and very sexy. I found the whole book romantic and ultimately joyful and I had a lump in my throat on more than one occasion. A wonderful book that certainly stirred my emotions."—*Kitty Kat's Book Reviews*

"*Courting The Countess* has an historical feel in a present day world, a thought provoking tale filled with raw emotions throughout. [Frame] has a magical way of pulling you in, making you feel every emotion her characters experience."—*Lunar Rainbow Reviewz*

"I didn't want to put the book down and I didn't. Harry and Annie are two amazingly written characters that bring life to the pages as they find love and adventures in Harry's home. This is a great read, and you will enjoy it immensely if you give it a try!"—*Fantastic Book Reviews*

A Royal Romance

"*A Royal Romance* was a guilty pleasure read for me. It was just fun to see the relationship develop between George and Bea, to see George's life as queen and Bea's as a commoner. It was also refreshing to see that both of their families were encouraging, even when Bea doubted that things could work between them because of their class differences...*A Royal Romance* left me wanting a sequel, and romances don't usually do that to me."—*Leeanna.ME Mostly a Book Blog*

Blood of the Pack

"[A] solid entry into the expanding Lesfic urban fantasy/ paranormal romance genre. I look forward to seeing more from the Wolfgang County series."—*Colleen Corgel, Librarian, Queens Public Library*

Soul of the Pack

"I enjoy the way Jenny Frame writes. Her characters are perfectly suited to one another, never the same, and the stories are always fun and unique...there is something special about her urban fantasy worlds. She maximises the butch/femme dynamic and creates pack dynamics which work so well with those."—*The Lesbian Review*

Heart of the Pack

"A really well written love story that incidentally involves changers as well as humans."—*Inked Rainbow Reads*

By the Author

A Royal Romance

Courting the Countess

Dapper

Royal Rebel

Unexpected

Charming the Vicar

Royal Court

Wooing the Farmer

Someone to Love

The Duchess and the Dreamer

Wild for You

Hunger for You

Longing for You

Wolfgang County Series

Heart of the Pack

Soul of the Pack

Blood of the Pack

Visit us at www.boldstrokesbooks.com

LONGING FOR YOU

by
Jenny Frame

2020

LONGING FOR YOU

ISBN 13: 978-1-63555-658-2

This Trade Paperback Original Is Published By
Bold Strokes Books, Inc.
P.O. Box 249
Valley Falls, NY 12185

First Edition: September 2020

Credits
Editor: Ruth Sternglantz
Production Design: Stacia Seaman
Cover Design by Tammy Seidick

Acknowledgments

Thank you to Rad, Sandy, and all the BSB staff for their tireless hard work. Thanks to Ruth for her guidance, patience, and advice. I'm deeply grateful to have you help me make my books the best that they can be.

Thanks to my family for their support and encouragement.

Finally, thanks to Lou and Barney for putting up with my craziness as I approach every deadline. I'll love you both forever and always.

To Lou

Always and forever

CHAPTER ONE

The sounds of laughter and happiness were making Alexis Villiers more down and depressed by the second. She should be happy. It was her best friend and mentor's wedding day. Byron Debrek had already been bonded by blood to Amelia Honey, but Byron wanted to honour Amelia's human side, and so they planned a lavish wedding.

The wedding was taking place at the Gothic and picturesque Debrek Castle in the Highlands of Scotland. Byron invited all of their paranormal allics and friends, including the four heads of the UK and Ireland werewolf packs—the Scottish Wulvers, the Irish Filtiaran, the English Ranwulfs, and the Welsh Blaidds— plus the BoaBhan Sith, all-female vampire-fae beings with whom the Debreks had a long alliance, who used the Debreks' Scottish residence as their home.

There were also representatives of the fae, the shapeshifters, and the witches, with whom they had a much more fragile alliance. And since Byron's cousin Victorija, the head of the Dred vampire clan, killed the leader of the French coven, relations between the vampires and witches had become even more strained than usual.

The wedding was the event of the century. Nobody, especially Alexis, ever thought that Byron would become bonded by blood, the vampire equivalent of marriage, but when Amelia Honey came along, everything changed. Alexis stood at the back of the banqueting hall watching the wedding guests dancing with a deep sadness and worry in her heart. She had been feeling it for months now and just couldn't shake it.

Alexis watched Byron pull Amelia closer as they embarked on their first dance, and the guests gave them a round of applause. Alexis could not share this happiness. She wandered over to the bar area and waited for service. Slaine, who ran The Sanctuary in London, had agreed to run the bar for this evening's special event.

The Sanctuary was a club where all paranormals could come together and have a drink in peace, no matter what grievances they had outside the door, and was the oldest bar in London. Slaine was part shifter, part fae, and it was the shifter part of her genes that gave her the six-foot-eight height and solid, imposing body. Slaine spotted Alexis and left her staff to handle the orders and made her way over to Alexis.

"What can I get you, Alexis?" Slaine said.

"Whisky, please."

Slaine grinned. "Try this." She brought out a bottle with a grey wolf on the front of the label from underneath the bar and poured Alexis a large drink. "Kenrick Wulver gave Byron and Amelia ten cases of this special reserve to mark their wedding day. Byron let us use one case behind the bar. It's a bit special."

Alexis took a sip and felt the satisfying burn as it travelled down her throat. It was really good, but she'd expect no less from the Wulver distillery. Kenrick was the new Alpha and not long mated herself. Everyone seemed to be destined for happiness except her. Alexis had lost her chance at love a hundred and seventy years ago, when Victorija killed Anna, the woman she was going to marry.

"It's good," Alexis said with little enthusiasm.

"Good? You can't describe that masterpiece as good, Duca."

Alexis swirled the amber liquid around her glass. "Really good?"

Slaine sighed. "You sound like you're at a funeral instead of a wedding."

"Slaine, the Dreds are turning humans at will to boost their boots on the ground, threatening to expose our world to humans, the witches are baying for blood, and the whole paranormal world is on a knife-edge. No one is taking the threat seriously," Alexis said.

"Look at everyone dancing and having a good time. Vampires, wolves, shifters, fae, witches, all in the same room, and not killing each other." Slaine pointed over to the small number of witches sitting together in a corner of the room. "At the moment the witches are baying for vampire blood, but because of this wedding, the British covens have sent representatives here and are enjoying a drink with vampires, who they probably trust as far as they could throw them. That's an achievement that only love can bring."

"Love?" Alexis snorted. "Please, love brings pain, not happiness."

Alexis's eyes flitted to a young blond woman, dancing not far from the Principe and Principessa—Katie Brekman, the Debrek head housekeeper, who was dancing with a female shifter. She felt her stomach twist with tension.

Katie's family had worked for the Debreks for generations, and her mother and father had headed up the Debrek household for years. When Katie came back from university to work for Byron, she'd joined the blood rota, as all the humans in the household did.

Alexis remembered every millisecond of her first encounter in the blood room with Katie. Katie offered her neck and Alexis groaned at the first scent of it.

For a vampire, going to feed in the blood room should be like eating a meal for a human—nice, but just a fuel stop to keep their vampire bodies going. Unless you were feeding from a lover. Alexis closed her eyes and she was back there, recalling the memory like a movie in her mind.

Alexis had a long morning and needed to feed badly. She unlocked her phone and opened the Debrek app. The app had been developed under Byron's leadership and modernized the Debrek way of life and business. She clicked on the icon to summon a blood host—a little like ordering an Uber—and made her way down to the blood room.

When she arrived at the old wooden door, she looked into the eye scanner to gain access. The security scanner released the lock, and she opened the heavy oak door.

She walked in and was surprised to see not one of the regular blood hosts, but young Katie Brekman, the daughter of the Debrek housekeeper and butler. Alexis knew that she had returned from university but didn't know she had started work.

"Duca?" Katie said in surprise. "I…I didn't know it would be you."

Alexis looked at the young woman silently. She appeared nervous, and Alexis's exceptional hearing could make out Katie's heart hammering in her chest.

Katie wasn't handling Alexis's silence very well and started to talk nervously. "This is my first time giving blood—well, I did give blood at university for the Red Cross, but that's a bit different—"

As she rambled on Alexis sighed internally. A blood virgin. Brilliant, that was just what she needed. Alexis wasn't like some vampires who liked to stop and chat, pass the time of day with their blood hosts. She didn't much like to pass the day with anyone. She had clan business to take care of, things to do, and people to organize within the clan.

She was clearly the wrong person to guide Katie through her first time and would just have to tell her so.

"I'm jabbering, aren't I?" Katie said, her cheeks blushing with embarrassment. "I do that when I'm nervous."

Katie's innocence and bashfulness lit an unexpected hunger inside of Alexis. Some vampires got off feeding from a blood virgin, to have the first taste of them, to be the one who would always be the human's first, but the idea never appealed to Alexis. So why this twisting of need in her stomach now?

Katie's mother and father were well-loved and extremely important to the Debreks, and Katie had grown up amongst them all. Usually, Alexis was barely aware of the human staff's children, unless they were getting in the way. But she had noticed Katie when she left for university as a young woman, and since she had returned. It was clearly a bad idea to indulge such a strong desire and satisfy an urge with someone so important to the family, so she was doubly sure to turn down this particular host.

"Katie—" Alexis was just about to turn her down when Katie interrupted.

"You want a more experienced host, don't you?" Katie's shoulders slumped, and she sighed. "You're the fourth vampire to ask for someone else."

"Oh, why is that?" Alexis said.

Katie popped her phone into her pocket, preparing to leave. "They're frightened of giving me a bad experience, I suppose, because of who Mum and Dad are. They probably think the Principe will be mad at them if it's not a perfect experience or something. I mean, I know Mum and Dad are close to the Debreks, but I'm still a human like everyone else here."

Alexis immediately felt guilty at the thought of turning Katie down, even if the vampire in her was a little too interested in drinking from her. She couldn't do that to Katie and supposed it her duty as Duca to guide her through this first time if no one else was brave enough to.

She caught Katie's arm as she started to walk away. "I'd be honoured to drink from you."

"What? Really?" Katie said.

"Yes."

The door to the blood room opened as another vampire came in ready to feed. Alexis turned around and gave them a hard stare. "Leave."

"Yes, Duca," the vampire said quickly.

The last thing Katie needed was an audience for her first time. Alexis locked the door with the key. "So we won't be disturbed."

Katie started to undo the first few buttons on her blouse. Alexis walked up to her and stilled her hand. "You do know *you* have the choice of wrist or neck?"

"Yes, Duca."

"The most important thing to remember is that in here, you are in charge. Don't let any vampire influence you about where to feed, or whether to feed at all. You always have the right to change your mind, at any point."

Katie nodded.

"And if any vampire in our clan does not respect your rights, or tries to influence you, report it to me, or your mother and father, understand?"

"Yes, I do."

Alexis felt the corners of her mouth rise into a smile. That was out of character. "Good." She walked around to Katie's back. "And you want to give me your neck?"

She saw Katie shiver and the pulse point in her neck pound. Alexis's teeth broke through her gums at the sight, and her mouth watered. The hunger she had felt in her gut was even more demanding.

This wasn't normal for her. She never needed someone like this—well, never since she had fed from the only woman she'd ever loved. That thought was ridiculous.

Just feed from her and get out of here.

Alexis took a step closer and pulled Katie's blouse around her shoulders. She inhaled sharply when her fingers touched Katie's skin and felt Katie shiver. This encounter was making her feel, and it scared her, but she couldn't turn back.

Just do it.

She moved closer so that her lips were next to Katie's ear. She closed her eyes and inhaled Katie's sweet perfume. It was intoxicating to her.

"Do you consent?"

"Yes, Duca," Katie said in such a breathy, wanting voice.

Alexis's hunger, and now her sex, burned with need. This wasn't about a lesson any more, it wasn't just feeding—it was a need. Alexis needed Katie.

She sank her incisors into Katie's neck, and before she even tasted her blood, Alexis was lost in the taste of Katie's skin. Then Katie's blood hit her tongue, and she experienced both shock and unbelievable bliss at the same time. Alexis sucked harder, and after

Katie's initial gasp, the feel-good chemicals hit, and she relaxed in Alexis's arms.

Alexis's head swam with what she could only describe as joy. She was sating a hunger that she didn't know she'd had since Victorija Dred first turned her and destroyed her humanity.

She should stop, but it just wasn't an option. Alexis stepped even closer and pushed her groin into Katie's bottom. Katie responded by groaning and slipping her hand into Alexis's hair and pulling her into her neck even more.

This wasn't feeding any more—this was a prelude to sex. Sex, love, and feeling like she hadn't since her fiancée was killed. The shock of the realization poured over her like cold water.

No. That couldn't happen again. She was never going to let herself feel that way again. Alexis pulled away from Katie's neck sharply, making Katie gasp, and like a coward, she ran.

"Alexis? You all right, mate?"

Slaine pulled Alexis back from her memories. She rubbed her face and said, "Yes. Give me some Debrek Special Reserve, will you?"

"Will do," Slaine said.

Alexis needed blood to calm herself. The memory of Katie never dulled in her imagination.

Slaine served her the glass of warmed blood, and she brought it to her lips. Katie's dance with the shapeshifter in female human form came to an end, and she saw the woman whisper something in Katie's ear that made her laugh.

Then Katie somehow sensed she was looking and returned her gaze. Alexis took a sip of the blood from the glass and whispered to herself, "No one will ever taste like you."

"Slaine? Your finest malt whisky. Great wedding, eh?" Bhal said, joining her at the bar.

"Hmm." Alexis nodded.

Bhaltair was leader of a group of warriors, bound by honour to serve the Debrek clan, and had been a mentor of sorts for Byron.

Slaine gave Bhal her whisky. Bhal said, "You don't seem too enthusiastic, Duca."

"I have reservations about a big celebration. Byron has taken her eye off the ball now that she is bonded. There is a war brewing between the witches and the vampires. After Victorija's last defeat, the Dreds are in a weakened state, but they are angry and eager to strike back."

"That may be so, Alexis, but Byron and the Principessa couldn't be safer here. We will deal with what we have to deal with tomorrow, for tonight we celebrate," Bhal said.

"There's nothing more dangerous than a wounded animal. My vampires on the ground in Europe tell me there are newly turned vampires flocking to the Dred banner, as well as some smaller European vampire clans."

Bhal patted her on the shoulder. "I know it's the job of the Duca to anticipate problems, but don't let life pass you by."

"Life? What life?" Alexis asked.

Bhal indicated over towards Byron. "Your friends, the people who care about you. Byron needs you as a friend, not just as her lieutenant."

Alexis snorted and took a quick drink. "Byron doesn't need me any more. She has the Principessa."

"Of course she needs you. More than ever now that she has a family to protect. You know what would happen if Byron lost Amelia? She would make Victorija and her father look like pussycats. It's our duty to keep them both safe and protected—for all our sakes. That's why she needs you."

"Maybe." Alexis wasn't entirely convinced.

"Besides, I think you have someone else to take up your attention."

"What are you talking about?" Alexis knew exactly what she was meaning.

Bhal indicated towards the dance floor. "Be careful though. If you don't grasp your chance, someone else will, and you'll be full of regret."

Pain or regret? She couldn't stand to have her heart broken again, so she would just have to live with her regrets.

❖

Katie almost floated back to the table escorted by her new friend Greda. They were soon joined by Daisy, who came back from the dance floor too and took a seat.

Ever since Katie had met Daisy through Amelia, they had become great friends. Daisy worked at Amelia's family's suit tailoring business but in her free time was a paranormal hunter.

Through her YouTube channel, Daisy and her small band of like-minded friends ghost hunted and interviewed whistle-blowers who said they had information on the paranormal world. But when Amelia had fallen in love with Byron, Daisy had finally found the paranormal world she had always believed in. Unfortunately, she now had to keep it secret herself, in order to keep her friends safe.

"They say never trust a shapeshifter, but Greda was lovely," Katie said.

"I could say the same about any paranormal in this room," Daisy said.

"I suppose it might seem that way, but I've been brought up in this world. It's normal to me."

"I can't believe those are Byron's parents," Daisy said. "Her mum is bloody gorgeous. If it wasn't for the grey streaks in her hair, you would never believe she was her mum."

Katie looked over to the middle of the dance floor where Michel and his wife Juliana were dancing alongside Byron and Amelia. Michel's hair and beard were carefully streaked with grey to take attention away from his much younger appearance, and Juliana was elegance personified, perfectly befitting vampire royalty.

"They are so nice too. They might look intimidating, but they couldn't be nicer to my parents and me," Katie said.

Out of nowhere Daisy grasped the table and closed her eyes.

"Are you okay? What's wrong?"

"Just feeling a bit dizzy. I think I might be coming down with something."

Katie beckoned a waiter over. "Can you get me a bottle of cold water, please?"

"Yes, miss."

Katie covered Daisy's hand with hers. "Do you want to go upstairs to your room?"

"It's okay. It usually passes in a minute," Daisy said.

Katie was concerned by that answer. "*Usually?* How long has this been happening?"

"Not long." The waiter returned with the water. Daisy clasped her hand to her silk neck scarf that perfectly suited her 1950s style dress.

"Are you sure you're okay?" Katie asked.

Daisy nodded. "Absolutely. Don't worry about me. Worry about the scary Duca."

"What? Why?"

"She hasn't taken her eyes off you. Every time you dance, her eyes are glued to you. I think she maybe wants to eat you," Daisy joked.

Katie laughed. "Hardly. She can't stand me, and I'm the last person she'd want to eat."

She turned around and tried to find Alexis, and there she was, standing at the bar, gazing over. When she saw Katie, Alexis turned quickly and spoke to Slaine.

"Hmm…she is a super scary vamp with everyone, but she really seems to get under your skin. Does she make you angry?"

"Infuriated, mostly. I think because she disappointed me. Can you keep a secret?"

Daisy rolled her eyes. "I'm a paranormal hunter who has discovered the paranormal world and can't tell anyone. I think you can trust me."

"True—well, the secret that I never told anyone was that I had a crush on Alexis Villiers ever since I can remember. Even before I understood why I found another woman so interesting. She strode through the Debrek estate, all-powerful and telling people what to do. She was exciting."

Daisy leaned in closer. "Oh, this is getting interesting. What happened next?"

Katie sighed. "People rarely live up to the pedestal you put them on, do they? I went off to university, then came back to work with the Debreks, and I was put on the blood rota."

"The blood rota?" Daisy questioned.

"All the humans who work for the Debreks provide blood for the clan's vampires. We are well rewarded, and we always have the right to leave or refuse. Blood rights are always about consent for the Debreks."

"Weird, but if it works for you, then great."

"I was called down to the blood room, and it was going to be my first time, and Alexis walked in," Katie said.

Daisy rolled her eyes. "Just your luck to get scary features."

"I was so nervous and yet so excited at the same time. The vampire who'd been my crush all my life was here to be my first."

Daisy took a drink and said, "I can imagine she behaved like an arsehole about the whole thing."

"That's the strange thing. She was so gentle, so caring, walking me through every step of my first time. It was like a dream. Then—"

"Then?"

A feeling of utter sadness descended on Katie. "Then she tasted me, tasted my blood, and was so disgusted that she tore her teeth away and ran out of the room, just leaving me there."

"She did that? I was right—she is a bloody arsehole, Katie," Daisy said.

"To this day I don't know what was wrong with my blood."

"There's nothing wrong. If I were a vampire, I'd happily feed on you."

Katie laughed. "Thanks, friend. At least I found out who she was. A cold, heartless vampire. Not worthy of my teenage crush."

She looked back round at Alexis. What she didn't tell Daisy was that in the brief moment Alexis was feeding from her, it felt better than any fantasy she'd ever had. She felt her everywhere. In her mind, her soul, her sex, everywhere. Katie remembered being so overcome with the need to touch and be touched that she'd reached back and grasped Alexis's dark hair.

But then Alexis ran like she was some cheap one-night stand. What was so wrong with her?

❖

"How long before we can slip away, mia cara?" Byron whispered into her wife's ear as they swayed to the music.

Amelia giggled and kissed Byron on the nose. "A little while longer. We have to be polite. So you'll need to put up with your hunger for the meantime."

"Fine, but I will be in misery until my fingers touch your body and my teeth graze your neck."

"Aww, you are sweet." Amelia tugged on Byron's stiff jacket collar. "I must say, I love your wedding outfit."

"Hmm. Debrek ceremonial wear. Thankfully I don't have to wear it too often," Byron said.

She wore a formal navy military jacket with large gold buttons and swirled gold braid on the sleeves, gold tassels on the shoulders, and matching navy trousers. A loose gold belt was slung around her waist with an old looking rapier hanging from it.

The outfit was similar to Byron's father's outfit, only he had different gold braiding. Amelia guessed that it signified their different ranks within the clan.

"I think you look very sexy," Amelia said.

Byron smiled. "Then wearing this uncomfortable uniform was all worth it."

Byron's mother and father swept past them as they performed some elaborate ballroom dance moves.

"Your parents really know how to dance," Amelia said.

"Yes, they very much enjoy dancing together. The Grand Duchess Lucia used to tell me of the great balls the family would host when the Debreks still lived in Vienna, and how they danced together."

Amelia sensed a sadness in Byron every time she talked about her great-great-grandmother, a sadness she'd be able to feel even if she didn't share a blood bond with her partner. Lucia was killed by Victorija in a terrible confrontation.

"You miss her a lot, don't you?" Amelia said.

"I do. It can be lonely when you're a leader, but I always had Lucia at the end of the phone."

Amelia kissed her cheek. "You know you're not alone any more, don't you?"

She pulled Amelia closer. "I know that."

Byron twirled them around and tipped her head to the bar at the back. "Look at my Duca, nursing a glass of blood and staring at Katie's table."

Amelia smiled. "She's lovesick, but she's never going to win Katie's love by mooching around the bar and looking so serious."

"She wasn't always so serious. At one time I had to caution her about falling in love so quickly and intensely."

"The girl that Victorija's vampires killed?" Amelia said.

"Yes, Anna. It broke her heart when she died. After that, she wasn't interested in anything but work and became harder and more serious."

Amelia trailed her fingernails down Byron's cheek. "So were you, and I melted your heart."

Byron's eyes started to turn red at Amelia's touch. "Are you sure we can't go upstairs now?"

Amelia laughed. "Not yet, but I promise it'll be worth waiting on. I have something special planned."

Byron was just about to reply when her sister, Serenity, danced up close to them with her dance partner, Angelo. Angelo was Byron's cousin, head of the North American wing of the Debrek bank.

Angelo was a younger vampire and biracial, African American on her father's side, but in most ways she was a kindred spirit and very like Byron in her tastes and her love of fashion, although

Angelo was more relaxed in her dress sense. Not today, though—today, she wore a dinner suit and looked extremely sharp as she danced Sera around the room.

"Sera, keep out of trouble," Byron said as the couple danced beside them.

"As always—anyway, I have my lovely cousin to look after me," Sera said.

"Are you enjoying yourself, Angelo?" Amelia asked.

"I sure am, Principessa. It's so much fun being with all the family again," Angelo said.

Byron smiled. "It'll be your turn next."

Angelo gave an exaggerated shiver. "God, I hope not. There are too many beautiful women out there to narrow it down to one."

"My thoughts exactly," Sera agreed.

Byron looked back to Amelia and deep into her eyes, "You might think that, but one day love will strike and never let go."

CHAPTER TWO

Victorija Dred let the human she was feeding on drop to the floor. It had been a waste of time. The blood she had gotten hadn't even touched the hunger she had. Nothing had touched it since leaving Britain.

In the months that passed since she killed her grandmother, her conscience and her hunger hadn't given her any peace. She'd retreated to her bedroom for the last few months. Victorija wanted solitude to torture herself with the memories of what she'd done.

Victorija never expected to feel this way about the Grand Duchess. She had always relished the idea of ending the Debrek matriarch, but when the time came, Lucia touched her and gave Victorija back memories she had repressed. Memories of being a child, being with her grandmother and her cousins, before her father had been banished from the Debrek clan for breaking their most sacred rule. Consent.

The memories of the little girl that she had been, happy and carefree, running around the Debrek estate, playing with her grandmother, chipped away at the ice inside her.

"Principe?" It was the voice of her Duca, Drasas, who stood in her doorway.

Victorija turned without making eye contact and walked over some bodies to get to her castle window. "What is it, Drasas?"

"I wondered if you could find the time to come and cast an eye over the new recruits I've been training."

"I'm sure you can handle it, Drasas," Victoria said without turning back from the window.

"Well, I can, but I just wanted you to see them. Our vampires are bringing home newly turned humans every day. We'll soon have the numbers to take on the Debreks and pay them back for what they have done to us and to take over their immense clan. You would be unstoppable with the Debrek clan under your boot."

"I'll leave it in your capable hands, Duca. I wish to rest for the moment," Victorija said.

"You haven't been downstairs for weeks, Victorija. Your vampires need your leadership."

The gnawing hunger was churning painfully inside her and driving her mad. Victorija flashed across the room and grasped Drasas's neck, pushing her up against the wall.

"I told you I want to stay up here," Victorija shouted. "Now get someone to clear up these bodies and send me *vampires* to feed from, from now on."

"Yes, Principe." Victorija walked back to the window. Drasas added, "Are you sure you're okay?"

"Yes, now send me some food."

Drasas bowed her head and walked out of the room. Victorija grasped her stomach and steadied herself against the castle wall. Then the cramps hit hard, and she doubled over in pain. Why was this happening? It had started after they returned to France.

She remained in her bedroom because she wanted to be alone with her thoughts, and not show any weakness to her clan. Her thoughts were almost as debilitating as her hunger for blood. Lucia hadn't just unlocked memories of Victorija with the family—the memories brought forth all the thoughts she had kept locked up tight behind her icy walls.

Victorija once told Amelia that she had experienced every shade of pain. Whatever Lucia had done to her mind, everything was melting, and facing those memories was terrifying. Between that and her unquenchable hunger, Victorija Dred feared she was going mad, just as her father Gilbert had done when he killed her mother, his blood bond.

The Debreks were vampire royalty. They were the oldest and most powerful vampires in the world because of one special ability—they could reproduce. Born vampires, as the Debreks were known, grew stronger with each new generation.

Victorija, Byron's cousin, was a born vampire, but when her father was banished from the clan, he and his descendants lost the ability to reproduce. It made the newly formed Dred clan weaker than the Debreks.

Victorija, like her father before her, wanted this ability back, not for the joy of bringing a new life into the world, but for building a powerbase of super vampires to rival the Debreks. She sought to find out what magic Lucia had stripped them of, but it wasn't until Victorija confronted her grandmother at the Debrek castle in Scotland that she found out the awful truth.

There was no secret magic or incantation that was taken from them—the secret was love. A pure unselfish love for another vampire or human would allow them to reproduce like the Debreks.

It was a shocking revelation, because Victorija knew she would never want or be capable of loving anyone.

Gilbert had fallen out of love with Victorija's mother after Victorija was born. He wanted to be rid of her, and a witch had promised him she could break his need for the blood of his bond, but the spell had never worked, and he began to lose his mind to the insanity of blood withdrawal.

Victorija wasn't bonded or ever likely to be, so why was she feeling like this? She recognized the symptoms of the same blood withdrawal Gilbert had gone through. Something was deeply wrong, and she was terrified of finding out the reason.

❖

Byron waited as patiently as she could in the ballroom downstairs while Amelia went up to their bedroom to get undressed and ready whatever she had planned. Just when her patience was ready to break, one of the staff brought her a note. It was Amelia asking her to meet her upstairs, and also one mysterious line: *Leave your uniform on.*

She sped upstairs without saying her goodbyes. There was more than enough time tomorrow to thank everyone for coming. Now she just needed to be with her wife. Byron hadn't spent last night with Amelia for tradition's sake, and she was hungry for Amelia's blood and her body.

Byron's heart was beating as if she was still alive with the anticipation of touching her Amelia. She arrived at the bedroom door, knocked, and then walked in and found the room bathed in only candlelight.

Her breath caught when she saw Amelia kneeling beside the bed, head down, naked, wearing ankle and wrist restraints. She had to stop herself from groaning out loud, because that wouldn't fit the atmosphere.

Amelia loved her dominance and light bondage play, and her request that Byron should keep her uniform on was part of that. She walked into the room and shut and locked the door. She noticed the leg restraints had a spreader bar between, keeping Amelia's legs open, and a soft corded rope waited on the bed.

She stood over Amelia and whispered, "I love you."

Amelia didn't look up but said, "I'm yours to serve, Principe."

Byron's mouth watered for Amelia's blood, and her sex was wet for her body. She craved Amelia, not just for what her body could give her, but also for her heart and how much she understood her needs and, even better, shared them.

She stroked Amelia's hair and said, "Look up at me."

Amelia did look, and her eyes were full of want. Byron was perfectly aware how much Amelia needed this side of their life as much as she did.

Byron picked up the rope and said, "Do you consent?"

"Yes," Amelia said in a breathy voice.

"Hands up then."

Amelia did as asked, and Byron slipped the rope through the

metal loops on the wrist restraints. Now, holding the rope in her hands, she could control Amelia's movements.

She pulled the rope and forced Amelia's face close to her crotch. Byron undid her belt slowly and let it hang loose. She knew how much that would tantalize Amelia.

Byron had worn a strap-on since she became a born vampire. It had suited her to pass as a man in the days when women weren't supposed to run businesses, far less banking groups. Then when female bosses became more acceptable, she came out as a woman, but who she was inside was still the person who identified with those masculine parts of herself.

Her strap-on was part of her, and Byron was eternally grateful that Amelia loved it just as much. Amelia touched her strap-on through her uniform trousers, then kissed her and fondled it.

Byron put her hand on her top button and paused. "Do you want it?"

"Yes. Please, Principe?"

Byron would love Amelia to suck her, but she sensed Amelia's request that she keep her uniform on was so Amelia could feel her pressed against her, taking her, using her. "Not just now. Get up."

Byron helped Amelia up and led her by the rope to the end of the wrought iron bed. She pulled Amelia close, so she could feel her hard strap-on pressing into her. Byron reached around and clasped Amelia's breasts.

They both groaned, and she pressed her face into Amelia's neck, and let her teeth graze the soft skin around her pulse point. "You smell so good, Amelia."

"Thank you," Amelia said.

Byron kept a tight hold of the rope, and of Amelia's wrists behind her back. She could feel Amelia pressing her bottom into her groin, and even moving her hips back and forth in small movements.

Byron ran her hand from the base of Amelia's spine and down into her sex. She was soaking wet. She allowed her fingers to wander briefly into Amelia's wet sex.

"You want this badly. Don't you?"

"Yes, yes," Amelia groaned.

She pulled out her fingers and offered them to Amelia's mouth. She greedily sucked them, and Byron knew she couldn't wait much longer. Byron moved her lips to Amelia's ear and said, "I'm just going to take you where you stand."

Amelia replied with a moan. "Oh yes."

Byron pushed Amelia forward over the wrought iron bedstead until she bent at the waist, undid her trousers, and pulled out her strap-on. She rubbed it up and down Amelia's wetness a few times and whispered, "I'm going to fuck you while I drink from you."

Amelia shivered. She loved it when Byron spoke that way to her, and being totally restrained was making her more turned on than ever before. They played with restraints all the time, but always very light ones—Byron's ties, scarfs, things like that.

But Amelia wanted to organize something special for their wedding night, something she knew they would both enjoy. She was probably enjoying it enough for both of them. The feel of Byron's uniform pressed against her was so hot. It made her feel like a camp follower, used for this officer's pleasure.

Amelia gasped when Byron pushed the tip of her strap-on inside her. Byron let her get used to the feel of it, whilst rocking her hips. Inch by inch, Byron filled Amelia up. They both groaned when it slid fully in.

Byron began to thrust, and Amelia felt so incredibly full, and so utterly taken. She tested her bonds to remind herself that she couldn't move, and she felt herself clench around Byron's strap-on.

Byron whispered, "This is what you wanted?"

"Yes," Amelia groaned, "I wanted your cock inside me—and your teeth."

Byron seemed to be overcome with lust at that last remark, because she bit into her neck straight away and began thrusting inside her faster. She could hear Byron's murmurs of pleasure as she drank her blood and took her body.

The feel-good chemicals from Byron's bite made her even more ready to come. Amelia's sex grasped the strap-on inside her, and her body started to shake. It felt like it was going to be too much—the feeling was overwhelming.

"Byron, it's too much. I can't—"

Byron dropped the rope and wrapped her arms around Amelia's middle, allowing Amelia to put her hands over Byron's. She felt safe, protected, and her orgasm started to tip over the edge.

"Oh God, oh God," Amelia repeated in a desperate plea.

Byron thrust faster and faster until she lost control and pulled her teeth from Amelia's neck.

"Fuck," Byron shouted. Byron collapsed over Amelia's back, breathing heavily. "God, I love you."

"I love you too."

Amelia reached her hand into Byron's hair and pulled her into a kiss and tasted her own blood. She then pulled back and smiled. "More, Principe."

❖

Drasas walked down the castle steps and out into the stable block at the back of the castle. She needed some air and to think. The Dreds' human estate workers and stable boys immediately put their heads down when they realized the Duca was there, and that gave Drasas a thrill. She wanted people to fear and tremble before her, the way they did when Victorija was around.

She walked up to one of the stable doors, and the horse neighed in distress and kicked the door. She hissed at it in return.

"Useless animals."

But the horses were safe and well maintained for Victorija. If there was only one thing in life Victorija took happiness in, it was her horses. Drasas didn't know why she cared for the filthy beasts, but everyone knew you would meet your end by the Principe's hands unless the horses were better taken care of than anything else on the Dred estate.

Leo, the vampire next in the chain of command, approached her. "Duca, how is the Principe?"

Drasas sighed. "I'm not sure. There's definitely something not right. She hasn't left her room in nearly a month."

"The blood hunger? Is it any better?" Leo asked.

Drasas shook her head. "No, it's worse. She's requested only vampires feed her from now on. Something happened to her in Britain, when she killed her grandmother. It left her—" Drasas wanted to say *weak*, but it was too dangerous to even say those words out loud. If her words got back to her Principe... "*Changed.* We need to get to the bottom of this, Leo. Our numbers have never been greater, and the Debreks never more distracted—and weaker, now that the Grand Duchess is dead. We need to strike them. The Debrek clan is our—Victorija's—birthright."

"The Principe is a born vampire. The most powerful vampire you can be. What could affect her so badly?" Leo asked.

"I don't know, but we must find out."

Drasas knew *she* would have already struck the Debreks by now. If only she had Victorija's powers. Victorija was her mentor and she had always revered her, but since the Grand Duchess had reduced her to tears, and Drasas had found her in a ditch running from the Debrek vampires, Drasas had lost a bit of respect for her.

"Organize a rota of vampires to feed the Principe," Drasas said.

"Yes, Duca. There's something else, an emissary has arrived and would like to talk to you," Leo said.

"An emissary from who?"

"A powerful ally, they said."

"And they wanted to see me and not the Principe?" Drasas asked.

"Yes, shall I fetch them?"

"Yes, bring them here."

Drasas paced around the courtyard. Why would someone want to see her and not Victorija?

A few minutes later Leo led a slightly built blond-haired young man into the stable block. Despite his youth and apparent lack of physical strength, he didn't look away in fear. He had the air of someone who was extremely confident in themselves and their safety.

"Are you Drasas, Duca of the Dred clan?" the young man said.

"Yes, and you are?"

"Asha." He bowed his head.

Drasas waved Leo away. "Well, Asha, there's not many who would walk into a vampire lair willingly."

"I have been sent as emissary from my mistress, Madam Anka. Have you heard of her?" Asha asked.

"Should I have?"

Asha chuckled. "Yes, you probably should."

Drasas didn't like his tone. She took a step towards him and bared her teeth. "Watch what you say."

Asha didn't flinch as she expected he would. "I mean no disrespect, Duca, but my mistress is probably worth researching. Anyway, she has asked me to convey this message."

Asha handed her a letter with an old-fashioned wax seal on it. She ripped it open and started to read while Asha said, "Madam Anka is a powerful, influential woman in the witch community. She would like to meet with you and discuss potential cooperation between the witches and the Dred vampires."

Drasas looked up from the letter. "Witches helping vampires? Are you joking?"

"No, Madam Anka never jokes," Asha said.

This was insane. "You are aware that my Principe just killed the high priestess of the Paris coven? The covens in France are baying for our heads, apparently."

"Yes, my mistress was most pleased to get Lillian out of the way. It only helps her cause. As for the other covens, there are different kinds of covens, Duca, some light and some darker."

"Why me? Why not talk to my Principe?" Drasas asked.

"We understand your Principe is having some…difficulties at the moment, and my mistress can help with that. Think about it. The contact details are in the letter."

Asha bowed and walked away. Drasas looked both ways to see who'd seen her talking to Asha, but everyone was busy with their own work. She should take this to Victorija, but then again, she wasn't herself.

Drasas stuffed the letter in her pocket and felt a small knot of fear in her stomach. Was this treacherous? No, Drasas decided. She was the only one capable of dealing with this new information. She would tell the Principe what she needed to know when she found out.

CHAPTER THREE

A lexis shut her bedroom door and walked along the corridor in the direction of the staircase. She was heading to the mess hall in the basement to talk with one of her vampires.

She came to the top of the grand staircase and looked at the throng of people below. The Principessa, with the help of Katie, was overseeing the revamp of the Debreks' London home, and for the last few weeks, since the wedding, the house had been filled with human decorators, plumbers, electricians, and joiners.

Just having these humans in Byron's home filled her with worry. How was she supposed to keep the Debrek secret world hidden and Byron and Amelia safe with all these human strangers milling about the house? She had tried to counsel Byron against letting so many in at once, and tried to limit the number, but Byron was relaxed about the whole thing. Too relaxed.

Alexis gripped the wooden banister. Byron had become less careful since she and the Principessa became bonded, but Alexis vowed she would not take her eye off the ball. It was her job to be vigilant, and to make sure everyone was safe.

For all they knew, one of Victorija's vampires could be down there, playing the part of a human and plotting right under their noses. Alexis had initially placed guards everywhere, determined the humans would see nothing they shouldn't, but both Bhal and Byron had said it made this seemingly normal private London home look even odder to have guards on every doorway.

Now there were just two on the entrance hall, but her security cameras were everywhere. No one was going to cause a security issue on her watch.

Something else caught Alexis's attention—the clatter of heels on the marble hallway floor. Katie had appeared from one of the downstairs rooms and walked across the floor towards one of the humans.

She hadn't spoken with Katie properly for a long time, unless it was to do with the house or Amelia and Byron, but that didn't mean Alexis hadn't taken notice of her. Alexis always noticed Katie, but she would never allow Katie to see that.

Her eyes caressed Katie, wearing a tight black skirt and white blouse. Alexis studied her so much that she knew every curve, every inch of Katie. Alexis asked herself time and time again why this one petite human captured her attention so much.

She had been surrounded by beautiful women most of her long life, she'd even been on the verge of marriage to one, but none had kept her attention like Katie Brekman. Katie wasn't glamourous— she was the girl next door with that simple, natural beauty that few possessed.

Alexis watched Katie talking to one of the painters. They were looking at paint colours, and Katie was laughing at what the painter said. She sometimes wished she had that kind of easy-going humour that would allow her to speak to Katie like that, but then her stoic personality was the one thing that protected her from getting hurt.

Then something changed. The male painter boxed Katie in against the wall and was entirely too close. Fortunately, Alexis's enhanced hearing was able to listen in on their conversation.

"No, I don't think it's a good idea. Let's just keep this professional now," Katie said.

The painter didn't seem to take no for an answer. "Just one drink, come on."

Alexis could feel rage building in the very pit of her stomach.

He leaned his face closer and put his hand on Katie's hip.

Seconds before Alexis was about to explode in anger, Katie ducked out of the painter's arms and moved away.

"Excuse me, I have to deal with something in the kitchens."

After Katie made a hasty retreat, Alexis watched the painter laugh with his fellow workmen and make a sexual gesture towards Katie as she walked away. Alexis leapt into action. She jumped over the banister and landed on the floor as if the height had been only a step. The painter looked at her in shock.

"How did you—"

He looked terrified, just as Alexis wanted. "Let's have a little chat."

❖

Katie walked down into the large Debrek kitchen. It was full of staff getting food prepared for lunch. A voice behind her said, "Cuppa tea, Katie?"

Katie turned around and smiled when she saw the Debrek executive chef coming out of her office.

"No, thanks. I can't stay long. I'm just trying to take a breather, Dane."

"What happened?"

Dane was a recent addition to the staff. Amelia had recruited her and revamped the kitchen. Everyone was enjoying the new meals she and her staff prepared. Dane had short shaved hair with a blue flop of hair on top. She was part human, part shifter and had come recommended by Slaine.

"Just an idiot guy trying it on," Katie said.

Dane crossed her arms. "Do you want me to go and have a quiet word?"

Katie smiled. "Don't worry—I can handle the likes of him. I'm just letting him cool off. In fact I should probably get back up there—thanks for the sanctuary."

"Anytime. See you at lunch," Dane said.

Katie walked back up the stairs. Hopefully painter Dave had

control of himself by now. She was only putting up with him because he and his team did such good work. Amelia had scoured London looking for the best painter and decorator. Dave was the best, so despite his hot hands everywhere, she had to calm things down and get him concentrated on work.

She opened the door that led from the kitchen staircase to the entrance hall and saw Dave and his crew hastily gathering up their stuff. A smug-looking Alexis was standing there, arms folded, watching Dave run out the door.

What had she done? "Alexis? What's going on? Where are the painter and his team going?"

"You don't have to worry. They will not be back."

"What? What are you talking about?"

"I saw what he did. I made it pretty clear to him what would befall him if he didn't leave."

"You scared him off?" Katie said angrily. "I was handling it, Alexis."

"It didn't look like it from where I was standing."

"What, so you were keeping your eyes on me? Watching me?"

Alexis never answered her.

"Amelia and I searched everywhere for him. He's the best, and now the refurb will be held up even longer."

Alexis's facial expression turned from smug to angry. "You shouldn't put up with any sexual harassment for the sake of keeping a good painter."

Katie felt hot fury burning inside her. Alexis was infuriatingly right. She shouldn't have to take that behaviour no matter how good he was. Still, it was her decision to make.

"You should have minded your own business," Katie said.

Alexis folded her arms. "This is the thanks I get for protecting you? Okay, the next time I see you being sexually harassed, I'll just walk away."

"I wish you would. You don't need to protect me from anything, Duca. Just mind your own bloody business in future." Katie poked an accusing finger into Alexis's chest. "Oh, and you can explain to the Principessa why her decorator walked off the job."

She turned and marched up the stairs trying to control her anger. Katie wasn't a disagreeable and angry person, but Alexis always manged to bring out her inner fury.

Bloody idiot.

❖

Byron was sitting at her old oak desk, a cigar smoking in the ashtray beside her, going through a box of papers. The Debrek solicitors in Venice had forwarded all of the Grand Duchess's papers. Most were legal and banking documents, but one plain envelope caught her eye.

She took her silver letter opener and sliced the white paper open. What she found was a handwritten letter from Lucia. It began: *If you are reading this letter, then I have passed to the other side...*

There was a knock at the door. "Come," Byron said. She was pleasantly surprised when Amelia walked in. "Mia cara, why are you knocking?"

"You might be having a meeting or something. I don't want to intrude."

"You could never intrude." Byron held out her hand to beckon Amelia over.

Amelia kissed her, then leaned over Byron's shoulder. "Are those your great-great-grandmother's things?"

"Yes, all her papers. I found this letter addressed to me. Take a look," Byron said.

Amelia took the letter and scanned it.

Losing Lucia was still raw for Byron. Lucia had been the matriarch and the life force of the Debrek clan, not to mention how much she was loved.

Amelia stopped reading suddenly and said, "She wants you to bring Victorija back over to the light before she destroys herself?"

Byron shook her head. That part of the letter had stopped her in her tracks. "How can she ask it of me? *Why* would she ask it of me? Victorija has just ripped my great-great-grandmother's heart from her body. I want to kill her, not help her."

Amelia sighed still reading over the letter. "She seems to think there's still good in her. Lucia says that she failed Victorija as a child. That she should have stepped in and taken Victorija away from Gilbert."

"She's a bloodthirsty killer, Amelia. Her upbringing can't be blamed for all her wrong deeds," Byron said.

Amelia took her eyes away from the letter and got a faraway look in her eye. "It was strange. That day we all met in the castle in Scotland, I got the feeling Lucia knew when she walked out to meet Victorija that day that she would die. Like it was part of her destiny."

"Hmm." Byron knew she was right. It had felt like that. "It still doesn't make her worthy of a chance to redeem herself," Byron said as she pulled Amelia down onto her lap.

"I will say one thing." Amelia placed her arms around Byron's neck. "The first time I met Victorija, when she faked the accident to get close to me, she talked about pain and said she knew every shade of it, and I felt that was true, despite all the other lies she told."

Byron sighed. "I always felt that if I had been unlucky enough to be brought up by Gilbert, I'd be exactly like Victorija."

Amelia kissed her on the lips. "I don't think so. You're the most noble person I've ever known."

Byron tapped the letter with her fingers. "I suppose I have to follow her wishes, but how I'll do that, I don't know. First things first, I have to find her. Since she ran after killing Lucia, Victorija has gone to ground. I'll need to put some people on the case."

"That's a start. Then if you find her, you can decide what happens next," Amelia said.

"I'll call Alexis to come and see me. She can put the feelers out for information."

Byron quickly dialled Alexis's number and asked her to come to her office.

"I meant to ask—have you found anybody who can help unlock my past?" Amelia asked.

Before she died, Lucia informed her that she had witch heritage, and it became apparent that the parents she grew up with had adopted her. Amelia had exhibited some magical powers, and she was determined to learn how to control them and to find out about her real family.

"I've asked my lawyers to make some enquiries, and Bhal has quietly put out the word asking for any information. Don't worry, we'll find out about your past."

"I need to know," Amelia said.

Byron took her hand and kissed it. "I know, and you will. Give me time. Anyway, on to more cheerful matters. It's your big night."

A huge smile grew on Amelia's face. Since leaving college she had worked in her uncle's tailors on Savile Row, honing her craft, but when the premises next door to her uncle's shop became available, she spotted a chance to make her dream come true.

Amelia had always most enjoyed tailoring for women, and as more women were turning to dapper suits and ties, she saw an opportunity to fulfil her dream and open a tailoring shop just for them.

Byron had handled the sale, and after outfitting the shop and recruiting staff, the opening night was here. The press, fashion designers, celebrities, and businesspeople likely to be customers were invited.

"Yes, I can't wait." Amelia leaned in to kiss Byron, but Byron stopped her.

She whispered, "Alexis is here."

Amelia got up from Byron's lap and joked, "What would we do without your super hearing?"

Byron smiled and winked. She had gained more strength than she could have ever imagined by being blood bonded to Amelia. Her very presence gave her strength and made her feel invincible. But she supposed that was only natural since Amelia was the Debrek life force, since Lucia died. She gave them strength and the ability to have children.

There was a knock at the door. "Come," Byron called out.

"Do you want some privacy?" Amelia asked.

"No, I have no secrets from you, mia cara."

Alexis came through the door and bowed her head briefly to them both. "Principe, Principessa, you called?"

"Yes, Duca." Byron knew better than to offer Alexis a seat. Alexis was always on duty, always on alert. "I've been going through the Grand Duchess's things, and I found this letter addressed to me. Read it," Byron said.

Alexis scanned the letter quickly. Her eyed narrowed, and then she looked up and said, "You're not seriously considering this?"

"It wouldn't be my first choice, but it's my great-great-grandmother's dying wish."

Alexis shook her head vigorously. "Have you forgotten what that vampire has done? She turned me, she killed some of our staff twice, and the Dreds murdered the woman I loved."

"I understand, but we're talking about finding her and talking things out, not forgiveness. Victorija will carry that guilt around until her last breath. In the meantime I want you to put out feelers, send out a recon team to find her."

Byron had never seen Alexis angry before. She felt Amelia put her hand on her shoulder in support.

"This is a mistake. You can't do this," Alexis said.

Byron leaned forward in her seat. She understood Alexis's objections, but she had to obey her orders. She said firmly, "Do as I have asked, Duca. I won't ask again."

Byron could see Alexis's jaw flexing as she most likely was trying to not lose her temper.

"Yes, Principe," Alexis said. "Excuse me then. I will give out the orders."

Then she stormed out the office door.

Amelia looked at Byron and raised an eyebrow. "That went well."

❖

Alexis was shaking with anger and a need for blood. How could the Principe ask this of her? She stopped dead outside the room where her Anna had her throat ripped out, so many years ago.

She stood and closed her eyes. When she tried to picture her

Anna in her mind, her face was blurred, and then Katie's face floated across her mind, and she could see every feature clearly.

Alexis's hunger for blood soared, so she got out her phone and requested a human staff member on the blood rota app.

She hurried down to the basement and cleared the security lock on the blood room door. When she walked in, she found Katie unbuttoning the first few buttons on her blouse to feed a waiting male vampire.

The scene before her felt like a dagger to her chest. Katie looked up with surprise. She clearly wasn't expecting Alexis to be here. The male vampire, called Tobias, acknowledged her with a nod. "Duca."

"Tobias." She then turned her attention to Katie. "You're not supposed to be on the blood rota."

"I had the rota changed. I don't want to be treated differently."

Alexis took a step closer and said, "You *are* different."

"Why am I different? You tell me why, Duca?" Katie said angrily.

Tobias asked, "Shall I just go, Duca?"

Katie said firmly, "You stay where you are, Toby."

Katie said again, "Why am I different?"

In her head Alexis knew clearly why she didn't want Katie on the rota—because she didn't want to see or even contemplate another vampire feeding on her—but she couldn't admit that out loud. So she said, "Katie, you are the head housekeeper of the Debrek household, a high position that means you should not be on the blood rota."

Katie sighed. "Rubbish. I shouldn't be treated any differently. The pact that the human members of the household have with the Debreks is that we offer our blood, and in return we get extremely well paid and looked after. I am no different."

The door opened again, and Alexis's human blood servant came in. "If that's what you want, Katie. Then have at it. I don't care," Alexis said.

James was the human who had answered Alexis's quest for blood. He got in position and unbuttoned his shirt. Alexis noticed that Katie hadn't taken her eyes from her. Tobias moved Katie's blouse from her neck, and Alexis was enraged watching him even touch her.

She could stop this right now, but then she would have to explain why, and she could never admit her feelings for Katie. It was hard to even say that to herself, far less outside.

Tobias's teeth entered Katie's neck and she gasped. Alexis followed suit and felt James's blood flow over her tongue.

After the feel-good chemicals took over, Katie opened her eyes and found Alexis's eyes staring at her as she fed on her host. Katie fixed her own eyes on Alexis. It was incredible. There was an energy pulling them together, and in her mind the two human hosts disappeared, and Alexis was feeding on her.

Katie's heart pounded and her mind went back to when Alexis first fed on her. She'd wanted Alexis that day, she would have given her anything. And now with every suck that Tobias took, in her mind, it was Alexis.

She was so turned on and everything inside her wanted to scream how much she wanted Alexis, that she couldn't stop her arm from rising, reaching out to make contact with Alexis.

Stop it. She doesn't want you.

Then, remarkably, Alexis raised her hand to meet hers, but then at the last moment closed her eyes, pulled away from her blood servant, and wiped the blood from her mouth.

"Thank you for your service," Alexis said to her blood servant and rushed out of the blood room again.

It was like cold water had been tipped on Katie. She was frustrated, angry, and annoyed.

Why couldn't she just be honest?

CHAPTER FOUR

B yron snagged a glass of champagne from one of the servers. Amelia was up on a small platform giving a speech for the crowd gathered at the opening of her new tailoring shop. Models dressed in suits designed by Amelia stood on either side of the stage.

Her uncle's shop next door was called Grenville and Thrang, and so to keep the tradition, Amelia simply called this shop Grenville, Thrang, and Debrek—For Women.

There was an excellent crowd out for the opening. Byron was pleased that their friends and a great number of acquaintances from the paranormal community had turned out tonight to support the opening of Amelia's new venture.

Byron was so proud of Amelia. This was her baby, and she, with Daisy by her side, put her heart and soul into it. Jaunty, her uncle, had helped as much as he could too. Byron had done everything she could discreetly, but she didn't want to be seen using her influence. Still, she made sure every fashion journalist worth their salt was there, as well as the LGBTQ media and social media influencers. Her sister Sera was entertaining one of those influencers at the moment with her smiles and chit-chat. Honestly, her sister found a woman to charm every place they went.

Amelia had been so nervous about this speech. She had practised it over and over for Byron, and Byron tried to give her pointers as she was used to talking to large groups of people. But as she'd reassured Amelia, everything was perfect on the night.

She had looked extremely nervous at the start but soon got into her groove and relaxed.

"And so, ladies and gentlemen, what I hope to create here is a safe place for women to explore bespoke tailoring and all it has to offer. Thank you."

The crowd broke into applause, and Amelia smiled with relief. Byron caught her eye and mouthed, *I love you.*

Then a voice she didn't recognize said, "I understand you are looking for information, Principe."

Byron looked to her side and saw a small man with round wire glasses and a suit and hat that had seen better days.

"I might be. Who are you, sir?" Byron asked.

He bowed his head and said, "Enoch Ratner at your service, Principe."

Byron spotted Alexis making her way over, to get rid of her new friend no doubt, but she waved her back.

"You have information for me, Mr. Ratner?"

"At a price. Of course I would normally give you anything I had free of charge, Principe, but times are hard."

Byron took her wallet out and extracted a large sum of notes but held on to them. "Tell me, then."

"There's a witch, runs a bookshop with her granddaughter. It's called The Portal."

"And why do you think this witch will be able to help?" Byron asked.

"Magda always knows what's going on in our community," Enoch said.

Byron handed him the notes. "This better not be a wild goose chase."

"It won't be, Principe. I promise."

❖

One of the models, a really good-looking butch named Will, was chatting up Katie in the corner of the room. She liked her, but the situation was getting uncomfortable. Every time she looked up, she saw Alexis scowling at her.

Then Daisy caught her eye. She was bracing herself against a chair and rubbing her temple.

"You'll have to excuse me, Will. I think my friend isn't feeling too well." She walked over and said, "Daisy, are you okay?"

Daisy put on a smile. "Oh yeah, fine. It's just been a lot of work getting this all ready for today. My head is a bit sore."

"As long as you're okay. You've done a great job here."

"Thanks. Amelia has appointed me manager—did she tell you?"

"No—congratulations, Daisy. That's great news." Katie gave her a kiss on the cheek.

"Thanks. It's going down well with the guests, isn't it? Are there paranormals here?"

"Oh, a few I'd guess, but none that will cause any harm," Katie said.

Daisy shook her head. "The things I could tell the world. It's crazy hard to keep secrets."

"I know, but it's to protect Amelia," Katie said.

Katie knew that Daisy wished she could tell the subscribers of her successful YouTube channel everything she had learned, but because of Amelia and her other new friends, she couldn't tell anyone. The outing of the paranormal world would put them in danger.

Daisy took a drink and pulled at the high collar of her jumper. "Hey, do you want to go out to The Sanctuary after this? I need to let off some steam."

"I'd love to," Katie said.

Daisy pointed to Alexis who was patrolling the room. "Super grumpy vamp is still gazing at you longingly."

"She dislikes everything about me, Daisy."

"I don't know. Hate and love are very close."

Katie thought back to the moment they shared in the blood room, while Alexis was feeding and she had a vampire feeding on her. The air was electric, and sex and need permeated the air, but then Alexis had run again. Like she always did.

"I don't care what she is or she isn't. I'm just sick of her scowling. Let's go out and have some fun. Oh, let's ask Sera too."

❖

The line of black Debrek cars pulled up in front of the house. Alexis got out and opened up the door for Byron, while Wilder, Amelia's guard, did the same for her. Byron waited for Amelia and took her hand.

"We're in for the night, Duca," Byron said.

"Yes, Principe."

Alexis waited while Sera and Katie got out of the car behind. She wanted to make sure everyone was in the house safely before she gave everyone their orders. As Sera passed her, she heard Katie say, "Are you sure you won't come out with us to The Sanctuary? I'm meeting Daisy there in an hour. Plenty of time to get ready."

"I'd love to. You know me—I never want to miss a party—but I'm flying out to New York at four a.m. It's my friend's art exhibition tomorrow night. The only way Byron's letting me out of the country since our little fight with the Dreds is if I take the Debrek plane and I stay with our cousin Angelo. Everything's been set, so if I miss my flight time, I'm in trouble."

"Oh, well, another time," Katie said as they walked up the steps.

Alexis was frozen on the spot. Katie was going out to The Sanctuary with Daisy. Two humans alone in a club full of paranormals, with things the way they were? She felt utter fear grip her heart.

"Duca?"

Alexis realized someone was trying to get her attention. It was Bhal, who was standing with Wilder.

"Sorry, Bhal. Could you give the orders? I need to speak to Katie."

"Aye, no problem."

Alexis ran up the stairs and into the entrance hallway. Katie was saying goodnight to Sera, and then Sera walked upstairs to her room.

Alexis's fear was turning into anger. How could Katie be so reckless, going to a paranormal club alone after everything they'd been through recently?

"Katie?" Alexis said sternly.

Katie turned around and sighed when she saw it was Alexis. "Yes?"

"Can I talk to you?"

"You are, aren't you?" Katie said sarcastically.

Alexis looked around and saw the entrance hall was filling up with the guards.

"A private word."

"If you insist."

Alexis led them into the drawing room and shut the door.

Katie said, "What have I done wrong this time?"

"I heard you were planning to go out to The Sanctuary," Alexis said.

"Listening in to my conversation, were you? Yes, I am. I'm getting ready and meeting Daisy there in an hour."

Alexis wasn't going to sugar-coat her response. Katie just had to be told it wasn't safe. "There is no way I'm letting you go to The Sanctuary. There's been case after case in the last few months of vampires attacking at will. Most likely the Dred vampires causing trouble in our home city."

Katie looked furious. "Excuse me? You aren't *letting* me? Who the hell do you think you are?"

"I'm the Duca of the Debrek clan, and when I give an order, it's followed," Alexis said matter-of-factly.

Katie stabbed a finger into Alexis's chest. "I'm not one of your vampires or Bhal's warriors. I answer to Byron and Amelia and no one else. You don't and will never have any say in my life, Alexis Villiers."

Why did Katie have to be so insubordinate?

"Listen, there are vampires turning humans and killing them

with impunity, and witches who hate vampires out there. Our world has never been more unstable in at least a hundred years, and you want to go out dancing. Alone?"

Katie looked her straight in the eye and said, "Why do you care if I'm safe or not?"

Alexis wasn't expecting that question. Her anger was making her flustered. "I'm responsible for the safety of the whole Debrek household."

"I don't buy it." Katie took a step closer to Alexis. So close that Alexis could smell her perfume and see the throbbing vein in her neck. There was still a mark from where the other vampire had fed, and Alexis hated it. It fuelled her anger and frustration.

Katie continued, "I don't ever see you trying to impose these rules on any other human in the household. So try again. Why does the safety of someone who you won't even feed from matter?"

Inside Alexis was bursting to tell Katie that she cared, that she wanted Katie, but instead she stared at her stiffly.

Katie said, "Just as I thought. I'm going now and maybe I'll meet a vampire who isn't repressed and emotionless."

Katie walked away, leaving Alexis alone. She looked over to the other side of the room, where long ago she discovered her Anna, dead by the Dred vampires' hands. Finding Anna like that had nearly destroyed her.

Alexis put her hands to her forehead and said, "No, I can't feel this again. I won't."

She had always been so determined that she would never let herself feel for another like she did for Anna, but it had crept up slowly on Alexis, and one taste of Katie's blood was enough to stir her heart again.

❖

At The Sanctuary club, Katie and Daisy were dancing with two werewolves who knew how to party. When the song came to an end, Katie said, "I think we'll sit down for a while. Thanks for the dance."

"We'll be here waiting for you if you change your mind, ladies." The werewolves gave a synchronized theatrical bow.

Katie took Daisy's arm, and they both chuckled.

"We've been popular tonight," Katie said.

They had been asked to dance by one person after another ever since they arrived. They took seats at the table.

"It's the novelty value, I think," Daisy said. "They don't often get humans in here."

"You know, Alexis was trying to stop me coming tonight."

Daisy grinned. "Oh, really. Someone feeling a little jealous?"

"Even if she was, Alexis is repressed up to her eyeballs. Besides she doesn't even like the taste of my blood. She just loves ordering me around."

Daisy raised an eyebrow. "You know, you haven't thought about one thing."

"What?" Katie asked.

Daisy leaned closer and said, "What if she didn't run because she didn't like the taste of your blood? What if she liked it too much, and it scared her?"

Katie's stomach flipped. Could that be true? Today when they had both been in the blood room, the feelings had been so intense. Did Alexis really—

Before Katie could contemplate further, Daisy doubled over in pain and grasped her neck.

"Daisy?" Katie took her hand. "There's something wrong. You're not going to dismiss this again. What's going on? Tell me the truth."

Daisy took a few breaths to calm herself, then pulled the scarf on her neck to the side. Katie gasped and covered her mouth with her hand. There was a fiery red vampire bite on Daisy's neck.

"Is that—"

Daisy covered over the bite again and nodded. "The bite Victorija gave me when the Dreds kidnapped Amelia? Yes."

Daisy had found Amelia in The Sanctuary, under the influence of Victorija's compulsion. She'd tried to help Amelia escape and to hold the Dreds off until Byron got there.

"The bite's never healed, and I keep getting spasms of pain from it. It's getting worse with every day that passes."

"Tell me exactly what happened when she bit you," Katie said.

"I got Amelia to the bathroom over there, and then Victorija and her Duca, Drasas, found us. I tried to protect Amelia. Victorija held me up by the neck, and I bit her trying to defend myself. She bled, and then Byron arrived at the club, and Victorija wanted to drink my blood before she retreated. She was angry, you see. She couldn't compel me. Victorija bit me, then stumbled back, looking at me funny."

Katie was shocked. "Oh God, you must be bonded by blood to Victorija."

"That's what I was frightened of. Byron's vamps said it would heal quickly, and it hasn't. It just keeps getting redder and sorer, but I can't believe that I could be bonded to an evil vampire."

"Daisy, do you know that not any human—or even any vampire—is compatible with a vampire for a blood bond?"

"What does that mean?" Daisy asked.

"It means that your DNA and only yours is compatible with Victorija's blood. She can't pick and choose who is blood bonded to her."

"That means…" Daisy looked terrified.

Katie moved her seat closer and squeezed Daisy's hand. "Remember what happened to Byron? The blood of the bonded is like a drug to the vampire. No other blood will sate their need. Every time you feel pain in your bite, that is Victorija's body crying out for your blood."

"Oh, shit," Daisy said.

"Daisy, you have to tell Byron and Amelia because when Victorija realizes what's wrong with her, when the Dreds find out, they will come for you and use you for your blood. She can't survive without it."

Daisy touched her hand to her head. "What, wait, I need to process this. Give me a little time to do some research and work out what this means, find out if there's a way to break this so-called bond. Then I promise I'll tell them."

Katie was reluctant. She knew Amelia would be angry that she kept this to herself, but if Daisy needed just a bit of time to get her head around it… "Okay, but just a short time. A few days."

"A week?" Daisy countered.

Katie sighed. She was going to get into big trouble over this. "Okay, but that's all, and you be careful."

Slaine approached them with a tray of drinks. "Here you are, ladies. Compliments of the two witches in the corner."

"Did they say why?" Katie asked.

"They just said to thank Daisy," Slaine said.

"What for?" Daisy asked.

Slaine shrugged. "They never said. Enjoy, ladies."

Katie looked over to the two witches, and they held up their drinks in a toast.

"We are popular tonight, aren't we?" Katie said.

CHAPTER FIVE

"It's your move, Alexis," Bhal said.

Alexis realized her thoughts had drifted away from her game. After Byron and Amelia retired for the evening, she and Bhal set up a game of chess in one of the upstairs sitting rooms.

They often played chess to unwind and discuss the day and the next day's security matters. But tonight Alexis's mind kept drifting to Katie alone at The Sanctuary. She was angry, worried, and frustrated.

"Sorry," Alexis said, then moved her pawn on the chess board.

"Alexis, why don't you just tell Katie you care about her?" Bhal said.

Alexis, who was taking a sip of whisky at the time, nearly spat it out. "What are you talking about?"

"You're angry she went out tonight."

"I'm only concerned for her and Daisy's safety, but of course Katie won't listen. She's behaving like a child."

"She's not a child any more, Alexis. You can't fool someone as old as me. I've seen your eyes follow her everywhere since she came home for holidays from university, and even more so since she began working with the clan."

"It doesn't matter how I feel—humans break and break our hearts. I saw the woman I loved dead in this house. Her throat ripped out by the Dred vampires. It destroyed me and it will not happen again. Besides, Katie can't stand me."

"I know what you went through. I was there to see your pain and grief, and believe me, I know how it feels to lose someone you love, but you can't fight love. Maybe she behaves like she doesn't like you because of the offhand way you treat her. You're trying to make her hate you, so you have every excuse not to love her."

Alexis knocked over her king in surrender. "I'm sorry, Bhal. I need some time to myself."

"Think hard, Duca. Some people aren't lucky enough to find love twice in their life."

Alexis didn't consider love luck. She walked out of the room and made her way back to her quarters. Was she really in love?

❖

Katie hugged Daisy outside The Sanctuary before she got into a taxi. "Are you sure you don't want me to wait until you get a taxi too?" Daisy asked.

"It's okay. Another will be along in a minute. Besides"—Katie pointed to the seven-foot-five doorman of The Sanctuary—"Otto will make sure I'm safe."

"Okay, well, let me know you get in safely," Daisy said.

"I will."

Katie waved as Daisy's taxi pulled away. She saw a few taxis stop further down the road, so she started to walk towards them. As she passed the alley at the side of the club, Katie heard moaning. She looked down the dark alleyway and wondered whether to go back and get Otto. Someone might be hurt. Alexis's warnings floated through her mind, but what if this was someone in trouble?

She looked down to the doorman again, and he was busy dealing with a pair of young, rowdy werewolves, so she decided to go down and see who needed help in the alley. As she started to walk down the dark alley, all she could hear was the clatter of her heels on the cobbled stones and moaning ahead. Fear gripped her. "What in God's name am I doing?"

Katie was about to turn back when the moaning got louder. Someone needed her help. She flicked the torch on her phone and started to walk again. All of a sudden, she saw a woman around her own age slumped against the wall of the building. Katie hurried over to her. She had a short blond pixie cut and a slim build.

"Hello, it's okay. I'll get you help."

"Help me, please," the woman mumbled.

Katie started to check her over and found a vampire bite on her and blood on her lips.

"I'm hungry, so hungry."

"Shit," Katie said. "She's been attacked and turned."

Katie had lived long enough with vampires to know the signs. This woman had been turned but hadn't completed the final step, feeding on a human. That's why she was in so much pain, and hungry. She had to make the choice to take the final step or die.

Katie needed to get her back to the house, so that she could be helped safely through the final stage.

"What's your name?" Katie asked.

"Josie," the woman wheezed.

"Okay, Josie. You're going to be okay. I'll get you help. Just stay calm."

Katie reached out and squeezed Josie's shoulder. Then everything happened so fast. Josie's eyes turned red, and she attacked Katie's wrist.

Alexis lay back on her bed staring at the ceiling. She had been in the same position since leaving Bhal and their chess game. All she could think about was Katie and worrying about her out on her own. Katie was so stubborn. Why couldn't she see that she was just trying to keep her safe?

Alexis had been shocked when Bhal called her out on her feelings. She didn't think anyone would have noticed, but then Bhal was an old, wise soul. Bhal was right about how much she cared for Katie. She consumed all of Alexis's thoughts. But it wasn't right—Katie was a young vibrant woman, while Alexis was a century-and-a-half-old vampire who'd had her heart broken in pieces before.

She sat up quickly and walked over to her chest of drawers. Underneath her clothes in the top drawer were a small painting of Anna and a lock of her hair. Alexis felt guilty about having feelings for Katie, but no matter how hard she tried, she couldn't shake them.

Alexis closed her eyes, and the movie of finding Anna dead, downstairs, at the hand of the Dreds, played in her mind as it always did, but then something different happened. Katie's smiling face came into her mind—her bright smile, her goodness, and the fire in her eyes when she and Alexis argued.

She took a moment and imagined giving Katie love. Spending her days excited to spend time with her, to share meals with her, to make Katie happy, to make love like any normal couple. The warmth of those thoughts started to fill her body with light and excitement.

She nearly jumped when she heard her phone ring. When she looked down at the screen it said: *Katie calling.*

Alexis answered immediately, tension and worry already gripping her. It was out of character for Katie to call her.

"Katie? What's wrong?"

"Alexis, I need help at The Sanctuary. I was just leaving to come home when I found a human injured. She's been forcibly turned. She needs our help."

"I'm coming. Stay with Otto at the front door."

She hung up and immediately called a group of her vampires to assemble downstairs. She wouldn't disturb the Principe until she had assessed the situation. True panic and fear gripped her heart and soul—she had to make sure Katie was safe. Newly turned vampires were volatile and unpredictable.

Alexis hurried downstairs to meet her team, and they set off quickly. When they arrived at the front door of The Sanctuary, Otto was standing by himself and looked none the wiser to the incident that was happening nearby.

When she got out of the car she could hear Katie down the side alley. "Luca, go and talk to Otto and see what he knows."

"Yes, Duca," Luca replied.

"The rest of you, follow me."

Alexis ran at super speed down the alleyway and found Katie

on the ground comforting the newly turned vampire. What was she doing by herself, down a dark alley, with a vampire?

Alexis's worry and fear were turning to anger. Katie just would not listen and was going to get herself killed.

Katie jumped in fright when Alexis appeared at her side. Alexis pulled Katie towards herself while her people checked over the newly turned vampire.

"Are you all right?" Alexis asked looking her up and down for injuries.

"I'm fine. Her name is Josie. She'd been turned and fed for the first time when I found her."

Alexis was thankful for that at least. The first blood a turned vampire drank was so overwhelming to their senses that they become possessive of the person they fed on, and addicted to their blood. It was a dangerous position to be in, as a new vampire could go too far and kill the person they fed on.

As a matter of policy, the Debreks always fed new vampires from another vampire, never the human staff, to keep everyone safe.

There was something strange about this scenario. Alexis sensed that Katie was nervous. Perhaps it was just the realization of the dangerous position she had put herself in. She needed to get Katie back to the car, so she was safe, and so she could read Katie the riot act. She wouldn't reprimand the head housekeeper of the Debreks in front of her vampires.

"Let's get to the car. My vampires will bring the young woman," Alexis said flatly.

Katie followed, and Alexis could hear Katie's heart beating so rapidly. Once they got into the car and shut the doors, Alexis turned to Katie and said with fury, "Once again you didn't listen to me and put yourself in a dangerous position. She could have attacked you, fed on you, killed you."

"I had no choice. I can't walk away when someone is injured," Katie said defensively.

"I'm not asking you to. You go and get Otto—he would have handled the situation—or you call me, and I'd be here as quickly as possible."

Katie pointed her finger at Alexis. "You always act like I'm a naughty ten-year-old. I can do what I want. I wanted to help a person in trouble. It's my decision how I do that, and it's none of yours."

Katie turned away from her quickly, but Alexis caught her arm and Katie hissed in pain.

"I'm sorry. I didn't mean to hurt you." Alexis didn't think she had grasped hard enough to hurt Katie.

Katie said coldly, "Just leave me alone."

Alexis sighed. If only she could tell Katie that she was angry because she was terrified of losing her. They rode back to the house in silence. Katie ran straight upstairs to her room, and Alexis could hear her bedroom door being slammed shut.

She and her guards took the new vampire down to the blood room where she would be fed and monitored until she was stable. Alexis rubbed her forehead. How different this night could have gone. She could have been carrying Katie's body back here, and she knew it would have destroyed her.

Alexis had to be tougher on Katie to keep her safe, and if that meant Katie hated her, then so be it.

❖

As soon as Katie got through her bedroom door, she tore off her coat to inspect her wound. Her wrist was a mess. This wasn't like in the blood room, where the Debrek clan vampires fed with respect and care. Josie had torn at her wrist in the frenzy of her need for her first blood.

The blood was seeping rapidly from her wound, so she hurried over to get the first aid box from her dressing table drawer. She quickly cleaned her wrist and bandaged it up tightly to stem the flow of blood.

She looked into the mirror—she looked pale. It must have been the blood loss and the stress of the incident. She had to hide the fact that Josie had fed from her, or Alexis would go crazy, and she'd never hear the end of it. Plus, Alexis would tell Byron, and then her parents would know. It would just be a big fuss over nothing.

Hopefully Josie would be happy with the blood available downstairs, and nobody need know.

❖

Alexis paced backwards and forwards in front of Byron's desk. She'd reported what happened to Byron when she got back, and Byron had dressed quickly and met Alexis downstairs.

"You have to have a word with her, Principe, because she won't listen to me."

Byron held up her hands. "Just take a breath, Duca. Katie is safe, but I will have a word."

"Katie forgets she is not like us. If she is attacked or killed, there is no second chance at life. She could be gone in an instant and I"—Alexis's emotions threatened to overcome her—"know how much the whole clan would be devastated if that happened."

"Yes." Byron sighed. "Her family is everything to me, so she must be well protected. I'll make sure she understands. Did you get any information out of our new vampire?"

"Nothing, she is having difficulties with the change. Her thirst for blood is extremely high. We found drug paraphernalia in her pockets."

"Good God. That's all we need," Byron said.

Humans with drug or alcohol problems always had a more difficult time turning, and their addiction often refocused to blood— always trying to get that first high of blood when they turned, chasing it relentlessly, and injuring and killing humans on the way, unless they got proper support.

"Okay, well, she'll need a tightly managed blood regime. I'll come down and see her tomorrow morning. Go and get some rest."

"Yes, Principe."

But as Alexis walked out of Byron's office, she knew she wouldn't sleep a wink. She would play tonight's events over and over in her mind, and the what might have been, like finding Katie drained of blood in the alley. The thought filled her with horror.

Alexis needed blood but didn't want to go downstairs to the blood room and disturb the medical care Josie was getting. A glass of blood and whisky would have to do.

Alexis walked to her room and poured out a glass of Debrek Special Reserve blood and downed it quickly. She then got a large glass of whisky to try to dull the aching want she had to be with Katie, protecting her, and the deep hunger she had for Katie's blood.

Her mind kept being tortured by images of finding Katie drained of blood and dead in that alley. Then a different memory struck her. When she'd tried to grasp Katie's arm, she remembered the discomfort Katie showed. Alexis didn't think she had grasped her that hard.

"No, it couldn't be, could it?"

Then the suspicion hit her: Had the newly turned vampire fed on Katie?

Alexis slammed down her whisky and stormed to Katie's room. She knocked hard on her door, and when Katie opened the door, Alexis pushed past her.

"What are you doing?" Katie demanded to know.

"Take off your dressing gown," Alexis ordered.

Katie crossed her arms defensively. "Excuse me? I don't take off my clothes to order, especially your orders."

Alexis motioned for Katie's arm, gently pushed up the sleeve of the dressing gown, and saw a bloodstained bandage on Katie's wrist. Josie had fed on Katie. Alexis felt a mixture of panic, jealousy, and anger. She didn't know what to say. Alexis's mind raced with all the emotions she was feeling and processing how dangerous it was to have Katie in the same house as Josie.

Katie gulped hard. She didn't know how to react to silence from a clearly angry Alexis. She cradled her wrist and said, "I kept it a secret because I knew everyone, especially you, would make such a fuss, and Josie couldn't help it, she was just following her instincts."

"You know what this means?" Alexis said. "Josie will now be ravenous for your blood."

"I'll feed her if I need to."

Alexis shouted, "No," and backed Katie up against the wall. Katie watched her eyes glowing red and her fangs erupted.

"I don't want *any* vampire feeding on you."

Katie gasped in shock. Alexis was jealous, demanding, and the look of want and hunger in her eyes was desperate. Katie's body reacted to her. Her skin tingled and tightened with need.

The want and sexual tension was palpable, and Katie was getting caught up in Alexis's need. She reached out and caressed her cheek, and Alexis groaned. Then she touched her finger to Alexis's fang and pierced her own finger, making the blood flow into Alexis's mouth. Alexis closed her eyes and moaned, sucking her finger into her mouth.

It was clear Alexis did like the taste of her blood. Had she been wrong all along?

Katie put her hand on Alexis's neck and pulled her close. Katie looked deeply into Alexis's eyes and saw fear, as well as want. Alexis looked like she was fighting what she wanted.

"Kiss me," Katie said.

"No, it's not right."

"It's right if we want it to be," Katie whispered.

Katie touched her lips to Alexis's and ran her tongue along her lower lip. Alexis met the tip of Katie's tongue with hers and then sucked in Katie's lower lip.

"Yes, kiss me." Katie lightly scratched the back of Alexis's neck. Her heart was pounding as well as her sex. She needed Alexis to touch her.

And then out of nowhere, Alexis pulled away from her. "No, no, I can't." Then she sped out of the room at super speed, leaving Katie trying to catch her breath.

"You ran from me again. What's wrong with me?" Katie shouted, knowing that the Duca would hear her with her exceptional hearing.

CHAPTER SIX

The next morning Amelia was sitting at her dressing table in her silk nightdress straightening her hair while Byron got dressed, and Byron told her about what happened last night.

"This woman—Josie—fed on Katie? Is she all right?" Amelia said.

"Last night all we knew was that Katie found a newly turned vampire. Alexis came to update me while you were in the shower."

"But is she all right?"

"Yes," Byron said straightening her tie. "Alexis took a team to The Sanctuary last night. Apparently, Katie didn't want to tell Alexis or myself because she thought we'd overreact, but she doesn't understand the severity of being a new vampire's first blood."

"What does it mean?" Amelia put down her straightener.

Byron walked over to her and put her hands on Amelia's shoulders. "Being newly turned is a dangerous time for a vampire. Remember what happened to me when I first became a born vampire?"

Amelia nodded and grasped Byron's hand on her shoulder. Byron had gone so wild that she had nearly drained and killed Katie's ancestors. Luckily Bhal got there in time and saved the family. That guilt always lay heavily on Byron, and since then the Debreks pledged to take care of Katie's family. "I know, sweetheart."

"If the care of the transitioning vampire isn't done within a clan, then the vampire will simply want to drain whoever provides first blood to them. It's like an addiction, that first shot of heroin, that first bottle of whisky—the new vampire's hunger for that human is insatiable."

Amelia sighed. "Katie."

"Exactly, but in this case things might be even more difficult. Alexis tells me that they found drug paraphernalia in this young woman's pockets. If she already has a problem with addiction, then her need for Katie's blood will be all the worse."

Amelia turned around on her stool to face Byron and said, "You're not going to let Katie near her, are you?"

"Of course not, mia cara." Byron took her hand and helped her up. "That would only encourage her addiction—besides, Alexis would kill her. Josie is being provided with rich vampire blood."

"You mean Alexis is actually showing how much she loves Katie?" Amelia smiled.

"You may have been right about Alexis and Katie, but all I know for certain is that Alexis doesn't want her anywhere near Josie. I've never seen her so animated about something in over a century."

"I knew it. I can always tell when there's romance brewing."

Byron slipped her hands around her waist and said, "Maybe it's the witch in you?"

Amelia remembered they were going to The Portal bookshop today to make contact with a witch who might help her. "Do you want to postpone today?"

"No, it's important. This is the first good lead we've had and the first witch willing to talk to us. I need to go down and speak to this new vampire, but then we can go whenever you're ready."

"I promised Alexis I'd talk to Katie too. What she did last night was far too risky."

There was a knock at the door. "It's Katie, may I come in? I have tea."

"Yes, come in," Amelia called out, then whispered to Byron, "I'll talk to her, okay?"

"Thank you, Principessa."

❖

Alexis felt like her skin was crawling as she paced outside the basement room where they were keeping Josie. Byron had promised to meet her here and talk to their new vampire.

Josie had been nothing but trouble all night as she struggled with her need for blood. The blood bags and vampire donors were not being received well.

The secure room was next to the blood room, and Alexis had relayed a message to Katie to not come down to the basement under any circumstances. Alexis also had the room and the basement under guard.

If it was up to her, they would have turfed this woman out onto the streets. She was too much of a risk under the same roof as Katie, but she knew Byron would always do the honourable thing, just as she had done for Alexis after she was turned.

Normally Alexis agreed with Byron's approach, but Katie's safety was everything to her, and her stress over protecting Katie was even more heightened after last night. She had tasted Katie's blood again and it was like tasting Elysium. She closed her eyes and listened to the heavy thud in her chest. Normally her heart beat only every so often, but since last night it had been pounding like a mortal's.

A crash was heard from inside the room, and Alexis heard Josie shout, "Get me that girl's blood now."

Alexis's temper was near breaking. She burst into the room and found blood bags burst over the floor, and one of her vampires trying to clear it up.

"Leave us, Nathan."

Josie was breathing heavily and leaning on the back of the chair. She didn't look good. Dried blood was all around her mouth, and she looked dishevelled and wild. "The big boss is back," Josie said with a sneer.

"I'm not the boss. Byron is our clan leader, and if you wish to become part of the Debrek clan, then you had better drink the blood we are giving you and start behaving properly."

"I don't want that blood. It's not working. I need the girl from last night—Katie. She's the only one who can satisfy me."

"Katie is not going to be an option for you, so you'd better get used to the blood offered to you," Alexis said.

"Why are you keeping her from me? I found her, I tasted her, she's mine."

Alexis grabbed Josie's T-shirt and pulled her up to her full height. "Katie is not yours and never will be."

"Why do you care so much?" Josie spat. Alexis stayed silent and Josie said, "Is she your girlfriend?"

"Katie is not my girlfriend, but she is off the menu for you and always will be, newbie."

A smirk appeared on Josie's face. "Oh, I get it. You'd like her to be, wouldn't you? Well you're out of luck. She's mine. I tasted her blood and claimed it. She tastes so sweet. I think I'll make her moan while I drink her."

Alexis couldn't hold her restraint any longer. She was sick of other vampires feeding on Katie and hiding her emotions. All of her repressed anger rose up in a flash, and she smashed Josie against the wall, still holding her T-shirt. Josie's body made an indentation in the wall, and the plaster crumbled to the floor.

She grasped Josie's jaw and squeezed tightly. "If you get within a hundred yards of Katie, I will take the head from your body, and you will die a vampire death. Do you understand me?"

"Put her down, Duca."

Alexis turned to the side and saw Byron standing in the room. She had been so caught up in her fury that she hadn't heard her enter.

"Duca?" Byron said firmly.

Alexis took a breath and the red mist started to fall from her eyes. She let go of Josie and went to stand by Byron.

Josie slumped against the wall. "Who are you?"

"Byron Debrek. Leader of the Debrek clan."

Josie got up and sat on the chair. "Is this how you treat all the people you help?"

"Your behaviour couldn't have been exemplary if you made

my Duca react like that. My people tell me you won't accept the blood we have provided for you."

"I want the girl from last night. I need *her* blood."

Byron straightened her tie. "That will not be possible. This hunger will get better if you let us help you, and we will give you safety and purpose within the Debrek clan. But it's up to you to take it. It's a dangerous world out there for a new vampire, but you have to want your place with us. The Debrek clan is run with respect and consent above all. Is that something you would like to be a part of?" Josie just stared at the ground. So Byron said, "I'll leave you to think about it. Duca? You're with me."

❖

"I know it was stupid, but..." Katie sat on the end of Amelia's bed talking about last night.

Amelia was sitting at her dressing table. "But what?"

"I just can't walk away from someone in pain," Katie finished.

"No one is asking you to. I couldn't either, but call Byron or Alexis or Bhal, even, and they will take care of it for you. Do you know what it would do to Byron if anything happened to you?"

"No, I never thought about it."

Amelia got up and sat beside Katie on the bed. "She would be devastated. You know how much she loves your family, and now that your mum and dad are away working for her parents, she feels it's her reasonability to take care of you. Not to mention how hurt our Duca would be."

"Alexis?" Katie snorted. "She took great pleasure in telling me what an idiot I was."

"She was concerned, Katie, as we all were. She asked Byron to remind you that you were mortal, unlike most of us, and if anything happens to you, there's no second chances. I agree with her. I think she really cares, Katie."

"She has a funny way of showing it, but I take your point. Tell the Principe I'll be more careful," Katie said.

Amelia hugged Katie. "Thank you. We all love you and care about you."

❖

Later that day Amelia and Byron travelled to the bookshop that the informant had told them about. The Portal was London's oldest occult bookshop, and Amelia had to admit that she was nervous, and somewhat scared.

Ever since the Grand Duchess told her she was half witch and that her parents weren't her true parents, Amelia had been desperate to find out about her past. But she was also scared about finding out the truth. It would change everything she felt certain that she knew about herself.

Amelia grasped Byron's hand tightly as they walked up to the bookshop door.

"Don't be nervous. I'm with you," Byron said.

Byron held the door open for Amelia and the bell on the door rang. They walked in and looked around at the shop. It was a typical old, dusty independent bookshop, which didn't look as if it had many customers. There was a counter and till at the other end of the shop.

Amelia and Byron walked up there and found an older black woman with salt-and-pepper coloured ringlets, and a young woman beside her, who was currently scowling.

"What do you want, vampire?"

"Piper, no," the older woman said.

Byron straightened her tie and said, "I'm Byron Debrek. I contacted you about some information we needed."

"Yes, yes. My name is Magda, and this is my granddaughter Piper."

"Charmed," Byron said somewhat sarcastically. "This is my wife, Amelia Debrek."

Magda suddenly looked very interested. "Tell me, what was your maiden name, Mrs. Debrek?"

"Honey, Amelia Honey."

Magda looked to her granddaughter in some kind of silent communication, then held her hand out to shake Amelia's in greeting.

Amelia took Magda's hand, and she felt a warm shot of electricity go up her arm. Magda herself shuddered.

"Welcome, Amelia."

Magda turned to Piper and said, "Bring some chairs for our guests."

Piper rolled her eyes but did as she was asked. Byron declined the chance to sit, but Amelia hopped up on a stool.

"You knew Rose, vampire?" Magda said.

Byron shifted uncomfortably. Amelia knew who Rose was—a former lover—and it was natural that Byron had many lovers over the centuries, but she didn't like to think about it too deeply.

"Yes, that's right," Byron replied.

Magda smiled. "One of the very best witches in our coven's history. She left extensive books and papers preserving her thoughts, view, spells, and insights, and in one such notebook, she told us to expect a woman named Amelia."

Amelia was too shocked to speak, but Byron said, "She did? What did she say?"

"Simply that whoever the high priestess was when Amelia came along was to help her because she had a very special future."

Amelia looked at Byron. This was what she was afraid of, learning something overwhelming. Byron took her hand and squeezed it.

"How did you find out you had witch blood in you?" Magda asked.

"The Grand Duchess told me," Amelia said.

Magda chuckled. "The most powerful witch in the world who married a vampire—a bit like yourself, Amelia."

There were parallels between her and Byron's great-great-grandmother, Amelia supposed.

The Grand Duchess, then simply Lucia, had fallen in love with Byron's great-great-grandfather Cosimo. She'd insisted that she would only be with him, and marry him, if he and his clan would vow to only take blood by consent. That became the Debreks' sacred vow.

"Can you tell me more about my past?" Amelia asked.

"First of all, have you ever used your power?"

"Only a few times, when I've been angry or threatened."

Magda looked at Piper, then back to Amelia. "We're starting from scratch then. Okay, first of all, do you know the New Forest area in the south of England?"

"Of course I do. I was brought up not far from there," Amelia said.

"I'm sure you have been there too, vampire?" Magda said to Byron.

"Yes, a few times in my travels."

"Excellent. Go to the New Forest. It's a place long associated with witchcraft and the occult. An ancient coven met there, and there are witches' cottages where they lived and worked. When you're there, open yourself up, listen, feel the energy. There's an ancient magic drawn from the sacred land of the New Forest. If you do that, come back, and I will instruct you in witchcraft and magic."

Amelia felt in that moment that if they went there, nothing would ever be the same.

❖

Drasas was nervous. She had agreed to meet Madam Anka, but she couldn't fight the feeling she was doing something behind Victorija's back. After Asha delivered Madam Anka's message, Drasas did as Asha suggested and researched the witch.

What she found were whispers of legends, a woman who wielded great power, a woman who drew her power from the ancient Celtic dark gods but hadn't been heard of in a long, long time. Drasas was intrigued and so agreed to meet her at a local park.

She went on her own and made sure no one knew where she was going. Drasas wandered over to a bench by the duck pond and sat down. The park was full of happy, smiling families, humans running, humans feeding the ducks. It was sickening.

"Hello, Drasas."

Drasas felt a shiver down her spine. That voice was like honey. She turned to the side and saw the woman to match the voice.

"Madam Anka?" Drasas croaked.

Anka smiled and held out her hand to shake hers. She had light brown skin and dark hair tinged with blond highlights. Drasas took her hand and gasped. Anka's eyes changed to yellow for a split second, then returned to normal.

Drasas's heart was pounding. This woman had such a powerful, sensual aura, and it was enveloping her.

"Please call me Anka."

Anka's bone structure, her dark make-up, and those eyes all drew Drasas in.

"Thank you for meeting with me," Anka said.

"My pleasure, Anka. How can I help you?"

Anka lifted her hand and indicated to all the humans around them. "Look at them, Drasas. What do you see?"

"Pathetic, weak humans," Drasas said.

"I see we are of the same mind, Drasas, and yet who is hiding in the shadows? Vampires, witches, fae, werewolves, all of us who are the most powerful creatures in the world are skulking around, when those humans should be worshipping at our feet."

Drasas turned around and said excitedly, "Yes, exactly my feelings."

Anka placed the tips of her black polished nails on Drasas's leg and stroked her thigh up and down. A fire was ignited in her sex with the barest touch. Drasas had sex on offer whenever she wanted from the vampires under her command and any human she fancied, but nothing had ever felt as exciting as that barest touch from Anka.

Anka suddenly pulled her hand away, and Drasas hated the loss. She wanted more.

"I represent a group that believes the time for living in the shadows is over," Anka said. "There was a time when the high priestess and other paranormal creatures were worshipped by humans, and now we are nothing."

"Who is in your group?" Drasas asked.

"Oh, small groups of dark witches, some werewolves, many shapeshifters, and more flock to us every day. We wish to bring a new age of darkness to the earth. One where we are the masters."

"How can I help?"

"I would like a powerful vampire clan to join our numbers. One without the sickening ideals of the Debreks," Anka spat.

"I agree with that wholeheartedly, but why come to me and not Victorija? She is a born vampire."

"Ah, yes. A born vampire, the most powerful vampires in the world," Anka said.

Drasas felt a pang of jealousy. She would never experience the fear of others that kind of power caused. She would always just be an ordinary turned vampire.

"I've heard that Victorija has been indisposed lately and that you have been virtually running the clan."

Drasas sat a little taller in her seat. "Yes, I have been. Ever since my Principe visited the UK and killed her grandmother, she's been different. She can't satiate her hunger and has no interest in striking back at the Debreks."

"The Debreks," Anka said with disdain. "They behave like the human world they are part of. They don't deserve the power that the Debrek bank brings."

"I've been telling my Principe that we need to strike against them while they are distracted, but she won't listen," Drasas said.

"Well, how about this. I visit your Principe, help you find out what's wrong with her, and help you—I mean, help your clan step out of the Debrek shadow."

Drasas got the feeling she shouldn't be planning this without Victorija's knowledge, but the Principe was ill, something was weakening her, so she had to step in.

Anka touched Drasas's cheek, and she shivered. "I can make you great, Drasas. Imagine dark witches fighting alongside your vampires. It could be great."

Anka had Drasas in the palm of her hand. She knew this was the perfect way into the Dred clan.

"*I* could be great…" Drasas said.

"Off you go then. I'll visit you and Victorija soon."

Once Drasas left her, Asha stepped out of the shadows. "Is she everything you thought she would be, Madam?"

"Oh yes. All that and more." She looked down at the gold ring with a purple stone on her finger. "I've collected werewolf, witch, and fae power, and now I need a born vampire's power. I need Victorija for that, but I'll control Drasas, and she'll make it so easy." Anka laughed.

CHAPTER SEVEN

Katie walked through the entrance hallway of the Debrek mansion. It was eleven o'clock and everything was quiet. Once Byron and Amelia retired to their room, most of the staff finished for the night, apart from a security team patrolling the house.

Katie had dismissed the housekeeping staff and was on her way to the kitchen to make a cup of herbal tea before bed. She walked downstairs to the kitchen, and only Dane and a junior chef were left.

"Evening, Katie, can I get you anything?" Dane asked.

"No, I'm just going to make a cup of tea."

Dane stretched her arms and yawned. "We'll leave you to it then. Goodnight, Katie."

Once Dane and her junior chef left, the large old kitchen was quiet as a grave. Katie pressed the kettle on and got a mug, teabag, and spoon. She brought them back over to the kettle and waited for the kettle to boil.

Katie liked this time of night for its quiet solitude. The Debrek house was always a busy place with vampires and housekeeping staff milling around, not to mention the decorators they had in at the moment causing mess everywhere.

But this was her quiet time. She would often sit here in the empty kitchen listening to the radio, alone and absorbing the quiet, but tonight she was tired, so she was going to take her tea back to her room and look at her iPad in bed.

The night before she hadn't had much sleep after the incident with Josie, the pain in her wrist and the nagging feeling that Alexis was right about being careful keeping her awake. It was annoying when Alexis was right—plus, she had to admit her body wanted Alexis. Since she was a teenager, she'd had complicated feelings over Alexis. Now her crush had developed into need and want, then hurt, anger, and frustration.

"Alexis." Katie sighed.

No matter what stage she was at, Alexis always managed to stir up her passionate emotions, whether anger or want.

Katie filled her cup up with water. Hopefully the camomile tea would soothe her to a restful sleep. She felt a breeze and the hairs on the back of her neck stood up.

There was someone behind her, and she felt fear. It couldn't be one of the Debrek clan—she would never feel fear because of them—and Alexis was more likely to make her heart speed up with excitement than fear, she was loath to admit.

She heard heavy breathing and forced herself to turn around slowly. It was Josie. She looked worse than when she had last seen her. Her eyes were red and dried blood was caked over her mouth and chin.

"Josie? Hi, aren't they looking after you in the basement?" Katie knew this was a dangerous situation. A dangerous situation of her own making, she heard Alexis say in her head.

She had to keep Josie talking and hope either someone came down to the kitchen or she found her chance to run.

"They were, *are*, but I had to see you, Katie. Last night is engraved on my mind, and I wanted to thank you for looking after me and giving me your blood."

Katie could see Josie's eyes fix on her jugular vein. Her heart beat furiously. This was bad. *How are you getting out of this one?*

"I'm happy to help. The Debrek clan is happy to help," Katie said.

Josie reached for her cheek and caressed it. "I need your help again, Katie. I'm so hungry, and I can't get your blood from my mind."

"But it's not a good idea. Didn't Byron and Alexis explain that to you?"

Josie slid her hand from Katie's cheek into her hair and grasped it tightly. "I know what I need, Katie, and it's in you."

"You have to have consent to take blood in the Debrek clan. That was explained to you, and I do not consent, Josie."

"I don't care about your stupid rules. I take what I need." Josie's teeth erupted, and Katie knew she was trapped. She pushed her hand behind her and felt her mug of tea. Maybe she had one chance to get away.

Katie grasped the handle of the mug, and just as Josie was about to strike, Katie threw the mug and its contents over her attacker. Josie squealed in pain and covered her face with her hands as the boiling liquid scalded her skin. Katie ran as fast as she could up the kitchen stairs and into the entrance hall.

She had to get upstairs to get help. Katie didn't look back but ran up the grand staircase and made it to the landing. She looked down and saw Josie below in the hallway.

"Come back. You're mine!"

Katie had to get to one of the bedrooms. Suddenly Josie jumped from below and landed right in front of her.

"You didn't think you could outrun a vampire, did you?"

Katie didn't have time to think. What happened next was a blur, until she felt Josie's fangs bite deep into her neck, and her strength ebbed away.

❖

Alexis was sitting at her writing desk making up this week's security rosters. The Debrek clan had gone computerized many, many years ago and had moved into using apps on phones and tablets for the running of the banking business and clan.

Byron took to these changes like a duck to water, but Alexis was an old-fashioned person at heart. Nothing felt better than using a scratchy fountain pen and paper. She looked up at the painted picture of her mother that she kept on her desk.

"If only you could see me now, Mama."

She often wondered if her mother would be understanding of her circumstances or if she would simply see her as a bloodthirsty vampire.

Not that she had a great deal of choice after Victorija had found her on the battlefield dying from her wounds. It should have been her fate to die with honour, fighting for King and country, but that was snatched away from her when Victorija fed her own blood to her.

Alexis put her pen in its holder and rubbed her face. She chose to believe that her mother would love her no matter what. She always had before, even when she found out about her interest in women rather than men, at a time when that was unthinkable.

Alexis was startled by a strange feeling passing over her body. The kind of feeling when it seemed like someone had walked over your grave. Then goosebumps erupted on her arms and legs.

She listened quietly for any sounds and then heard a woman scream from the other side of the house. Then a realization hit her in the chest. It was Katie. Alexis ran for her at full speed.

The staff rooms were on other side of the house from the staircase, and so she couldn't be there instantly with her vampire super speed, but she was soon approaching the main staircase.

What she saw there made her feel like she was having her guts wrenched out. Katie was lying on the floor with Josie feeding on her neck. "No!"

Alexis pulled Josie off her, and without any thought, snapped her neck and threw her off the staircase. Josie landed on the marble floor below.

She fell to her knees and cradled Katie, looking for signs that she was okay, but her lips were turning blue. "No, no! Don't leave me, Katie," Alexis roared.

Suddenly Byron was by her side. "What happened?"

"Josie was feeding on her." Alexis couldn't stop the tears from rolling down her face.

Byron felt for a pulse on her neck and Amelia arrived by her side.

"Katie? Is she okay?" Amelia asked.

"There's barely a pulse," Byron said.

Alexis pulled up her sleeve and bit into her own wrist. The only way Alexis could see to save her was to turn Katie into a vampire. She was just about to drip her blood into Katie's mouth when Byron caught her wrist to stop her.

"No, Alexis, she hasn't consented," Byron said.

Alexis wasn't thinking about anything apart from Katie's well-being and the rage and panic inside her.

Amelia gasped and said, "I...I think I can see her spirit leaving her body."

Alexis growled, "I don't care. I'm not losing someone else I love to a vampire. Let me go."

Byron let her go, and Alexis brought her wrist close to Katie's lips. "I'm only doing this because I love you. if you hate me for it, I'll just have to live with that."

"Don't be like Victorija, Alexis. Remember what she took from you, and don't take Katie's humanity."

Alexis looked up at Byron through tear-filled eyes. "I have to."

"Stop." Bhal came barrelling towards them. "Let me, Duca." She kneeled down next to Katie and poured some liquid from her whisky flask. It looked like plain water when it pooled in her hand.

Bhal looked up at Alexis and said, "Trust me, Alexis."

Alexis nodded and Bhal dribbled the water from her hands onto Katie's lips and into her mouth. Alexis couldn't breathe as she stared at Katie's lifeless body.

After an anxious few seconds, Amelia said, "Her spirt is going back—it's going back into her body."

Alexis pleaded, "Breathe, Katie, breathe."

Then Alexis heard the best sound she'd ever heard, Katie gasping for breath.

"She's alive, she's alive," Amelia said.

Alexis had never felt such relief in her life. She took Katie's hand and kissed it.

Byron stood and said, "Right, let's get her to bed, and I'll call the doctor."

Alexis felt shattered inside but would allow no one else to lift Katie. She hesitated and said to Bhal, "Thank you, Bhal. I owe you everything."

"You owe me nothing, Duca." Bhal smiled.

Alexis had heard the rumours about Bhal's so-called super-powers but had never seen them in action apart from her incredible strength. Clearly, she could bring life back from the brink too.

Alexis carried Katie to her room, followed by Byron and Amelia, and laid her down on her bed. When she took a step back, the realization of what had happened, and what she nearly did, hit her. Her hands started to shake and she twisted and turned.

"Alexis? Are you all right?" Amelia said.

"I need some air." Alexis sped off down to the kitchen and opened the back door, just in time to vomit onto the ground.

Once she finished she wiped her mouth with her shaking hand. "What did I nearly do?"

Guilt descended on her like a cloud. Consent was sacrosanct in their clan, and she'd nearly violated it, violated everything she believed in. She was just like Victorija, and the scary thing was, she'd do it again if it meant saving Katie.

Alexis had to face it—she was in love with Katie and would do anything to make her safe and keep her alive.

❖

"How is she, Doctor?" Byron asked.

Dr. Tyler McKenzie took off her stethoscope and ruffled her short blond hair. "It's remarkable that she's even alive."

Amelia gripped Byron's hand tighter. Tyler checked the lines on the blood transfusion bag that she had set up by the side of the bed and looked up at the housemaid standing by the door. "Could you get Katie as many hot water bottles as you have?"

"Yes, Doctor." The maid quickly left the room.

"Despite the fact that she should be dead," Tyler said, "she's doing as well as can be expected. The blood transfusion should make her stronger, but she will need time to recover."

Tyler's family had been serving as the Debreks' private doctors for two hundred years. They were another human family who had earned the Debreks' trust. Not that vampires needed much medical care, but they did from time to time, and the humans in the household certainly did.

Byron was thankful for Tyler. Otherwise they'd have to find a way to explain to the accident and emergency department at the hospital why Katie was drained of blood and had bite marks on her neck.

"What do we need to do for her?" Amelia asked Tyler.

"Mostly give her time and complete bed rest. Whatever Bhal did, I don't know, but Katie was dead and had her soul literately ripped from death, then put back into her body. That shock will take its toll on the body and mind. Katie will be weak and will need to regain her strength slowly."

"We'll take care of her, Dr. Tyler," Amelia said.

Byron nodded. "Like the finest of china. You have my word."

Amelia said to Byron, "I'd better go and tell Alexis. She's waiting at the door."

"Of course."

Amelia walked to the door and slipped out quietly. She found Alexis pacing up and down.

"How is she, Principessa?"

Amelia had never seen such panic, such strength of emotion, from Alexis since she had met her. In fact until now, Amelia thought Alexis would never let anyone see the strength of the feelings she had for Katie. She was in love and had announced it to everyone as Katie lay dying. "She's doing okay. Dr. McKenzie says she will recover, but it will take some time and a lot of care. What happened to Josie?"

"By the time our guards were alerted, she had fled," Alexis said with anger.

"But you snapped her neck and threw her off the stairs. She must have broken every bone in her body."

"She's a vampire."

Even though Amelia knew that logically, this was all still

new enough that the vampires' healing ability still caught her by surprise.

"She will be fully recovered?" Alexis said anxiously.

"What?" Amelia had been lost in her thoughts.

"Katie, will she be fully recovered?"

"Yes, Katie's getting a blood transfusion now to help her recover. Come in and see her."

Alexis had a look of fear on her face. "No, I'll leave her to rest. Thank you, Principessa."

She gave Amelia a bow of the head and walked away quickly. Amelia sighed. Alexis was one loved-up vampire, but she was terrified of it.

Alexis awoke with a start, her heart pounding incredibly fast. She was sitting at her desk and must have fallen asleep. Alexis rubbed her face and then looked at the time.

"Five in the morning."

She couldn't remember what her nightmare was about exactly, but she woke up screaming Katie's name. *Katie.* Now, what happened last night and what she had nearly lost and done hit her like a ton of bricks.

Guilt enveloped her, and she hurried over to the whisky decanter and poured out a large glass, to take the edge off her emotions and hunger to feed. As she lifted the glass, her hand shook.

"Shit." Alexis put her hand to her forehead in frustration. "I'm just like Victorija."

She could have changed Katie's life forever. She fully expected Byron to take her position as Duca from her and banish her from the clan. Alexis had broken their most sacred rule and she deserved everything she got.

But her banishment from the clan would be nothing compared to not seeing Katie again, even if it was only from a distance. How could she live with this love and not act upon it, bare her soul to Katie, and beg her forgiveness for nearly turning her into a vampire?

❖

Katie slowly became aware of voices around her. She opened her eyes and saw Amelia beside her bed, talking to some woman she didn't know. Then she felt the pain in her neck and deep cold right down into her bones.

"You're awake." Amelia smiled.

"Yes," Katie said hoarsely.

"How do you feel?"

"My neck hurts, and I'm so cold." Katie pulled the covers right under her chin.

The woman she didn't know said, "I'm Dr. Tyler McKenzie. May I take your pulse?"

"McKenzie? I know that name," Katie said.

Tyler smiled. "You probably remember my father. He was the Debrek family physician. I've taken over from him."

When Tyler lifted her hand she felt the drip in her arm for the first time. Then what happened last night hit her.

"Josie," Katie said with panic.

Amelia stroked her hair. "It's okay, stay calm. She's gone."

"But she caught me and was feeding on my neck…What happened after that?"

Amelia looked at Tyler, "Could you excuse us, Doctor."

"Certainly. You're doing fine, Katie. Just get lots of rest."

Tyler gathered her bag and left the room. Amelia sat down on the chair at the side of Katie's bed and took her hand.

"What's the last thing you remember?"

Katie squeezed her eyes shut and saw Josie looming over her in the kitchen. She opened her eyes and looked at Amelia.

"I was in the kitchen making tea—" Katie rubbed her throat with her other hand. It was raspy and sore.

"Take your time," Amelia said.

"Josie came in and wanted my blood. I threw my cup of boiling hot tea on her and ran. I got to the landing and then up the stairs, and

Josie was already there. Then I just remember her biting my neck and drifting out of consciousness. What happened after that?"

"Alexis found you," Amelia said.

"Alexis?" Katie had been dreaming about her for a reason.

"Yes, she pulled Josie off you, broke her neck, and threw her off the stairs."

"And I was okay?" Amelia hesitated, making Katie suspicious. "Please tell me? I want to know the truth."

"Byron and I got to you after that and I saw…I saw your spirit lifting out of your body. That only happened to me once before, when my grandmother was dying, when I was a little girl, but my mum always told me I was dreaming. It must be one of my abilities, being part witch."

Katie felt even colder than she had before. "I was dead?"

Amelia hesitated to tell Katie the truth. It would be upsetting but Amelia would have liked to know if it was her. The only thing she wouldn't tell her was that Alexis tried to turn her in order to save her. That was not her truth to tell—it was up to Alexis, and she didn't want to make things worse between them.

"Very near, but Bhal saved you before we lost you."

"The same way she saved my ancestors?" Katie said.

Byron had told Amelia that Bhal had saved Katie's ancestors after Byron lost control and attacked them.

"Yes, it seems to be one of Bhal's superpowers to bring people back from the brink of death by drinking water from her hands."

"And Josie?"

"Escaped once she recovered enough from her injuries. Everyone was distracted by gathering around you. But she won't get near you again, I promise." Amelia noticed Katie was shaking badly. "Are you okay?"

"I'm so cold." Katie's teeth were chattering too.

Amelia picked up her phone and dialled. "I'll get your hot water bottles refreshed. Norah is looking after the house management while you're not well. Hi, Norah? Could you refresh Katie's hot water bottles? Thanks."

Amelia got up and took a blanket from the armchair on the other side of the room. "In the meantime, this will help a bit." She tucked the fleece blanket around her. "The doctor said being cold is a side effect of being brought back from the edge—"

"Of death?" Katie finished for her.

Amelia nodded. "Yes, but don't dwell on that. You're here now, and we're going to look after you. Byron will come and see you soon. Is there anything you'd like?"

"Hot tea please, oh, and could you ask Bhal and Alexis if I could see them. To thank them?"

Amelia smiled. "Of course I will."

She didn't know how Alexis would react to that. She was so emotional after what happened last night.

"Alexis was right," Katie said.

"Right about what?"

"About The Sanctuary being too dangerous for humans alone, at the moment. I caused all this because of my stubbornness, by not listening to Alexis."

"No," Amelia said firmly, "it happened because you have a kind, loving heart and wanted to save someone who had been attacked and turned by a rogue vampire. You weren't to know that Josie would struggle to cope with her blood hunger. You're a kind soul, Katie."

❖

Alexis got a message from Byron to come down to her office. After last night she didn't even know if she would still be the Debrek Duca. She had broken their most sacred rule, or at least tried to.

She hesitated on the top landing and looked along to Katie's room. There were members of the household staff coming and going, taking care of Katie as she should have done. Her security measures had failed and allowed Josie to escape.

She didn't blame the guards on Josie's holding room. She had slipped out while the guard was changing shift.

Alexis blamed herself. She should have been there, guarding

that vampire every second, and protecting the woman she loved. There was no point hiding it or burying it deep down any more—she loved Katie Brekman, and she'd nearly lost her.

God knew what Katie thought of her now—probably despised her now that she knew what Alexis tried to do. Alexis despised herself for it. She shook her head and carried on downstairs to Byron's office.

Alexis took a breath, knocked, then entered. Byron was working on her computer, her lit cigar burning in the ashtray. Without looking up Byron said, "Sit down, Duca."

This was it, she was going to lose her place in the clan, and her life would have no meaning.

Byron lifted her cigar and took a puff, then sat back in her leather chair. "Have you been in to see Katie?"

"No. How is she?"

"Dr. McKenzie tells me she is in no danger but is extremely weak and will take some time to recover."

"I'm glad to hear she's well," Alexis said.

"I wanted to talk to you about two things—"

"You don't have to, Principe. I'll resign and make the way clear for you to appoint your new Duca."

"What are you talking about?" Byron said with a confused look on her face.

"I broke our most sacred rule last night," Alexis said.

"You didn't break it."

"I was about to and would have if Bhal hadn't stepped in. I was going to keep Katie alive without her consent and only to stop the pain I would feel if she died, and to tell you the truth, I'd do it again. I'm no better than Victorija. That's exactly what you said to me last night, and you were right. So I'm not fit to be Duca."

Byron put her cigar in the ashtray and leaned forward. "I said that to try and bring clarity to your mind, but you and Victorija were doing it for very different reasons. Victorija turned you for the sport of it and to add to her foot soldiers. You were doing it for love."

Alexis hated to acknowledge her love for Katie out loud, but she had already betrayed her feelings the previous night.

"The result is the same. I didn't have Katie's consent to turn her. She could be waking up this morning having to choose whether to take the final step and turn or let herself die. I know what pain you go through making that decision, while fighting the insatiable need for blood. It was unforgivable."

Byron stood up and walked around to the front of the desk. She crossed her arms and leaned on the desk.

"Consent is what we live by, both for taking blood from humans and turning them. They are high ideals, what we strive for, but we can make mistakes. I took blood and nearly killed Katie's ancestors when I first became a born vampire. Where would I be without their forgiveness?"

"That's different."

"It's not. I failed to reach our high ideals, and I was punished for it, and I keep making up for it to their family every day, and I have to say, if that had been Amelia before we became blood bonded, and she could have gained immortality through me, I would have probably done the same thing. Love drives us and makes us defend our lovers no matter the cost."

"I love Katie, and I will try to make up to her for letting her down, but she could never accept me as her lover after what I nearly did. Besides, I'm not brave enough to try and love again."

"What if the best thing for Katie, the thing that would make her happiest, make her safest, was your love?"

Alexis was caught cold with that remark. It made sense. Maybe putting Katie's happiness first was more important than her fear of getting involved with a human again. She needed to think about it more. "It's all academic anyway. I am Katie's least favourite person, and after what I tried to do, even less so," Alexis said.

She thought about being in Katie's room the other night, angry at her for putting herself at risk, and they'd shared something so deep it shocked Alexis. Katie asked to kiss her. Did she truly share her feelings?

Byron said, "She doesn't know what happened. The Principessa and I decided to leave that to you. You can explain it to her, and I'm sure she will be more than understanding."

Alexis almost wished someone else had told Katie. How she was going to do that, she didn't know.

"So, Duca, on to the second reason why I wanted to see you. Amelia and I have decided to take Magda's advice and go to the New Forest. Try to find some answers about Amelia's past."

Alexis was relieved. At least she'd get away from here, away from facing Katie and her own guilt.

"When would you like to leave, Principe?" Alexis said.

Byron returned to her chair and said, "Soon. When Katie is strong enough to travel."

"Katie? Why—"

"Katie is going to take time to recover and get her strength back, and Amelia thought it would be nice for her to have a break with us in the country."

Alexis gulped hard. "Is that wise? It could be dangerous."

Byron looked up and smiled. "We're not expecting a battle, Duca. This is a fact-finding expedition."

What could Alexis say without letting Byron know what a coward she was? It was pathetic. She had been in huge bloodthirsty battles, the odds against her, nearly dying more than once, and she was more frightened of one human lying upstairs.

"Yes, Principe. We'll be ready to leave whenever you are."

"Thank you. That's all for now."

Alexis bowed her head and left her office. She was about to head downstairs to her own office in the basement when she heard Amelia shouting her name. She looked up and saw Amelia running down the stairs.

"Principessa, how may I serve?"

Amelia smiled, "Good morning, Duca. I've just been in to see Katie."

"How is she?"

"Oh, bearing up. She tells me you haven't been in to see her yet."

What could Alexis say? *Yes, I've been hiding from her like a scared child?*

"Yes, I've been busy."

"I think she'd really appreciate if you did, Duca. Give her some closure on the whole event. Bhal's been to see her."

That was because Bhal was a hero, not a coward like her.

"Would you go and see her? For me, Alexis?"

Dear God. She couldn't get out of a direct request from the Principessa.

"Of course, Principessa."

Chapter Eight

K atie hugged the bedcovers up under her chin. She just couldn't seem to get warm, despite the three hot water bottles, the central heating in the room, and an electric heater Amelia got for her.

She finished with the blood transfusion and was now hooked up to a drip giving her fluids and some essential vitamins. Dr. McKenzie said she was almost back to health and her old self, but regaining her strength would take some time.

Katie didn't feel like her old self, that was the thing. She heard a knock at the door. It was probably Norah with her breakfast.

"Come in," she croaked. Even her voice didn't seem like her own.

The door creaked open ever so slowly, and then to her surprise, Alexis popped her head around it.

"Katie, the Principessa said you wanted to see me."

"Yes, come in."

"I can come back if this is a bad time—"

"No, no, come in," Katie said.

She tried to push herself up onto her pillows so that she was sitting upright, but her muscles were devoid of energy.

Alexis hurried over to her bedside. "Here, let me help you."

Katie felt Alexis's strength making it easier to move. "Thanks."

"Your voice?" Alexis said.

"The doctor said it will return to normal soon, amongst other things. Sit down, please." Katie pointed to the chair by the bed.

Alexis looked at it warily, then pulled it closer and sat down awkwardly. Alexis looked nervous. She didn't think she'd ever seen a nervous Duca, but then recently she'd seen another first from Alexis. When they'd nearly devoured each other in her bedroom, Katie had seen lust, directed at her.

Alexis crossed and uncrossed her legs and shifted around the seat. Her nervousness almost made her sweet.

"Thanks for coming, Alexis. I wanted to thank you for saving me."

"I didn't save you, Bhal did," Alexis said firmly.

"Of course you did. If you hadn't come to me, then I would have been too far gone for Bhal to save me."

"Any vampire would have done the same."

Grumpy, awkward Alexis was back, and it was bloody annoying. "Look, I've offered you my thanks—would you just accept it graciously?"

"Don't get all upset. Save your strength," Alexis said.

"Well don't be so bloody-minded then, and accept my thanks."

"I'm sorry. Of course I accept your thanks."

Katie started to cough and pointed to her bottle of water by the bedside. Alexis got it quickly and helped her take a sip.

"Thanks," Katie said.

Alexis put the bottle down and returned to her seat. She watched Katie pull the covers around her tightly. She didn't look at all well. Katie's skin was so white apart from the dark circles under her eyes.

To Alexis, Katie looked so small and helpless lying there. She had an urge to wrap her arms around her and hold her till she felt better. "How are you?"

Katie looked her in the eyes, then stared back down at the pattern of her covers. "I'm okay. Be back to normal in no time."

Somehow Alexis didn't quite believe that answer. What was Katie hiding? There was an awkward silence while Alexis tried to pluck up the courage to tell Katie about what really happened last night. "Katie, I..." Alexis hesitated.

"What is it?" Katie asked.

Alexis couldn't spit the words out. She was too frightened and fearful of the hurt and disgust she was sure Katie would show her. So Alexis chickened out.

"Is there anything I can get you?"

Katie gave her the smallest of smiles. "No, it's okay. How did you know I needed help last night? Did you hear me screaming?"

"Not at first. I felt something was wrong, and then I heard you scream."

"You felt it? Have you had intuitions like that before?" Katie asked.

Alexis couldn't bring herself to lie about a second thing. She looked into Katie's beautiful eyes and said, "No, I never have. I just felt you needed me."

Katie looked back at her, clearly surprised, but something else was passing between them in that moment, something deeper.

"Wow—I mean, that's great. By the way, I wanted to apologize to you," Katie said.

Alexis was surprised. "What do you have to be sorry for?"

"I caused all this mess, Alexis. You told me it wasn't safe for a human, and I was stubborn and wouldn't listen."

Alexis sighed. "I've realized now that I can't lock you up and protect you twenty-four hours a day, as much as I'd like to."

"You'd like to protect me?"

Alexis nodded and whispered, "Of course I would. You're very important to m—the clan."

Katie reached out her hand, and Alexis looked at it for a few seconds before taking it. Touching Katie made her heart thud hard. The feel of Katie's skin also showed her how cold Katie was.

"You're cold."

"Yeah, I can't seem to get warm," Katie said.

Without thinking Alexis moved her chair closer and said, "Give me your other hand."

Katie moved to the edge of the bed and gave Alexis her other hand. Alexis put her hands over Katie's clasped hands and started to rub them vigorously.

Katie smiled, "That's nice."

"My mama used to do it for me when I was a little girl," Alexis said and then kicked herself. Why had she said that? She never talked about her hurt and her family.

"I haven't heard you talk about your mother before—mind you, I haven't ever heard you talk about anything apart from giving me trouble." Katie smiled when Alexis stopped her rubbing motion and looked a bit flustered. "I'm just joking, Duca. How about we call a ceasefire on all our squabbles from before last night."

Alexis returned her smile but didn't let go of Katie's hands. It felt nice to be touching her, after she thought she'd lost her last night. She stroked her thumb across the back of Katie's hand.

"I'd like that."

Katie's smile at that comment shattered any remaining hardness around Alexis's heart. In that moment Alexis promised that she would help Katie back to health and guard her to make sure no harm would ever touch her again.

"I'm sorry Josie got past my guards. They have been reprimanded. She managed to sneak out when the guards were changing shift, then made off."

"It's not your fault. You can't be everywhere." Katie hesitated. "But Josie is still out there."

"I don't want you to worry about her. I will keep you safe." Alexis was getting lost in Katie's eyes and her touch.

"You know," Katie said, "when I was unconscious last night, I dreamed about you."

Alexis's heart thudded even harder, and she tried hard not to show how much Katie's touch was affecting her. But goosebumps had broken out up and down her arm. "Oh?"

"I was looking for you, shouting your name, but I couldn't find you."

That was a bit too close to the dream she'd had. She had been screaming Katie's name, desperately trying to find her. She pulled her hand away and stood up quickly.

"I'd better get back to my duties."

Katie's face fell. "I wouldn't want to keep you from your work." Alexis knew she was being gruff and dismissive, but it was her way of coping with this emotional situation. She turned and walked to the door urging herself to not look back, but she couldn't stop herself. Alexis had so much to make up for. She would have to beg for Katie's forgiveness once Katie found out what she'd done.

Alexis turned back around and said, "I do have to go now, but may I visit you this evening?"

Katie's smile was back and it made Alexis feel good.

❖

Victorija had to get out of her room. The walls felt like they were closing in on her, so she walked downstairs and out of the castle to the stable block. Her horses reminded her of a happier time when she was young.

She patted the horse named Angel on the snout, and it whinnied. Her horses were the only creatures that weren't afraid of her.

Victorija had only just finished drinking blood, and the gnawing hunger was back again. She hated feeling like this, constantly hungry and her body jittery like she was some kind of drug addict.

But there was fear too, for there was nothing Victorija hated more than being out of control, and this hunger was out of control. An image of Victorija ripping the heart out of Lucia, her grandmother, came to the forefront of her mind.

The movie in her head of the event was torturing her and had taken its toll on her. The childhood feelings of happiness, sadness, and love were debilitating. She had banished love from her heart centuries ago, but now she could remember how they felt.

Victorija looked down at her hands and saw they were shaking. She pressed her head against the stable door and pleaded with herself, "You have to conquer this."

"Principe?" She heard Drasas's voice behind her.

Victorija turned around and saw Drasas with a woman she didn't know. An attractive, intriguing looking woman.

"Who is this?" Victorija asked.

"This is Madam Anka, the woman I said may be able to help you feel better."

Anka held out her hand. "Principe, it's an honour to meet you." Victorija took her hand. "Who are you?"

"I'm a very powerful witch who can help you. I contacted Drasas to broker this meeting. I want to propose a deal. I have dark witches, werewolves, and fae all on my side. So I should like to propose a mutually beneficial arrangement to allow us both to take on the Debreks."

"I don't care about attacking the Debreks just now." Victorija started to walk away.

"What if I could tell you what's wrong? Why you can't seem to sate your hunger? Why you feel like you're becoming lost in your mind?"

Victoria stopped and looked back. "Tell me."

Later that evening, after Alexis finished with her duties, she went down to the kitchen to get Katie a cup of tea. Alexis knew this was Katie's nightly ritual and probably no one else noticed, and she didn't know if Katie would ask for it in her current state.

She bounded up the stairs in a flash and walked along the corridor towards Katie's room. There was a guard now stationed outside on Alexis's orders. Josie had run, but she might be stupid enough to return if the lure of Katie's blood was too strong. As she approached, she heard a voice in Katie's room and it put her on alert.

"Who's in there?" Alexis said to the vampire on the door.

"Dr. McKenzie, Duca. Katie had a bit of an incident when the doctor arrived to check up on her."

Alexis tuned her hearing into the room.

"I know it can be a frightening world, living amongst vampires. If you'd like to get away to recover, I mean, it could be arranged."

Alexis had heard enough. No one was taking Katie anywhere. She walked straight in the door without knocking and saw Tyler

McKenzie seated on the bed. Katie had pushed herself up against the headboard and was using her covers as a barrier.

Tyler jumped when she heard the door open. "Ah, Duca. I came to check on Katie and take out her IV line, and she seemed to think I was Josie coming back to finish her off."

Alexis gave her a hard stare. "I'll take it from here."

At first the doctor met her stare for a few seconds, then looked off to the side. "I'll just get my bag. I'll be back tomorrow to see how she is."

Tyler gathered her bag and started to walk to the door. Just as she was about to leave, Alexis said in a low voice, "Ms. Brekman will not be going anywhere, Doctor. A vampire attacked her, and only vampires are the correct ones to keep her safe from further danger."

Tyler gave her a false smile. "Of course."

Once the doctor left, Alexis approached the bed and put the tea down on the bedside cabinet. "I brought you your tea. What happened to make you so frightened?"

Katie's knuckles were white from hanging onto the bedcovers so hard. "The window."

Alexis looked over to the window, but she didn't see anything amiss. She reached out her hand, asking Katie to take it. Katie looked at her hand, grasped it, and as she did let out a breath. Katie's hand was still feeling cold.

"Everything's not right," Katie said.

Alexis remembered this afternoon when Katie said she was fine, she'd felt Katie was hiding something. But she had to get her to relax before she could talk properly.

She lifted the mug of tea and put it into Katie's hand. "I've got your cup of tea. I know you don't go to bed without it."

Katie felt the warmth of the mug enter her hand and travel up her arm. It along with Alexis's presence made her taut muscles relax, and she slid back down the bed. She brought the hot tea to her lips and the warmth seeped into her bones, brought her back to the present.

"What happened, Katie?"

Katie rubbed her forehead. "I was dreaming, I think. I thought I could see Josie at the window, and then I woke up and Tyler was standing over me. I thought it was Josie."

"Listen, Josie can't get in here. I have a guard on your room door, and I'll put two guards on patrol under your window. She won't get near."

"Thank you, and thank you for the tea. How did you know I have it every night?"

"I noticed," Alexis said simply.

Katie was taken aback. "I didn't think you noticed anything about me."

"I notice everything."

Katie's thoughts and emotions were so mixed up, she didn't know what to think about that answer. She would think about it more deeply another time.

"When you said everything's not right, what did you mean?" Alexis asked.

How could she explain how she had been feeling since she woke up after the attack? She hadn't articulated it to anyone. Could she now? How could you explain that you felt like you had lost a part of yourself?

"I don't know how to explain—I haven't told anyone this."

Alexis gave her a lopsided smile. "We may not have always been the best of friends, but I think you've always known that you could trust me."

That was very true. Despite butting heads on occasion, Katie had looked to Alexis since she was a little girl as the protector in the clan, and one who was steadfastly loyal to all in the Debrek family, be they vampire or human.

"I do trust you. It's hard to put into words. I feel disconnected, out of sync."

"In what way?" Alexis asked.

Katie put her cup down on the bedside cabinet and held up her hand. "When I look at my hand, it doesn't seem like my own, like I'm not fully in my body, like I'm in a movie watching myself from above."

"It's probably a symptom of being pulled back from the brink—"

"Of death? That's what worries me. I feel like I lost a part of myself to death, and I'm frightened that I'll never get it back."

"You've been through such a lot of trauma. I'm sure it's just a way of your brain coping with what's happened to you. I'm confident you haven't lost anything, and that part of you that you think is lost will come back to you as you heal."

"Is this what it feels like to be a vampire? Like you've lost a part of you to death?"

Alexis nodded. "Sometimes. Becoming a vampire means losing a part of your humanity, and it's a lot to lose. When you are turned, the blood hunger is driving you to complete the change, while your humanity is pleading to die with dignity."

"Is that why changing someone without their consent is forbidden?"

Alexis looked away quickly. She looked nervous all of a sudden. Then she changed the subject, saying, "Well, your parents will be here tomorrow. I'm sure seeing your mother and father will help ground you back to this reality."

As soon as they heard about the attack, her mum and dad insisted on travelling back to see her. She couldn't wait to have a hug from her mum.

"Once they make sure I'm okay, they are going to be mad at me for going out to The Sanctuary."

"It's only because they care. Always appreciate having your parents still in your life. I miss my mother every day, even after all this time."

Katie wanted to ask about her mother, but that would be pushing her too far, she suspected.

"Well," Alexis said, "I'd better go."

"Alexis? I'm sorry you feel like this all the time. I'm sorry Victorija did this to you."

Alexis was silent, but Katie could see a lot going on behind her eyes. "I don't feel like it all the time. There are moments with people I care about that make me feel alive."

"With all people?" Katie asked.

Alexis felt like Katie had a direct line to her heart. "No, not all. Very few. Goodnight, Katie."

❖

"I cannot be bonded by blood," Victorija roared and kicked the small table by the couch in her room.

Drasas watched as Madam Anka never flinched. That intoxicated her. Someone who didn't fear a born vampire must be extremely confident in their abilities. Drasas craved just to be allowed to touch this woman.

"Whether you like it or not, the facts remain the same. You once relied on a witch called Lillian's advice, I believe? I am more powerful than she could have ever dreamed, so I would take my word."

"You believe this witch, Drasas?" Victorija said.

"Yes, Principe. I do. Anka wishes to partner with us to bring humanity to its knees, but she needs our clan, and so she needs you to be back to full health. Anka is not going to give us bad advice."

"Then how do I conquer this? Byron fell in love with her blood bond, Amelia, but that is never going to happen to me. If I don't drink their blood, then I will go slowly mad, like my father did when he killed my mother."

"Who have you exchanged blood with? One of your vampires here?" Anka asked.

"No." Victorija began to pace in front of the fireplace. "I don't allow anyone to feed on me."

"Then think long and hard, because that person will need to be brought here to feed you. In the meantime, I must go."

Victorija didn't even notice when Anka got up and Drasas followed her out.

Anka stopped outside the door and took Drasas's hand. "She knows who it is, somewhere in her subconscious."

"I'll bring whoever it is to her as soon as we find out who," Drasas said.

Anka leaned in and stroked her cheek, lighting fires all over Drasas's body. "In the meantime, we cannot halt our plans. I need your vampires to help my witches."

Drasas hesitated. "Victorija—"

Anka ran her fingers down Drasas's chest and lingered on her belt buckle. Drasas groaned, and then they heard a great crashing noise from Victorija's room.

Then Victorija shouted, "Get me some blood now!"

"Your Principe is in no fit state to make these decisions. Look how long you've wasted already."

"Victorija might see this as treacherous," Drasas said.

"No, you are taking care of the clan while she cannot. I know who you are, Drasas, and who you long to be."

"What do you mean?" Drasas asked.

Anka slipped her hand down to Drasas's crotch and grasped it. Drasas leaned forward looking to kiss Anka, but she held her at bay.

"I know how you felt sitting on the street, homeless. Humans passing you by, spitting on you or worse. When Victorija turned you, you wanted to feel power over those humans, didn't you?"

"Yes." Drasas would never forget the fear of living on the streets. It drove her to be the powerful vampire she was.

Anka brought her lips to her ear and rhythmically squeezed her sex. Drasas closed her eyes and concentrated on the feelings Anka was giving her.

"I can make you even more powerful than a born vampire, Drasas. Follow me and do as I say."

"Yes, Anka."

When Drasas opened her eyes, Anka was gone. She slammed her fist against the wall, making the plaster crumble. She had been on the edge of orgasm.

One of her female vampires came walking down the corridor. "Can I serve you, Duca?"

She grabbed Meg's hand and pulled her into one of the adjacent castle rooms. "Yes, you can, Meg."

Meg was a femme-presenting newly turned vampire who was eager to please. Just what she needed.

"I need to fuck you and drink from you."

"Anything, Duca."

Drasas guided her over to an old oak table in the room and bent her over it. She pulled her trousers down and did the same with Meg's. Drasas opened herself up and began to thrust herself onto Meg's buttock.

She closed her eyes and pretended Anka was touching her. It felt so real. She heard Anka's voice say, *I can make you so powerful, more powerful than Victorija, more than Byron Debrek, just follow me.*

Drasas's orgasm overtook her and she shouted, "Yes, Anka."

CHAPTER NINE

A week later Katie was deemed well enough to travel. Amelia was pleased—they would finally be able to start her journey to discover who she really was. As was their habit, when Amelia wasn't rushing for work, she joined Byron in her dressing room to help her get ready.

Amelia picked out a selection from Byron's tie rack and brought it over to Byron. She slipped it around Byron's neck and started to slowly tie it.

"This is one of my favourite times of day," Byron said.

"One of?" Amelia smiled.

Byron lifted her hand and trailed her fingers across Amelia's cheek, making her shiver. "Yes, one. As well as waking up next to you, that first feed of the day, and making you come in your favourite way."

Amelia got a flashback to earlier when Byron was feeding from the artery on the inside of her thigh. The pleasure of having Byron's teeth in her, so close to her sex, as she stimulated Amelia's clit with her fingers was one aspect of her marriage that she adored.

She shook the memory away and play-slapped Byron on the chest. "Don't get me all hot and bothered again. We have to leave soon."

Byron grinned with satisfaction. "Very well, what shall we discuss?"

"How about where we're going, Burley in the New Forest. Have you been there before?"

"A few times. There's always been a coven there. It's a sacred forest to the witches."

"And you had dealings with them?" Amelia asked.

"One or two."

"My mum and dad—sorry, my adoptive mum and dad—were always worried about the supposed witches and Satan worshippers there."

Byron laughed. "No Satan worshippers. Nature worshippers, more like."

"Mum and Dad had some pretty far-out fundamentalist Christian beliefs, and anything outside of that, like women worshipping nature, was evil," Amelia said.

"They were not dark witches in the New Forest," Byron noted. "In fact, they did more to help the human population than any other paranormal group."

Amelia folded Byron's collar down and went to pick up her waistcoat from the hanger and helped slip it on her.

"How so?"

"Well, a lot of covens are insular, not welcoming to newcomers," Byron said.

"You mean for humans like me who discover they have powers?"

"Exactly, they welcomed them in and taught them, not only gifted humans, but humans who simply had a strong interest in witchcraft and what it could do."

"They sound nice."

"Yes, Rose—" Byron hesitated. "It doesn't matter."

"It's all right. You can talk about her," Amelia reassured Byron.

"I didn't want to upset you."

Amelia cupped Byron's cheek. "You don't have to censor yourself. I know you love me. You have a past, but I have your love."

"I just don't want to hurt you. Rose's sister was the leader of the

New Forest coven, and the welcoming nature of the coven provided cover to let them hide in plain sight."

"How so?"

"Well one of the humans they trained, Gerald Gardner, founded Wicca. He gained a lot of publicity and notoriety, leaving the general public to think the witches there were nothing more than that, human. The village of Burley in the New Forest where they met is still a tourist attraction to this day, because of the witches and the birth of Wicca."

"So how did they help humans more than most?"

Byron walked over to a chair and beckoned Amelia to sit on her knee, which she did.

"During the Second World War, I worked in intelligence, the Secret Service."

"You did? You never fail to amaze me. I always forget you've been living a very long time."

"The world was on the brink. It didn't matter if you were human or a paranormal—we all had to do our bit. So I was contacted by the cunning folk, which is what the coven became known as over the years. They wanted to try to use magic to help the war effort. Things were looking bleak at the time, the government was worried that Hitler would invade any day, and the cunning folk wanted to help."

"Wow, that's amazing. What did they do?" Amelia asked.

"First of all, I had to get my superiors to agree, as the witches needed secret information on Hitler's whereabouts and his forces. Luckily, I wasn't the only paranormal in the British command structure. I was tasked with conveying the secret information and observing how it was used," Byron said.

"Was the other side using vampires, witches, and the like?"

"I'm quite sure. The Nazis were very interested in studying the occult, so I'm sure they found help of their own. It was August 1940 and my secret mission was called Operation Cone of Power. The witches cast a circle, then performed the ritual with the information I gave them. They sent a powerful message to Hitler: *You cannot come, you cannot cross the sea.* Whether this actually worked, we will never know. He didn't cross the sea, but whether it was with the help of magic, who knows."

"That's amazing. You have had the most interesting life," Amelia said.

"Interesting but lonely, until I met you."

Amelia smiled and kissed Byron tenderly. "Good answer. Let's go and find out about my past."

She stood and Byron followed suit.

"Oh," Amelia said, "a certain someone has been visiting Katie in her room every night, taking her tea."

Byron raised her eyebrows. "Interesting. I've only seen Alexis's softer side once before. She was a younger vampire and didn't see the danger in loving a fragile human. I warned Alexis loving a human would always end in pain, and now look where we are."

"Katie is besotted with Alexis. I'm sure she is. That's why she bickers so much with her, but will Alexis take her chance at happiness? I don't know."

"Sometimes," Byron said, "love doesn't give you a choice."

❖

Victorija was crawling in her skin, her hands shaking, as she tried to type on the laptop on her desk. She'd remembered the girl in The Sanctuary, the girl who bit her when they were fighting to take Amelia, the girl she couldn't compel.

Amelia had called her Daisy, and it didn't take long to find out she worked beside Amelia, and her name was Daisy MacDougall. A whole litany of hits turned up on that name—blogs, interviews on human–paranormal websites—all calling Daisy a monster hunter.

Victorija clicked on a YouTube link and found herself watching Daisy and a group of friends, ghost hunting in an old churchyard. She paused the video, took a screenshot, and enlarged it.

"Daisy MacDougall." She reached forward with her shaking hand and said, "Why you?"

When she had tasted her blood in The Sanctuary, it had been

like a punch in the chest, and when she looked in her eyes there was something so familiar about them.

On a hunch she went to the births, marriages, and deaths website for the UK. The results would take her hours to go through, but Victorija knew she had to trace this girl's family back in time, and she had a sinking feeling of where that might lead and what it would mean for her. Death or a broken vow.

❖

A line of black SUVs and a classic Rolls-Royce ambled through the English countryside. In one of the black SUVs was Katie, who was now well enough to travel. She was still weak, but the doctor thought a change of scene would help.

Katie pulled the blanket under her chin to try to comfort herself. The moment she stepped out of her room this morning, she realized how different she still felt. As she passed the spot on the landing where Josie had attacked her, she had to conceal the panic she felt.

If she had shown the terror and fear that was deep inside her bones, Byron might have left her at home, and she couldn't bear that. Since her mother and father had flown in to be by her side, she'd hardly been able to breathe.

Her mum especially had not left her bedside, fussing over her. The only respite she got was when Daisy came to visit her. She could understand her parents' reaction—their daughter had been essentially dead, if not for Bhal's actions—but the constant talking about it, and no privacy to come to terms with how she was feeling, had only made her confusion over the trauma worse. The other thing was that since her parents arrived, Alexis hadn't been near, and she couldn't understand why.

She had gotten used to—indeed, looked forward to—Alexis's nightly visits with a cup of tea. Katie had to admit it was the only time of day she felt safe, anywhere near grounded, and not filled with anxiety.

Near grounded, that was a joke. Katie gazed out of the window and watched the hedgerows and leafy trees of the countryside whizz by. When she saw the trees, the leaves, the sheep and cows in the field, it was like a scene from a movie she was watching, observing from some point outside herself.

When Bhal had ripped her back from death, death had left its mark on her, and she didn't know if she would ever be the same again. If Katie thought about it for too long, her anxiety went sky high.

"Katie? You okay back there?"

Katie looked away from the scenery and saw Wilder, Amelia's personal guard, turned around in the front passenger seat.

"Yes, I'm okay," Katie replied.

"Good, we won't be too much longer," Wilder said. "The Duca said we'll stop in the village for a short while to pick up the keys to the cabins, and then we'll get going."

The Duca. Was she the same person as the one who helped save her and brought her tea each night until her parents arrived?

Katie had thought she was finally seeing beneath that protective wall Alexis kept around herself, but then she just disappeared. Maybe she had just felt sorry for her after the attack and come back to her senses. If that was the case, then the truth would sadden her. Maybe the connection Katie thought they finally had was all an illusion.

The village of Burley hadn't changed much over the years, Alexis thought as she stood beside the Rolls-Royce. They had stopped in the centre of the village to pick up the keys to the cabins Byron had booked from the pub owner.

One thing that had changed in the small village was the embracing of all things witch and paranormal. From what she could see, there were two witchcraft shops that appeared to be popular with the tourists coming and going. Nowadays the paranormal was vaunted by humans—they were desperate to know the truth of this world, but if they did, it would keep them up at night.

Alexis looked to the SUV parked behind them and had to fight the urge to go check on Katie, but she couldn't. She knew that Katie would most probably be angry at her lack of visits over the last week.

The truth was that she couldn't face Katie's parents, knowing that she nearly forcibly turned their daughter. It was unforgivable, and Alexis almost wished the Principessa or someone would tell Katie what happened. Then she'd only have to avoid her, not face her.

As it was, everyone was leaving it to her, but she didn't have the courage.

Byron emerged from the pub carrying keys.

"Any problems?"

"None," Byron said.

She passed a set of keys to Alexis. "These are yours."

Alexis took them and nodded.

When Byron had told her the plan to only take Amelia, Katie, and herself into the forest and leave the guards at the coaching inn and hotel in the village, she had been dead against it for security reasons, but the more she thought about it, the more she realized that it would give her the chance to look after Katie and try to make up for her mistakes.

"Thanks, I'll take good care of her."

Byron smiled and slapped her on the shoulder. "I know that. Let's get going."

Behind Byron she saw a middle-aged woman standing outside the witch and witchcraft shop.

"We have company," Alexis said.

Byron turned to look. "So we do."

"Do you recognize her?"

Byron shook her head. "No, but it's a long time since I've been here. They can detect a vampire at a hundred paces, can't they?"

"Do you think that shop is run by real witches or witch enthusiasts?"

"That woman is a real witch—I can feel it. Okay, let's go. We need to get Katie settled. It's been a long journey for her."

They travelled into the forest, and the trees became denser as they went. This was a perfect place for witches to have a coven. Deep cover on ancient ground, a perfect match for magic and mayhem. The Rolls-Royce went down a side track, not especially easy for a car such as that.

Finally two log cabins came into view, and the line of cars parked up. The rest of the guards would be staying at the hotel under Bhal's command.

The car came to a halt and Alexis jumped out and opened Byron's door. Byron stepped out and looked down at her expensive leather shoes, now covered in mud and God knew what else.

"Welcome to the country, Principe," Alexis joked.

"Indeed," Byron replied.

Amelia joined them and laughed. "It's the perfect chance for you to try the new country clothes I got you."

Byron rolled her eyes. "I can't wait."

Alexis looked over at Wilder helping Katie out of the car, and before she could say anything, Byron said, "Go, Duca. Look after her."

"Thank you, Principe."

She hurried over to the SUV. "I'll take it from here, Wilder."

"Yes, Duca."

Alexis took Katie's arm, and she shot Alexis a look. "You want to help me too now?"

All the other guards were looking at them, so she decided to wait until they got inside.

Alexis said to the guards, "You're dismissed. Go and check in at the hotel and keep your heads down with the locals."

"Yes, Duca," they shouted, and the line of cars began to back up and leave.

"Why aren't you going with them?" Katie asked her.

She was clearly annoyed about her disappearance over the last week. "Didn't the Principessa tell you?"

"Tell me what?" Katie said.

Faced with Katie's clear annoyance, she lost some of her usual confidence. "I'm staying here with you. To look after you."

"You? You want to help look after me? You stop visiting me

and don't even check how I am, and now all of a sudden you want to help take care of me?"

Alexis felt so awkward and put on the spot. Luckily, Amelia came over to them and put her arm on Katie's.

"I can explain—"

Alexis interrupted, "Let's get you inside."

"I'll get the bags," Byron said.

Alexis snapped her head around. The Principe should not be carrying luggage. "Just leave it, Principe, and I'll come back out and get it."

"Relax, Duca. I can carry a bag from time to time," Byron said.

Amelia laughed. "Yes, we need to put her to work for a change. Come on, Katie."

Alexis had no choice but to follow, holding Katie by the elbow.

They walked up onto the porch, and Alexis did the honours, unlocking the door and holding it open.

The cabin was simple and cosy looking, even without the fire going. They walked into an open plan living area and kitchen off to the side. The living area had a comfortable couch facing a fire, and the kitchen was just to the side. At the back of the living room was a corridor, which led to what Alexis presumed were bedrooms.

"This is nice, isn't it?" Amelia said.

"It's really sweet. Thanks for bringing me along," Katie replied.

"Couch or bed?" Amelia asked.

"Couch, I'm sick of lying down."

Byron came in with the bags. "I'll put them into the bedrooms."

Katie got settled on the couch, and Alexis stood awkwardly, unsure of what to say or do. Then the fire caught her eye.

"I'll light the fire." She kneeled down and arranged the logs from a basket beside the fireplace. She was so glad to be facing away from Katie. Katie was clearly annoyed with her. If she was annoyed at her not visiting for a week, then what was she going to think when Alexis admitted to nearly turning her?

After chatting for about ten minutes, Amelia and Byron started to leave. Byron said, "If you need anything, just call me, but I'm sure Alexis will look after you."

Alexis could hear Katie sigh under her breath. But she ignored it and walked the Principe and her wife to the door. When the door shut, and they were alone for the first time, Alexis felt nerves fill her.

How on earth did she think she could ever do this? The last person she had looked after when she was ill was her mother, and then they had a housekeeper to help.

But despite her nerves and worry, she was determined to take care of Katie. It was her duty to try to make things right as best she could.

Alexis gulped and said, "I'll just finish making the fire, and then I'll get you a cup of tea. Okay?"

Katie hugged her blanket from the car and nodded. This was awkward.

Katie watched Alexis making the fire with ease, as if she'd done it a thousand times. She couldn't believe she was here with Alexis like this. This kind of behaviour, looking after someone, was not usual for Alexis, although since her attack she thought Alexis had softened, visiting her every night. But then she disappeared. What was going on with her?

"You seem to know what you're doing," Katie said.

Alexis looked around. "What, you mean the fire?"

"Yeah."

"Remember, we didn't have heating when I was a young woman. I've lit fires like this for years," Alexis said.

"I can't imagine you living in the past," Katie said.

Alexis got up and turned to Katie. "What do you mean?"

"Every time I try to picture you back then, it just doesn't work. I mean the type of strong, tough, butch soldier, in a time of petticoats and corsets. It was such a restrictive time."

"I got away with breeches most of the time when I lived at home with Mama, but if anyone came to stay, or Father came for dinner, then I had to suffer the whole corset and big dress affair."

Katie was surprised that Alexis mentioned her family again.

Alexis was so closed off and guarded Katie almost thought she didn't have a family.

Wait, *Father came to dinner?* That was a strange thing to say.

❖

Byron could feel Amelia's tension as she lay with her head on Byron's shoulder.

"What are you thinking?" Byron stroked Amelia's long brown hair.

"I'm thinking about too much." Amelia sighed.

"Well, pick one thought, and tell me about it."

"Why we're here, I suppose. How we're going to find out any information about my past, and if we find the truth, I'm frightened of what the truth might be."

"First of all, remember Magda said the knowledge of your past would find us, and two, whatever the truth is, we'll get through it because we are a team, and we can face anything."

Amelia turned around so her head was now on Byron's chest. "I'm so lucky to have you, Byron. You don't just make me feel safe, but you make me feel like I can face anything. When I met you…"

"What?" Byron asked.

"I was full of anxiety, generally felt afraid of what people would think of me. My parents told me I wasn't good enough for so long that I started to believe them. You make me feel good enough."

"I'm glad you feel like that, but I'm the lucky one," Byron said. "You always were good enough—you just had to see yourself through my eyes. A beautiful woman who makes my blood run hot, and now a businesswoman in your own right."

Amelia smiled. It meant so much to her to open her own shop, making her own money and giving jobs and apprenticeships to young women entering the tailoring business. Now she wasn't Amelia Debrek the wife of the billionaire businesswoman, she *was* the businesswoman.

"I hope Uncle Simon is okay."

Since Amelia was going away so soon after opening, she didn't want to leave Daisy on her own. Uncle Jaunty was busy running his tailor shop next door, so his husband Simon was insistent on helping out.

Byron had been friends with Jaunty for years but had never met Simon until she and Amelia got together. She and Jaunty had built a mutual respect and trust, but Simon took nothing on trust. He was at first highly sceptical of Byron as a suitor for Amelia, whom he thought of as his daughter, but Byron respected that. Anyone who put Amelia first and had the strength of character to go up against a born vampire was to be admired in her book.

"Simon will be fine. He'll be fussing around Daisy and having a whale of a time."

"So, what is the plan for tomorrow?" Amelia asked.

Byron rolled them both over so she was on top of Amelia. "I'll take you to all the places that are related to the New Forest coven and see what happens, but don't be scared. I'll be with you."

"I won't. How do you think Alexis and Katie are getting on?" Amelia asked.

"Alexis is probably tiptoeing around Katie, afraid she'll say the wrong thing."

"Do you think she'll tell her about that night?" Amelia was referring to Alexis nearly turning her.

"Yes, she may be frightened, but Alexis is as honourable as they come," Byron said.

Amelia ran her fingers through Byron's hair. "Was she like this the first time she was in love?"

"The Alexis back then was a very different person. She was open, optimistic, too optimistic perhaps. When she met Anna, a witch in a local coven, she fell head over heels. I'm not proud of the fact that I counselled against the relationship."

"Why?" asked Amelia.

"Because as an immortal, you are always going to have a broken heart when the human or witch grows old and passes away. She was besotted by Anna, and she had to be prepared to watch her age and die. Alexis already had her fair share of pain," Byron said.

"And was that how you felt when you met me?"

"Initially, but then I saw things from Alexis's point of view. Love was worth the risk of losing someone. Luckily things changed, and our blood bond will keep you alive as long as I am."

"I think they both look lost," Amelia said.

"Let's hope they find each other."

❖

Katie woke from her slumber to the smell of cooked breakfast. She hadn't been eating much, but the smell was making her mouth water. She got up slowly and put on her dressing gown.

With the aid of a walking stick to support her weak legs, Katie made her way out to the living area of the cabin and followed the smell. She came out to the open-plan living area and caught the sight of Alexis making food at the cooker.

Alexis was wearing jeans and a sleeveless T-shirt. Katie was immediately attracted and intrigued. She hadn't ever seen the Duca so casual before.

Alexis turned around and said, "Oh, you're up already. I was going to bring you breakfast in bed."

What? Had she entered some sort of other dimension where Alexis was open, helpful, and nice?

Katie was too shocked to say anything. Alexis hurried over to her. "Let me help you sit down."

"Breakfast? You can cook?" Katie asked.

"I wouldn't go that far, but every soldier can knock up bacon, eggs, and sausages." Alexis went back to the kitchen and lifted a plate and brought it back to Katie. "Eat up. There's bacon, eggs, sausages, fried bread, and beans."

Katie looked down at the plate and then up at Alexis. She gazed at her silently. What on earth was happening here. The cold, stoic soldier and vampire had made her a cooked breakfast?

"What's wrong? Don't you like it?"

"No, it looks lovely. Thank you," Katie said.

"Eat up then. It'll help get your strength back."

"Are you eating?" Katie knew that vampires liked to eat for

the pleasure of it sometimes, even though they didn't need food for survival.

"No, I'll probably eat dinner later, but now I thought I would try the herbal tea you like so much," Alexis said.

"My herbal tea? Did Amelia organize the food and drink for the cabins?"

Alexis returned with her cup of steaming hot tea and sat down. "No, I made sure everything we needed would be here on arrival, including your teabags."

Katie was touched that Alexis remembered her tea. She seemed to notice her in the smallest of ways, like which brand of tea she liked. Alexis was watching her, eagerly awaiting her verdict on breakfast. She picked up her knife and fork and tasted her food. "Mm. Really tasty. Thank you, Alexis."

What happened next rocked Katie to the core. Alexis smiled, openly and brightly. So brightly that Katie could feel the warmth invade her heart.

"I'm glad you like it."

Katie then felt frustrated. Why was Alexis behaving like this when she ignored her last week? This was just weird. She put down her knife and fork and lifted the warm cup of tea Alexis had given her.

"I thought after breakfast," Alexis said, "we could sit out on the porch so you could get some fresh air. There's a nice rocking chair, and I can get you some blankets—"

"Okay, stop." Katie couldn't listen to any more weirdness. "Why are you doing this?"

Alexis furrowed her eyebrows. "What do you mean?"

Katie indicated her plate. "Cooking me breakfast, looking after me, when last week you wouldn't come near me."

Alexis cleared her throat. There it was. The question she knew Katie would ask eventually. Katie had clearly been annoyed by her behaviour. What could she say? That she couldn't face Katie's parents knowing that she had tried to forcibly turn their daughter, that guilt was eating away at her very soul?

"Your parents were here." Alexis hoped that would be enough to stop Katie's enquiries.

"And that stops you visiting how? I mean, I'm used to being ignored by you. You've ignored me since I came home from university and started working for Byron, but after the attack..." Katie hesitated, then looked down at the table sadly. "I thought we had a better understanding. You came to visit me every night, and I thought we could be friends at least."

Friends? If only Katie could see inside her heart. She had to cover for her actions somehow.

"I didn't want to get in the way. Your mum was there every night, and she probably wouldn't approve of me being your friend," Alexis said.

"Why? You worked alongside them for years when they were the Debrek butler and head housekeeper."

"Yes, and they only knew me as the Duca. A single-minded, work focused, dismissive, cold vampire. They'd probably think I'd upset you, and I doubt they'd believe the other side of me you'd seen."

"I've seen another side?" Katie questioned.

In her mind Alexis could see the hot kiss they had shared before she ran, and the bloody finger Katie had pushed into her mouth.

"Yes, you have. Listen, I'm sorry I stayed away last week. Maybe I was wrong, but it wasn't my intention to upset you."

"Fair enough." Katie picked up her fork and continued to eat.

Alexis had gotten away with it for now, but the bigger thing, what she had nearly done to Katie, was not going to stay hidden forever.

Byron walked into the living room, and Amelia frowned when she looked up from the book she was reading.

"I left your clothes hanging up for you, and it wasn't a tweed suit."

Byron had agreed back in London to wear something more appropriate for walking in the forest, jeans and walking boots. Amelia bought a few different kinds of jeans to bring with them, and had left an outfit hanging up for Byron while she had a shower, but when it came to it, Byron couldn't wear it.

"I just couldn't do it. I've never worn a pair of jeans in my life. I wouldn't feel appropriately dressed, and besides"—Byron straightened her knitted red tie—"a gentleman always wears a tweed suit in the countryside."

Amelia laughed and shook her head. "I despair of you, vampire."

"What are you reading?" Byron asked.

"A history of witchcraft in the area. It's strange—I come from a village just thirty minutes from here, and I didn't know anything about the witches here, besides what my mum and dad told me."

Byron sat on the arm of the armchair. "That they were devil worshippers?"

"Yeah, it used to scare me, but now that I realize I have witch ancestry, I can't wait to find out more."

"Then let's go. I'll take you to all the places I can remember," Byron said.

Amelia stood and put her book in her shoulder bag. "What if nothing happens?"

"It will. Magda said you would get some insight, and I believe her. There's no love lost between vampires and witches, but I don't think they were lying to us. Let's go and see what happens, mia cara."

❖

Alexis finished speaking to Byron and walked back to the cabin, where Katie was sitting on the porch.

"Everything all right?" Katie asked.

"Yes, Byron and the Principessa are going to visit some of the witch sites."

"And you're not going with them?" Katie asked.

"No, the Principe wants to be alone with the Principessa."

"You normally don't give in so easily, Duca. Normally you fight tooth and nail to make sure Byron takes security with her."

"I trust that she is safe enough walking around the forest paths. Besides, Byron isn't my only focus on this trip. I'll go and get you a blanket."

"Wait a minute," Katie said. "What is your focus?"

Alexis was going to be truthful. She didn't need any more secrets. "You."

She didn't wait to see Katie's reaction and just walked inside the cabin.

❖

Amelia and Byron had been walking in the forest for about twenty minutes, and Amelia was loving it. They hadn't found anything yet, but it was such a luxury to be alone with Byron.

"What are you smiling about?" Byron asked.

"It's just nice to have you all to myself, without an entourage around following us."

Byron smiled. "Yes, quite right. It is beautiful here."

"Where are you taking me first?" Amelia asked.

"The place I visited during the War. Where the witches cast their spell to try to repel Hitler. I presume that such strong magic would leave a trace of energy that maybe you could tune in to."

Amelia sighed. "It sounds like a good plan. Only thing is that I haven't a clue how to tune in."

"Follow your instincts." Byron pulled back some branches. "It should be right through here."

Amelia walked into a small clearing and saw a circle marked out by small rocks and, in the centre, one worn-down rectangular stone. Amelia's body—all of her nerve endings—began to buzz.

"I can feel something, Byron."

"What?"

"An energy, electricity in the air," Amelia said.

Byron slipped her arm around Amelia's waist as they approached the perimeter of the circle.

"I'm right by your side," Byron said.

Amelia gripped Byron's hand tightly. "Will you come in with me?"

"I can't. A vampire can't step inside a witch's casting circle, but I'll be right here," Byron said.

Amelia's heart started to thud. So much had changed for her in such a short time—meeting Byron, learning she was a vampire and about all the paranormal world, discovering that her mother and father were not her real parents, and taking her place as the immortal matriarch of the Debrek clan. Not to mention the fact that she had witch blood in her. But through it all she had the strength of Byron right by her side. Did she have the courage to take this step alone?

She held out her hand, and it shook as she reached into the perimeter of the circle. Amelia looked back to Byron, who smiled and nodded.

"On you go."

Amelia's pushed her fingers that final few inches across the perimeter. She immediately felt a warmth that welcomed her in.

"Here goes." Amelia took a few steps, and she was in the circle entirely.

The warmth she had felt on her fingertips now enveloped her whole body. She gasped and lifted her arms to see all her hairs standing up on end.

"How do you feel?" Byron shouted.

Amelia looked over to her and smiled. "Good. I feel warm, calm, but at the same time…"

"What?"

Amelia turned in a circle and closed her eyes. "It's like there is an energy surrounding me. It doesn't feel scary." Amelia opened her eyes and looked at Byron. "It's almost like a happy energy, if energy can be happy."

"The power that made that casting circle is pleased to see you,

I'm sure." Byron smiled. "The witches touched that stone in the centre when I was here. Maybe you could try that?"

Amelia nodded and walked over to the simple looking grey stone. She kneeled down and held her hand above it. The sensation of electrically charged air intensified the closer her hand came to the stone, and her heart began to pound. Somehow in the back of her mind, Amelia knew something was about to change.

She pressed her hand to the stone, and an energy pushed her off her feet, and she landed on her back. Amelia heard thunderous noise all around her, and when she opened her eyes she found she was in the centre of what looked like a tornado.

She stood slowly. The noise of the wind whipping around her was deafening, and she couldn't see Byron any more. She started to walk back over to the stone. As she did, she could hear what sounded like voices in the midst of the noise of the wind.

The voices got louder and stronger. She kneeled by the stone and shut her eyes to concentrate on the voices, but she just couldn't catch the words.

Almost as quickly as it happened, it stopped. The howling winds disappeared, and she could see Byron standing calmly outside the circle. That was odd. She expected Byron to be going crazy trying to get to her.

"Anything?" Byron said.

"What? Didn't you see any of that?" Amelia marched out of the circle.

Byron looked confused. "Any of what?"

Amelia explained about the winds and the voices. "You didn't see that?"

"No, nothing. To me it just looked as if you were touching the stone in quiet contemplation."

"It was anything but quiet. What do you think it means?" Amelia asked.

"I don't know. If only the Grand Duchess was still alive. She would know what it meant."

"I wish I could talk to her." Her death had left a huge hole in the paranormal world.

Byron took her hand. "Let's go back to the cabin, and we'll talk about it."

As they walked away from the circle, Amelia heard a voice whispering behind her. She turned around quickly but there was nothing there.

"What's wrong?" Byron asked.

"Nothing. Let's just get back."

Amelia shivered. The voices had followed her out of the circle.

CHAPTER TEN

W hat are you doing on your feet?" Alexis said. Alexis had found Katie pouring herself a drink from the fridge. As soon as she said the words, she knew they were said too harshly, like the way the old Alexis used to talk, and judging by Katie's scowl, her words hadn't gone over well. "I'm sorry if that sounded harsh. I simply meant that you should ask me for what you want. That way you can rest."

"I can get a glass of juice. Besides, I'm feeling a lot better, a lot stronger."

"As you wish, but come and sit on the couch, so I can change your dressing. Dr. McKenzie said I had to change it once a day."

Katie took Alexis's arm and walked back to the couch. Alexis had a first aid kit and put it on the coffee table, then kneeled in front of Katie.

Katie reached out and touched her mouth. Alexis caught her breath. Why was Katie caressing her? Katie gazed deeply into her eyes, and Alexis's mouth went dry. No enemy she had ever come up against had ever been able to disarm her the way this human did.

Then Katie's eyes narrowed and she held up her finger with a spot of blood on it. "You missed a bit."

Instead of licking it off Katie's finger, which was what Alexis wanted to do, she took a handkerchief from her pocket and wiped it away. She had drunk some blood from the bottled supply she brought with her.

"You don't have to look so terrified when I touch you," Katie said with annoyance.

"I wasn't. I was simply—"

Katie sighed. "You were. Anyway, how are you feeding while you're here?"

Alexis opened up the first aid box. "Bottled, and some blood bags in the fridge."

"You can't be satisfied on bottled alone. Byron has Amelia, and I could feed you."

"No way," Alexis said, "you're recovering from a physical and mental trauma. I'm not taking blood from you."

Katie couldn't help but feel a little hurt. "I forgot—you don't like my blood."

"Of course it's not that. I'm trying to do the right thing here. Can you let me?"

"You never will answer that question, will you?" Katie asked.

Alexis took out the bandages and said nothing. Alexis got the alcohol wipes ready to clean the wound and began to reach for the bandage around Katie's neck, then hesitated.

"I have to take off your old bandage. May I?"

Katie didn't know whether she was coming or going with Alexis's behaviour. One moment she was barking an order at her, the next falling over herself to take care of her, not to mention being terrified when Katie touched her.

She thought when Alexis had shown her passion in her bedroom, after their argument over Josie, that she had finally broken through those tough layers of steel Alexis had around her, but it hadn't turned out that way.

Katie had been so angry at herself for ever finding Alexis attractive, far less having the biggest crush on her since she was a teenager, but the way Alexis had saved her from Josie and taken care of her since had made her think maybe her heart was right all this time.

"May I?" Alexis asked again.

Katie shook herself from her thoughts. "Yes, sorry."

Alexis tenderly unwrapped her neck bandage, and Katie winced as the pad covering her bite was eased off.

"Sorry," Alexis said.

"It's okay. How does it look?"

Katie watched as Alexis examined her wound, and her eyes started to flame red, the colour a vampire's eyes became when they felt extremes of emotion.

"What's wrong? Is it that bad?" Katie asked.

Alexis stared silently at her wound, becoming tense with utter fury, it seemed.

"Alexis? Is the wound worse?"

Alexis closed her eyes and shook her head. When she opened them, Alexis looked at her and said with passion and anger, "I hate seeing her bite on you. If I ever find Josie, I won't break her neck—I'll sever her head from her shoulders, so she'll never harm a human again."

Katie was taken aback with her honesty. Her heart beat heavily, and her stomach flipped in response to Alexis's passion. Alexis did feel deeply—she was sure of it now.

Alexis must have seen her silence as fear of her fury, because she took a breath and said, "I'm sorry. I hate to see a vampire use such violence in an attempt to feed. New bloods often do, and some vampires never learn to take what they need with care and respect."

"I know—some are rougher than others, but my best experience came to me when I was new to giving blood."

Alexis looked away, clearly not wanting to hear about an experience she'd had with another vampire.

"Alexis?" Katie touched Alexis's chin and made her look up to her. "It was you. I was a blood virgin, and you slowly, kindly eased me through my first experience. I've never had anything close to that feeling that gave me"—Katie moved her hand to caress Alexis's cheek—"but then you ran."

Alexis covered her hand with hers and took a breath. "Katie, I ran that day because…"

Finally, Alexis was going to explain, to tell her the truth about that day. "Why, tell me?"

Alexis shuffled forward on her knees and put her arms on Katie's waist. "I ran because—" Suddenly Alexis's phone started to ring and the intense moment was gone. Alexis pulled the phone from her pocket and said, "Sorry. I have to take it."

Alexis got up and walked over to the fireplace to talk.

Katie could have screamed. Alexis was so close to acknowledging what happened that day and talking about her feelings, and the moment was gone.

❖

Amelia was back at the cabin sitting at the kitchen table, while Byron made a phone call. Something had changed inside her, but what she didn't know. The voices that she had discovered and heard in the circle were still there but were only a muffled whisper, a mishmash of voices, and she couldn't tease them apart.

She tapped her fingers against the kitchen table incessantly. Since she'd left the circle, it felt like she had brought the energy from it with her. Her nerves were buzzing. It was most intense in her sex and her nipples and made her long for the touch of her lover to ease her need.

Byron walked back in the door and Amelia jumped up.

"Everything all right?" Amelia asked.

"Yes, I just had to call the office. Are you okay? You look a little tense and jumpy."

Amelia walked over to Byron, unbuttoned her coat, and slipped it off. She loosened Byron's tie and slipped her hands under her collar. "I just feel full of energy. Do you need to feed?"

Byron smiled. "Do you want me to feed?"

Instead of answering Amelia kissed Byron and jumped, wrapping her legs around her waist. They kissed feverishly, and Amelia just felt hotter by the second. There was a torrent of energy inside her, and it was desperate to get out.

Byron carried her into the bedroom, and between kisses they

pulled at each other's clothes. Amelia saw Byron's eyes were red, and it just made her want her all the more.

Amelia was naked, but Byron still had her jockey shorts on. Amelia couldn't wait and pulled Byron onto the bed on top of her. The need inside her was stronger than she had ever felt, and the utter bliss she experienced when Byron sucked her nipple and grasped the other breast was painfully good.

"I need you inside me, Byron. Fuck me, or I'm going to explode."

Byron grazed her teeth down her neck, teasing her for that first bite and suck of her blood. It wasn't fast enough for Amelia. She was overwhelmed and needed to set the pace herself.

She pushed Byron onto her back and straddled her. "Let me?"

Byron smiled. "Whatever you want, mia cara."

Amelia slipped Byron's strap-on out of her underwear and pumped it with her hand a few times, making Byron moan as she watched her.

"I need your cock," Amelia said in a low voice.

She was so turned on that her hands had a slight quiver in them. All she knew was that she needed Byron inside her, or she would explode.

Amelia eased the strap-on inside her and didn't take her time getting used to the feel. She pushed it deep and started to thrust. Bryon reached up and squeezed her breasts. They were on fire at her touch.

She leaned over and kissed Byron, sucking her lip and teasing her fangs with her tongue.

"You feel so good, mia cara," Byron moaned.

The muffled voices were getting louder in her head and seemed to increase with every thrust she took. Amelia's heart hammered like it was going to explode.

"I need to come," Amelia said in a desperate voice. She sat up and leaned against Byron's legs.

"I love you," Byron said.

"I love you." She held out her wrist to Byron and said, "Feed from me when I come."

Byron nodded and took her hand, peppering it with kisses, then scratching her wrist with her teeth.

Amelia closed her eyes, and her head fell backward. Her hips had settled into a slow, deep rhythm, and with each thrust the voices in her head got louder. Her head was starting to swim, her body to shake, as her orgasm approached.

It was going to be too powerful, too much, but she couldn't stop, not any more. Her hips sped up, and she moaned deeply, almost as if in pain. All the need and desperate want was ready to explode in her.

Just before she fell over the edge, Amelia told Byron, "Bite me, bite me now."

Amelia's hips started to jerk as a searing heat surged from her sex and speared all over her body. Her vision went white, and she heard a high-pitched whistle in her ears. Suddenly all the energy she had disappeared, and she fell forward onto Byron. Her body started to shake, and Byron wrapped her arms around her.

"It's all right. I'm here, you're safe."

Amelia opened her eyes, and she heard a clear voice in her head say, *Welcome, Amelia. We've been waiting for you.*

Alexis lay on her bed staring at the ceiling. She never slept much as it was, but after today, she was never going to sleep. She had come so close to telling Katie the truth of how she felt about her. Katie had this knack of looking in her eyes and finding the truth, but verbalizing it was different.

Things just seemed to get more complicated every day. She had finally had a phone call from her informant in Paris, and it was not what she had expected to find. Victorija had become a recluse and her Duca, Drasas, appeared to be the figurehead for the Dreds since their encounter in Scotland.

She'd shared this information with Byron earlier this evening, and neither of them knew what to make of it. Victorija was not one for delegation. She liked power and control, so there must be something else going on. There were also smaller vampire families, clans, newly turned vampires going to the Dred banner. They were building their numbers, but to what end?

Alexis was shaken from her thoughts when she heard a low moan coming from Katie's bedroom. Katie was dreaming.

But then the moan became, "No, please don't. Josie, no."

Alexis was by the side of her bed in seconds. Katie was thrashing around, quite distressed. She fell to her knees and took Katie's hand.

"Shh, shh, it's all right. I'm here."

Suddenly Katie gasped and her eyes popped open. "Alexis?"

"You were having a bad dream."

Katie turned over on her side to face Alexis. "Josie was chasing me, and I couldn't get away."

Alexis put both hands around Katie's and kissed her knuckles. "She can't get you. I'm here."

"Will you stay?" Katie asked.

"Of course I will. Just shut your eyes. You don't have to be frightened when I'm here."

CHAPTER ELEVEN

Victorija had been staring at the computer screen for hours, in between feeding from her vampire blood hosts. She had followed the trail of birth, death, and marriage certificates back through the years, from Daisy MacDougall's birth. She had nearly given up many times.

The way she was feeling, on the constant edge of hunger, was driving her insane. Victorija just wanted to get up and smash her head against the stone castle wall. But she resisted and finally found what she was looking for.

It was a parish record from 1810, a marriage in Glasgow between Marie Anne Brassard and Thomas MacDougall.

"Fuck." Victorija let her head fall to the desk in frustration. She had a hunch, followed it, and it had been right. The French Brassard family had married into the MacDougalls.

She sat up quickly and unlocked a drawer in her desk. Victorija pulled out an old leather diary, monogrammed *Angele Brassard*.

Victorija brought the diary to her lips and kissed the name on the cover. "My Angel. What do I do now?"

A feeling of panic surged through her body. It wasn't something Victorija was used to feeling, nor the pain of first love and fear and grief and despair that came along with her memories of Angele Brassard.

Victorija had shut down her heart and kept these raw, desperate emotions locked up so tight in a dark corner of her soul. So locked up that she had almost forgotten they were there, but with this blood hunger and the feelings that her grandmother had released with her touch, those overwhelming emotions came bursting out.

How could she cope with these feelings? On top of that, how could she be bonded by blood to Angele's descendent, the young woman who had destroyed the last part of light in her heart, and ushered in the darkness?

She was suddenly hit with an intense hunger pang, and she cried out.

❖

Amelia awoke with a gasp and sat up quickly. She could remember voices in her dreams but not the muffled ones from the stone circle. Clear voices asking her to go somewhere, but where she wasn't sure.

When she and Byron had made love last night, it was as if some switch had been clicked, opening up her mind to the voices.

She looked to the side and saw Byron sleeping soundly. It always made her happy to see that Byron was sleeping so deeply, so contentedly. Byron told her she'd never slept through the night when she was on her own. An hour or so was all that she could manage.

Amelia was proud and fulfilled that she could be that for Byron and give her the comfort that she deserved. Then she heard it. The voices from her dreams were ringing in her head.

Go to her. Go to her.

She looked at the bedside clock. It read five thirty a.m. Amelia scrubbed her face. Something had changed since last night. The muffled voices were loud, chattering, and clear.

Amelia sat up on the side of the bed. Now that she was fully awake, the voices were even clearer.

Go to her. Through the trees.

Before she could think about it too deeply, Amelia had pulled on her jeans and a jumper and was writing a note for Byron. *Gone for a walk.*

When she got outside, the voices got louder. Every step she took, they got louder still. She walked into the cover of the trees.

"You are such an idiot," Amelia told herself.

This was the kind of situation in a horror film that had you screaming at a character's stupidity. Yet here she was. She had been walking for about five minutes, the voices getting louder all the time, when she came out to a clearing.

There in the clearing was a perfect little cottage with smoke coming out of the chimney. Amelia got chills running down her spine. It felt like she was in some twisted fairy tale, and a wicked witch or a wolf would eat her all up. But she had to keep going now—whatever these voices were, they were willing her to this cottage, and she had to find out why. Even if Byron would kill her for it.

The door of the cottage was slightly ajar, and as she got closer, she could smell the breakfast cooking. In her horror movie Amelia would be shouting even louder at the screen, *Get out of there! Turn back!*

As she turned to walk away, she heard a voice from inside saying, "Running away, dear?"

Whoever lived in that cottage knew she was there. She would look stupid to walk away now.

Amelia turned and climbed the stairs at the front of the cottage and eased the door open. She found a kitchen table groaning with breakfast items, enough to feed an army, and there by a wood-burning stove was a grey-haired woman busy making more food.

The woman didn't turn around but said, "Sit yourself down, Amelia. I'll be right with you."

She knew her name? This was getting creepier by the second. Amelia sat on the edge of the seat, ready to run out of there if need be. Finally, the elderly woman turned around and gave her a huge smile, followed by a head bow.

"Principessa, my name's Sybil Westford. The Grand Duchess said you would be coming."

"Lucia? My partner's great-great-grandmother?" Amelia said.

"Yes." Sybil carried over a plate and put it in front of her. "I hope you like scrambled eggs."

"But she's dead."

Sybil smiled and poured out two cups of tea. "True, but you can still hear her if you're open enough." Sybil sat down next to her. "I think you know what I mean. Don't you?"

Amelia hesitated. "I've been hearing voices since I was in a casting circle yesterday."

"And what did they say?" Sybil asked.

"I couldn't tell. They were all talking over each other and too far away. I couldn't make out the words."

"And now?"

"It's all so clear. The voices wouldn't stop telling me to come here. I couldn't sleep."

Sybil smiled. "Those are the voices of our ancestors, your ancestors. All the witches who came before give us our power."

"So I am a witch? Really?" Amelia said.

When Sybil nodded, Amelia asked. "Did you know my mother and father?"

"I knew your mother. I was close to her."

"Who was she? And what about my father?"

Just as Sybil took a breath to answer, Byron burst through the door in a flash. "Stay back from my wife—" Byron stopped dead. "Sybil, you're still—"

Sybil laughed softly. "Alive?"

Byron caught her breath. "No, here."

Amelia looked back and forth between the two of them. Byron had dressed really hastily, having pulled on the jeans and T-shirt that Amelia bought her. How did she know Sybil?

"You two know each other?"

Sybil nodded. "We've crossed paths over the years. We first met when I was a girl, and Byron came to us during the War, although she was much better dressed back then."

Byron looked down at what she was wearing. "Please forgive me. I had to dress in haste. Amelia, why did you leave without me?"

"I didn't think I'd be in danger. The voices wouldn't stop talking, and I could hear them clearly after last night."

Sybil smiled at her, clearly understanding what had happened between them. "The power of love and communing with your partner in the flesh can open up a blocked mind to the ancestors."

Amelia felt heat radiating from her cheeks. Byron crouched down and took her hand.

"You shouldn't have left without me."

"It was something I felt I had to do on my own."

"Your guards are staying in the village?" Sybil said.

"You heard?"

"One of our coven—Catherine, who runs the shop in the village—spotted you," Sybil said.

Byron slipped into the seat beside Amelia. The panic she had felt when she had wakened to an empty bed was starting to subside.

Byron had met Sybil many years ago, during the War, when she was sent by the Secret Service to liaise with the coven here in the New Forest.

"Bhal is staying in the village, and Captain Villiers is staying in the cabin next door to us with a friend."

"Captain Villiers? Is she still as serious as she always was?"

"She is mellowing slightly. We think love is working its magic on her," Byron said.

"There's no greater magic than love," Sybil replied.

Amelia turned to Byron and said, "Why didn't you say you knew Sybil? We could have come to her straight away."

"I honestly didn't know she'd still be living here. I'd heard the coven wasn't as strong in numbers as it had once been."

"Yes," Sybil said, "we cunning folk were once the biggest and most powerful coven in Britain, but through one thing and another our numbers have dwindled."

"You are their leader now?" Byron asked.

Sybil smiled. "Yes, hard to believe that little girl you met then would grow up to be the leader?"

"Please, tell me about my birth mum, my dad, who were they? Do I still have family?" Amelia was sounding frustrated.

Byron put her arm around her. "Give Sybil time."

"More tea?" Sybil picked up the teapot.

"No, just tell me who I am." Amelia smacked her hand down on the table.

Sybil sat down again. "I will answer your questions, but first I need you to visit your adoptive mother and father."

"What? Why?"

"I need you to understand why things were done the way they were before I tell you everything," Sybil said.

"Why can't you witches stop talking in riddles and just speak the truth? The ones we met in London said I had to come here to find out the truth, these stupid voices in my head tell me to find you, and now you tell me to go back to my adoptive parents? When will it end? When will anyone give me a straight answer?"

"Amelia—" Byron said.

"No." Amelia shrugged away from Byron, and a flash of light came from her hands and knocked a chair across the room.

"You are a powerful witch, Amelia. But you can't control yourself or that power," Sybil said.

Byron looked at Sybil. "Please, Sybil. If you could tell her more. She is distressed about this."

"She?" Amelia said. "Who's *she*? The cat's mother? I have a name."

Byron knew Amelia was simply frustrated. Amelia's life had been turned upside down since the minute she'd met Byron, and every time Amelia thought she had a handle on this new world, this new existence, the rug was pulled from under her.

Byron took a breath and said. "*Amelia* is distressed. Could you please tell her some more?"

"I have my reasons. Go and see your parents, then come back to me. Now, let's have some more tea."

"I know you won't like this, Alexis, but these are my orders. Bhal and my guards will go with us to Amelia's parents' home tomorrow. I want you to stay here and guard Katie."

After leaving Sybil's cottage, Byron and Amelia went to Katie and Alexis's cabin and had dinner with them. Now Byron and Alexis were enjoying a glass of whisky and a cigar on the porch of the cabin.

"I think you're right, Principe."

"You do?" Byron was totally surprised—she'd expected a fight over this.

"Yes. Katie needs me. She wouldn't be ready for travelling there and travelling back, and I can't leave her here to fend for herself. Especially now. Did Bhal report the intelligence she was hearing?"

"Yes, many of the smaller European covens are joining the Dreds. Why on earth would they do that, after Victorija killed Lillian, the French coven high priestess? It makes no sense."

"For whatever reason the paranormal map of Europe is changing after a long period of calm. The change has already reached our shores," Alexis said. "We haven't encountered forced transitions for many years, but there are more and more at the moment. Like Josie."

Byron sighed. "Yes, that's true. Forced transitions cause havoc and pain to the human community and compromise our relationships with the wider human population."

"I can't risk Katie being alone," Alexis said.

Byron smiled. "Sounds as if your priorities are changing."

"You are still my Principe," Alexis said.

"I know that, but it's all right that your priorities are changing, Alexis. It's natural when you're in love. You are in love, aren't you?"

Alexis nodded and looked down at her boots.

Byron put her hand on the back of Alexis's neck and squeezed it hard. Byron looked her in the eye and said with slight menace, "You know what Katie's family means to me?"

"Of course I do."

"Then you be honest and don't hurt her, or I'll have your head."

"Yes, Principe. Of course I'll treat her with respect, but just because I have these feelings doesn't mean I'll act on them, even if

Katie would want me to. She won't want to know me after I tell her what I did, Byron."

Byron scoffed. "Tell her. I think Katie will surprise you."

❖

"You're feeling stronger?" Amelia asked Katie.

Katie was sitting on the couch with Amelia, talking after dinner. "Stronger with every day. Just being here, so close to nature, is helping," Katie said.

"And Alexis? Is she helping?" Amelia asked.

"She's falling over herself to help me. I don't know why."

"She cares, Katie."

Katie touched her bandaged neck and remembered the care Alexis had shown her. "Yes, I think she does, but I don't know if she's capable of admitting it."

Katie didn't mention that Alexis sat on her bedroom floor, holding her hand all night. Neither of them had mentioned it since.

"She will, I'm certain. You've known her longer than me. Is this taking care of you normal to her?"

"No, but she seems to blame herself for Josie attacking me. God knows why."

The door to the cabin opened and Byron and Alexis walked in.

Amelia whispered, "Just give her a chance, no matter what she tells you."

That was a strange thing for Amelia to say. What did she mean?

CHAPTER TWELVE

Katie gazed at Alexis as she filled up the dishwasher in the kitchen. It was such a novelty to see this stoic vampire suddenly doing domestic tasks.

She chuckled, and Alexis turned around. "Why are you laughing?"

"Finish up what you're doing, and come and sit with me," Katie said.

Alexis started the dishwasher, washed her hands, and came into the room holding two ice-cold bottles of water for them. She put both of the bottles down on the coffee table and went to stoke up the fire.

"It's nice having a real fireplace. So calming," Katie said.

"Real fires were all we had for most of my life, but they do give a nice atmosphere." Alexis joined her on the couch. "So, why were you laughing?"

"I hadn't ever seen you being domestic before. It was sweet," Katie said.

"No one has ever accused me of being sweet."

Katie laughed again. "It's not a bad thing. Besides, don't worry, I won't tell anyone. What did Byron want?"

"Amelia and Byron are going to visit Amelia's family. It's only a few villages away," Alexis said.

Katie felt sadness envelop her. She didn't want Alexis to go. "I see. When do you leave?"

Alexis raised a questioning eyebrow. "I'm not leaving. I need to be here to make sure you're safe and to look after you."

Katie was so surprised, but happy. She knew how important Byron's life and security were to Alexis and was amazed that she was staying.

"Thank you," was all she could think of to say.

The room was filled with silence for a minute or so, but Alexis didn't seem uncomfortable. The quiet of the room was nice, especially with the crackle of the flames in the background.

"How are you feeling, Katie?" Alexis asked.

"Much better. You know that feeling I told you about? That I wasn't quite here, like I was a step out of time and place?"

"Yes," Alexis replied.

Katie had to be brave and honest. How could she expect it of Alexis when she wasn't herself?

"Since I've been here with you…"

Alexis turned around on the couch so she was facing Katie. "Yes?"

"It's hard to put into words. I was in limbo, floating between life and death, and you are grounding me in life, in hope." Katie took Alexis's hand. "You've been my anchor."

Alexis turned away from her and rubbed her forehead with her finger. She looked stressed, uptight.

"I don't deserve such praise, Katie," Alexis said.

"You do, you saved my life."

Alexis just shook her head. Katie didn't think she would get Alexis to open up at the moment. She was beating herself up over something, but it would take time for her to feel safe enough to talk about it, Katie guessed.

Katie leaned back on the couch and said, "Tell me a story."

"Tell you a story? About what?"

"Where you were born, your family, how you became Captain Villiers? How you became Duca? Anything."

Alexis crossed and uncrossed her legs, ran her hand through her hair, and questioned whether she could tell her story. Katie must have sensed how uncomfortable she was, because she said, "You don't have to tell me if you don't want to."

"No, I'm just not used to talking about it. I haven't..."

Alexis thought of Anna. She was the last person to hear her story, but she wanted Katie to know who she was.

"I was born in 1792," Alexis said.

Katie's face lit up with interest. "Wow, I can't imagine what it's like to live through all those years."

"You just adapt. There isn't much choice. My mother's name was Jane Villiers. She used the title *Mrs.*, but she was never married."

"That was a big deal back then," Katie said.

"Yes, she pretended to be a widow and got away with it until near the end of her life. I lived a comfortable life with my mother. We had a nice house, servants, everything paid for by Father."

"You said your mother wasn't married?" Katie said.

Alexis cleared her throat. "No, she wasn't. She was the mistress, or kept woman, as some people might have said then, of the Duke of Branwick and Bowater."

"You're a duke's daughter? That's amazing. Was he a nice man?" Katie asked.

Alexis sighed. "He was a man of his time. Strict, and didn't much like the fact I behaved and dressed like a boy. I had to dress up when he came on Friday and Saturday. He spent the rest of the week with his other family. His proper family."

"He had a wife and other family?"

"Yes, Lady Branwick and his son, James."

"You said your brother's name with anger in your voice. Did you not like him? Did your father's wife and your half-brother know about you and your mum?"

Alexis gave a rueful laugh. "Oh yes, I met James quite often, and he went out of his way to remind me that I was illegitimate."

"That's horrible. What a pig!"

Alexis opened up her bottle of water and took a mouthful. Telling her truth was hard, but Katie deserved it.

"I wasn't upset for myself—I've always had a thick skin—but

my mother had to put up with a lot of looks and gossip behind her back. But she adored my father for some reason and put up with that life."

Katie moved closer. "I suppose love makes us do things we never imagined."

Alexis gulped hard. It was as if Katie knew, but she *couldn't.* "Yes, it does."

This would have been a great chance to tell her about the attack and what really happened, but she bottled it.

"Anyway, most of the time Father left us alone, and my mum made sure I was well educated, and I had a father figure in my mother's brother who taught me everything a girl wasn't meant to learn. Sword fighting, shooting, hunting. It was in those moments that I felt mostly like the real me. My brother was jealous of me, I think. He wasn't a natural fighter or hunter like I was, and it frustrated him if Father gave me praise. Then one day everything changed. My whole life turned on its head."

"What happened?" Katie asked.

"Father died, and my brother inherited everything. My father had left a stipulation in his will that my brother James must take care of me and my mother, but he had a different idea about *care* than our father."

Katie took Alexis's hand and furrowed her eyebrows. "What did he do?"

"Cut us off without a penny."

"Bastard," Katie said angrily.

"That's what he thought I was. Anyway, it was quite a shock. The staff had to go, and we hardly had enough to live on from my mother's savings. It wasn't long after that, that Mother grew ill. Very ill. The doctor gave her only a few months." Alexis's voice cracked with emotion.

Katie lifted her hand and kissed the knuckles. "I'm so sorry, Alexis."

Alexis wanted to bury her head in Katie's neck and sob away all her pain and guilt, but she couldn't.

"Thank you. But I was able to pay back my brother James with a little shame of his own. When my mother was in her last few days, she asked me to fetch a pile of letters from her safe. They were between my mother and father, and some were from his wife, Lady Branwick. James wasn't my half-brother, he was my full brother. My father had two children with my mother, but his wife was unable to have children. Thus the title and the lands belonging to my father's family would go to some distant cousin. To stop this happening, my mother agreed to allow James to be brought up as Lady Branwick's son. He would then be the legitimate heir and carry on the family title and lands."

Katie gasped. "That must have been devastating for your mum."

"Yes, it hurt her so badly to watch another woman bring up her son, especially when he got older and looked down on us as my father's shame, when he was part of it."

"So what did you do?" Katie asked.

"When my mother passed away, I took the evidence to James. He was terrified of the consequences of losing his dukedom and agreed to pay me a proper inheritance. I made him sign a letter at his lawyer's so he wouldn't weasel out of it. I was then able to buy a commission in the army and live the life I wanted. Of course I had to pretend to be a man, and I passed successfully and made the rank of captain during the Napoleonic Wars."

"You're so brave," Katie said.

"I'm anything but, believe me."

"Did you ever see him again?"

"On his deathbed. I had been turned by Victorija decades before then, and when I heard he was dying, I felt I had to see him."

"How did explain your appearance?" Katie asked.

"I told him the truth. He was pretty out of it on drugs at the end, and no one would have taken his words seriously. I was glad I went. He apologized for what he had done and said that the guilt had eaten away at him over the years. That gave me an ending to that chapter of my life."

"Ready for the next chapter of your immortal life?" Katie's smiled.

"Yes, quite so," Alexis said.

❖

Katie was gobsmacked at Alexis's former life. She would never have believed it. It was like something from a Jane Austen or a Charles Dickens novel. No wonder Alexis was so guarded emotionally—she was hurt so very badly.

Alexis had gone to make Katie her nightly cup of tea, which, Katie knew, was also an opportunity for Alexis to retreat and recover a little after exposing so much of her past. When she returned with her tea, Katie said, "You must be so bored, stuck here with me, instead of out there doing your duty with Byron."

Alexis sat down and said simply, "You are my duty."

Katie was taken aback and didn't know what to say next. Surely Alexis couldn't feel that guilty. What was going on in this mixed-up vampire brain of hers?

The silence between them hung so heavily that it felt it was going to be ended with either a passionate kiss or a passionate argument. But Alexis stepped up before any of that happened.

"It's your turn," Alexis said.

Katie, who was enjoying the warmth of her tea mug, snapped her head around to Alexis.

"My turn? What do you mean?"

"You wanted a story from my life, and now it's your turn to tell me one from yours."

"A story?" Katie said with surprise. "I haven't got any interesting stories. I've just lived my life with the Debreks."

"You do. For instance, what was it like to grow up in a household full of vampires? I imagine it didn't feel normal."

"Normal? What is normal? Anyway it was normal to me. When I look back, the most overwhelming feeling I remember was of safety. I had a whole clan full of immortal vampires to make sure I was safe. They played with me, were very indulgent with their time, and entertained me as I ran around the estate. It's strange when I think about it. The vampires that played with me back then haven't changed, but now I'm grown up and basically the same age, and when I'm old and grey they'll still be the same age."

"I don't remember that—I mean, I remember some of the children of the human staff running around, but I don't remember my vampires playing with you," Alexis said.

"You were too busy with your mind on clan business." Of course, when she had the biggest crush on Alexis as a teenager, Katie often wished Alexis would notice.

"What was it like at school?" Alexis asked.

Katie chuckled softly. "That was a little strange, I suppose. As you know, the human staff get the best of everything, even more my family, because of our history with Byron. I was sent to the finest private school by Byron. The other children were sons and daughters of aristocracy, rich businesspeople, and celebrities, and there I was, my mum head housekeeper for the Debreks and my dad butler. There was gossip and lots of rumours about why I was really there."

"What kind of rumours?" Alexis asked.

"That I was Byron's father's love child, that Byron *was* really a man, and I was her illegitimate daughter, but nothing was as wild as the truth."

"I suppose not." Alexis laughed.

Alexis was enjoying listening to Katie talk so much. She couldn't believe she had kept herself distanced from Katie for so long. Katie was such a wonderful young woman, but that was why she kept herself away, because Katie terrified her.

"I wish we had talked like this sooner," Alexis said.

"So do I. My teenage self wished that too," Katie said softly.

"Why?" Alexis noticed a change in Katie physically. Her breathing became shallower, but her heart was increasing in speed. "What is it?"

Katie cleared her throat and looked away. "It's a bit embarrassing."

Alexis sat closer. "You don't need to be embarrassed with me."

Katie searched her eyes, then took a breath. "I had the biggest crush on you since I was about twelve. I spent all my time trying to get your attention, but to no avail."

Alexis felt like she was punched in the chest. All these years they had been arguing and sniping at each other, and all that time there had been something between them.

"Then I left home and went to university."

Did that mean she grew out of her crush, she had no feelings any more? But that night in Katie's room. Alexis was sure Katie reciprocated her passion. Alexis knew what she should say—*I feel the same way, I hope you still feel that for me, kiss me, let me make love to you, the first time I tasted you, I knew I wanted you*—but instead, like an idiot, she went on to tell her why she couldn't handle feelings of love and passion.

"I've been in love before."

Katie's eyes widened at that. "You have?"

"Yes, back in 1850. I fell in love with a witch from a London coven," Alexis said.

Katie gulped. "What was her name?"

"Anna. Byron warned me against falling for or having a relationship with a mortal, but it was first love, I was too wrapped up in it, and too young a vampire to understand the consequences."

"What happened?"

It was so hard to tell this story, even though the pain in her heart was being eased by her love for Katie.

"Byron and I had been called away on some business that evening. We were supposed to be having a dinner party with friends, and I was going to propose to Anna."

"You?" Katie said with shock. "Get married?"

"Yes, well, I was still passing as a man in those days, and Byron was going to slip the vicar a few quid in case he was suspicious. But it never got that far. We returned back to the London house and found it had been attacked. Byron lost her lover, and I found Anna with her throat ripped out."

Katie gasped and put her hand to her mouth. "Oh God. Like

that night when the London house was attacked and my friends killed when we were at The Sanctuary?"

Alexis nodded. "I didn't want to take the chance that would happen again."

Katie took Alexis's hand. "I'm sorry. I shouldn't have argued and behaved like a brat."

"You didn't. I should have explained myself, instead of ordering you like one of my vampires," Alexis said.

Alexis loved the feel of Katie's fingers caressing the back of her hand. She realized being truthful was their only way forward.

"That night when I held Anna's dead body in my arms, I promised myself I'd never let myself fall in love or have a relationship with a mortal again."

Katie stopped caressing her hand and went stiff. She'd clearly said the wrong thing.

Katie let go of Alexis's hand and stood slowly. "I'm really tired. I think I'll go to bed."

❖

Alexis paced up and down in front of the fire, her hunger for fresh blood gnawing at her nerves like a million rats.

She downed the glass of blood she had poured herself and prepared another from the bottle on the mantelpiece. Going without fresh blood wasn't pleasant, but she could normally cope for this short a period, but this wasn't a normal situation.

Being in such close proximity to the woman she loved, the woman who fuelled her thoughts, her fantasies, her needs, was driving her hunger. Now she knew how Byron had felt when she fell for Amelia.

Alexis was trying to keep it together for Katie's sake, but she was stumbling with every word and had hurt Katie.

It was clear Katie had feelings for her. That had become especially clear in light of Katie's admission that she'd had a crush on her as a young woman.

And instead of telling Katie the truth about her own feelings, she'd done her best to convince Katie that she wouldn't be interested in love or a relationship again. Alexis leaned against the mantelpiece and glared at herself in the mirror.

"You're a bloody fool."

But wasn't she correct? She'd vowed she didn't want to love anyone again, but did she? She had to do something. She put down her glass and sped to Katie's room's door and felt even worse. With her enhanced hearing she could identify the snuffles of tears.

Those tears were her fault. "Katie?"

She heard Katie blow her nose in an attempt to cover the fact she had been crying, Alexis suspected.

"What is it?" Katie said with anger in her voice.

"Er, tomorrow...would you like to go a walk with me?" Alexis smacked herself in the head. *That's what you come up with? Seriously.*

"If you want," Katie replied.

At the very least, hopefully a new day would bring Alexis more courage.

CHAPTER THIRTEEN

Byron was worried about Amelia. She'd hardly said a word since they left their forest cabin, and she doubted she'd slept much last night. Her mind had been left reeling from this new information from Sybil, so goodness knew how Amelia felt. One thing that continued to surprise Byron was how much Amelia had been wrapped up in Byron's world all this time, and she never realized it.

The weather matched the sombre mood in the car as the rain bucketed down outside, and in the silence, the pounding of the rain was all the more pronounced.

They pulled up beside a farmhouse outside the village they had just passed through, and Amelia grasped at her hand.

"Is this it?"

"Yes, I can't believe I've come back here. I vowed I never would."

Byron cupped Amelia's cheek. "This time you have me with you. No one can do you any harm while I'm around. I promise you that."

"Words can wound as deeply as any physical blow," Amelia said. "I've become everything Mum and Dad warned I would when I ran to the big city and bright lights. I'm in league with the devil, or so they'll think when they see you."

"Well, perhaps, but you know differently. Just get the

information, and let them think what they like. They'll never know I'm a vampire anyway."

Amelia snorted. "They bloody will. I'm telling you—I grew up with this. For some reason they believed in your world, the paranormal one. I thought they were mad and their fundamentalist Christian ideas were as cuckoo as them, but here we are—they were right."

"Maybe that has to do with your past? Maybe they were let into our secret because of you?"

"Maybe," Amelia replied.

"Shall we get it over with then?" Byron asked.

Amelia wrung her hands. "Let me gather my thoughts. Just another few minutes?"

Byron kissed Amelia's hand. "Anything you like, mia cara."

❖

Katie had been waiting patiently since this morning for a break in the weather. She was determined to get out for their walk, just as Alexis had promised her, and finally the rain had stopped for the moment.

She was waiting by the front door for Alexis while she finished up a phone call with one of the vampires that Byron had left in the village hotel. Katie sat in the chair on the porch and watched the water drops that the rain had left dripping off the roof.

There was something calming about the forest scene after the rain, something soothing, fresh. Katie was feeling more connected to life with each passing day. It was a great idea of Byron's to invite her here, and of course being close to Alexis was helping. Alexis, who she knew was her anchor, despite Alexis's assertion last night that she wasn't interested in love.

That had hurt her feelings. Every time they seemed to get closer, Alexis either ran or said the wrong thing. Maybe she had overreacted last night, but it was hard to hear all about the woman that Alexis had loved.

Just thinking that made Katie feel guilty. After all, the poor woman was killed, but it was hard knowing that the person you loved wouldn't or didn't want to move on from the past. Because she did love Alexis, every annoying, bad-tempered part of her. She always had.

The cabin door opened and Alexis walked out. "Sorry to take so long. I just had to check in with the troops."

"Troops?" Katie questioned.

"Vampires. I'm an old army officer. It's hard to shake off sometimes. Are we ready?"

"Yes, is everything all right?" Katie asked.

Alexis looked confused. "Sorry, what?"

"With Byron and Amelia?" Katie said.

"Oh, sorry. I see what you mean. Yes, they set off earlier, and Bhal checked in a short time ago to say they were nearly there."

"I hope Amelia will be okay and find the answers she's looking for."

Alexis helped Katie up and offered her arm. "I'm sure she will. Shall we take our walk?"

Katie was glad to take Alexis's arm. She was getting better but wasn't at her full strength. They walked down the steps and down one of the forest paths beside the cabin. Katie looked at all the colours of the leaves and inhaled the fresh scent of the woods after the rain. She sighed.

"Is there something wrong?" Alexis asked.

"No, it's beautiful. I'm so glad to be out in the fresh air."

Alexis smiled. "Good, I'm glad. Listen, I'm sorry if I upset you in some way last night."

"Why would you upset me?"

"I thought—" Alexis would have to admit listening at Katie's bedroom door. "It doesn't matter."

They walked on in silence. Alexis was desperate to talk and open up about her feelings. The love she had inside her had grown so large that it was so hard to keep contained.

But what to come clean about first? That she loved her or that she almost tried to forcibly turn her into a vampire? Both could destroy any kind of new friendship or feelings they shared.

They crossed over a little bridge with a stream flowing underneath. "It's so pretty here. Yes, pretty and…"

"What?" Alexis asked.

Katie guided them over to a bench made out of tree stumps. "Let me catch my breath. I can't wait till I'm fully fit again. I've usually got so much energy."

"You'll be back full of vim and vigour in no time. What were you saying before? It's pretty here and—?"

Katie didn't know to explain it exactly. "Um…it has a feeling of something more ancient, something otherworldly, close to the spirits, I suppose."

"It is. A witch once told me that the veil between our world and the next is very thin here. Like a portal where the two worlds intersect. That's why the cunning folk based themselves here."

"The cunning folk?" Katie asked.

"The witch coven who lived here. They were called the cunning folk. An ancient coven of witches, very powerful ones at that."

"And that old woman Amelia met. She's one of them?"

Alexis nodded. "Sybil, yes she's one of the few left."

Katie rubbed her neck.

"Are you okay?" Alexis said. Alexis felt bad. Maybe she could offer some of her blood to help Katie heal more quickly. Vampire blood was rich and could ease all manner of physical harms, but she couldn't offer her blood without telling Katie the truth. Maybe it was now or never.

"Shall we keep walking, or do you want to go back?" Alexis asked.

"No, I'd like to go a little further." Katie took her arm again and they walked onward.

Alexis closed her eyes and took a breath. She was going to do it. "Katie, I'd like to talk to you about something."

"What is it?"

"It's about the night Josie attacked you."

Katie sighed. "Do we have to relive it again? I'm trying to forget it."

"Yes, I have to tell you what happened," Alexis said.

"Okay then, tell me."

This was it. She would relive her shame and lose any chance she had with Katie.

"When I found you that night, you were—" Alexis stopped dead. She could hear something. She had tuned out all of the usual forest noises, but this was different. There were lots of voices coming from all around.

"What is it?" Katie asked.

Alexis held her finger to her lips, then guided Katie into the bushes to keep out of sight.

Amelia held Byron's hand tightly as they walked up the path to her parents' front door. Behind them, Bhal and Wilder followed, leaving the rest of the guards at the cars. The nerves in Amelia's stomach doubled as they got near the door.

What would she say, would she manage to keep it together? Her parents always managed to make her doubt herself. She looked down at the Grand Duchess's ring on her wedding finger.

You're strong now. They can't hurt you.

Suddenly Byron stopped and pushed Amelia's hand away from the door.

"What are you doing?" Byron pointed to the broken lock on the front door. "Oh no."

"Wilder? Stay here with the Principessa. Bhal, you're with me."

"Yes, Principe," Wilder said.

"But Byron—" Amelia tried to stop her.

Byron gave her a serious look. "Please, Amelia. We need to check that it's safe first."

Amelia finally relented and walked back to the car with Wilder.

Byron could smell the unmistakable odour of fresh blood and heard a low moaning noise.

"Blood, inside," Byron whispered to Bhal.

Bhal nodded and drew the large Celtic sword from her back. "Let me go in first, Principe."

Byron nodded and watched as Bhal pushed open the front door slowly. She followed Bhal in and pointed her in the direction of the blood. When they got to what looked like the drawing room door, Bhal held up three fingers and counted down.

On one, Bhal kicked open the door, and what they found shocked even Byron. Two people, who she presumed were Amelia's adoptive parents. The male had his entire throat ripped out and was as still as the grave, but she could see and hear the woman's shallow breathing, despite her injuries.

Byron sped over and dropped to her knees beside her. "Mrs. Honey?"

Byron's eyes must have turned red, as she had been expecting a fight, because Amelia's mother looked absolutely terrified.

"Vampire?" She wheezed.

"I am, but I'm a friend of Amelia's. She wanted to come and visit you. What happened?"

"Vampires, witches, they came looking for us. What's your name, vampire?"

"Byron Debrek."

Mrs. Honey grabbed her arm. "Don't let them get her. The witch said you would come one day, that you would protect..."

Byron was starting to get even more fearful now. She had to know who they were. "Bhal? Check on Amelia and Wilder at the car."

"Yes, Principe," Bhal replied.

Byron turned her attention back to Amelia's mother. "Who are they? Why do they want Amelia?"

"She's...descendent," Mrs. Honey rasped.

"Descendent? What does that mean?"

"Safe..." Mrs. Honey said.

"I will, but what does *descendent* mean?" Byron asked.

"Tell her we always loved her, and find Sybil…"

Then she went limp. Mrs. Honey was gone. It was then that Amelia rushed into the room and screamed at the sight.

❖

"What the hell is going on?" Katie said softly. They were crouched in the undergrowth since Alexis said she heard something.

Alexis again shushed her. "Please, let me listen."

Katie wanted to say something snappy back, but she kept quiet. Alexis had her captain-of-the-guard voice on again.

After a few minutes Alexis turned to her and said, "They've passed now."

"Who's passed now?" Katie asked with annoyance.

"You still need to be quiet—a vampire could hear us. I heard a lot of voices approaching. They were talking about finding someone quickly and eliminating them."

"Killing them?" Katie said with shock.

Alexis nodded, and then her phone rang. She grabbed it quickly to stop the loud ringtone.

Katie worried more and more as she listened to Alexis's side of the conversation.

"But the Principessa is unharmed?…Yes, yes, of course. Katie is with me…No, I won't let her out of my sight…Yes, Principe." Alexis ended the call.

"What's happening?" Katie asked.

"When they arrived to see the Principessa's parents, they had been viciously attacked by vampires. Byron has a suspicion that they may go to Sybil next, and after what I heard, I think that's a safe bet."

"Don't think you're going to leave me behind while you deal with this," Katie warned.

"I can't. As much as I'd like to, you wouldn't be safe."

"So what do we do?"

"Bhal has ordered any of our vampires left in the village to meet us here, and then we'll go to Sybil's cottage. Then you will just need to keep behind me with no arguments." Katie did open her mouth to argue, but Alexis said firmly, "No, I don't care what you say. You mean too much to me to risk you getting hurt."

That did shut Katie up.

❖

Amelia sat on the couch gazing at her adoptive parents' bodies covered with a sheet. She wasn't crying, she couldn't. Amelia felt numb and cold.

Byron finished talking to Bhal and joined her on the couch. "How are you feeling?"

"Numb. I want to cry, but I can't. I know they were harsh to me, and I couldn't wait to get away from them, but they were still my parents. They gave me a roof over my head, and I never wanted for anything materially. Emotionally, yes, but—"

Byron put her arm around her. "I understand. They were a big part of your life, and they didn't deserve this ending. You are right to grieve them."

"I know. We'll make sure they have a decent funeral?" Amelia said.

"Of course we will. The police will be here soon, and we'll head back."

"What about Sybil?"

"I've let Alexis know, and there are vampires on their way to her."

"This is a mess, Byron. Not long ago I was opening my first business, enjoying the start of married life, and now—everything's unravelling."

Byron pulled Amelia to her. "All of those good things will be waiting for us when we have sorted out this situation. We have an immortal life to look forward to, and I promise you will be safe to enjoy it. We will grieve your parents and deal with whatever comes to us."

Amelia grasped Byron's lapels and hugged her tightly. "There's no way I could cope with this without you."

Byron kissed her head. "You'll never have to."

❖

Alexis edged closer to the perimeter around Sybil's house, with Katie close behind her. They heard bangs and shouts as they got closer, and when they could finally see what was going on, they saw Sybil at the door of the cottage trying to hold back a group of attackers.

"Who are they?" Katie whispered.

"Vampires and witches together, I sense," Alexis said.

"Why are witches helping vampires?"

"I've no idea. Look."

Alexis pointed to Sybil when they were close enough to the cottage. Sybil was pouring her power into a dome of protection around her cottage, which wasn't allowing the vampires through. Some of the witches helping the vampires were casting spells to try to break through Sybil's spell.

"You can't hold us out forever, witch!" one of the vampires shouted.

Alexis turned to Katie and put her hands on either side of her face, then stared directly into her eyes. She used her telepathy skills to speak directly to Katie's mind.

Can you hear me? Nod if you can.

Katie nodded.

Good. I don't want the vampires to hear my voice. I'm going to help Sybil, but I want you to promise that you'll stay hidden here, no matter what you see out there.

Katie started to protest but Alexis stopped her, out of the blue, with a kiss.

I can't help Sybil if I'm worrying about the woman I deeply care about being in danger.

Katie was taken aback at both the kiss and the admission that Alexis cared about her. Instead of protesting and because she couldn't speak, she placed her hand on her heart to show her feelings. Alexis smiled and returned the gesture exactly as Katie had done and smiled.

Katie could hardly watch as Alexis headed out into the fray in a flash. Alexis dispatched the witches quickly, with them not even knowing she was there. Alexis then began hand-to-hand combat with the other vampires. Katie was mesmerized by Alexis. Watching her fight was something to behold. She was so quick, a master of unarmed combat. She could picture her on the battlefield in the days before she was a vampire, serving in the army.

When Alexis disabled all but two of the vampires, the Debrek vampires burst onto the scene. The two remaining vampires ran, leaving the injured ones on the ground. Alexis was breathing heavily and shouted to her people, "Get these vampires out of here before they heal."

Then Alexis turned her head to Katie and, with blood-red eyes, winked at her. There was such passion and heat in that look that if there had been no one else about, Katie would have run out from the trees and leapt on Alexis. She wanted her.

It was the first time since being attacked that she had felt such aching need, such hunger and passion for someone—okay, *Alexis*. It had always been Alexis.

❖

"Why didn't you tell me what I wanted to know? Instead of letting me find my parents like that?" Amelia paced up and down inside Sybil's cabin.

Byron and Amelia had come straight to Sybil on their return.

"I never expected them to be attacked, Amelia. I'm sorry you had to see that."

There was a short silence, and then Sybil said, "I'll make some tea."

Sybil stood up slowly with the aid of her walking stick and Amelia said, "Why always tea? I don't want any bloody tea."

Byron tried to comfort her, but she pushed her hand away.

Sybil didn't bat an eyelid and walked over to her cooker to put on her kettle.

Amelia immediately felt guilty and covered her face with her hands. "I'm sorry—it's just been too much. I don't know what to think, to feel, to say. I ran away from Mum and Dad at my first opportunity. Their religion and beliefs were suffocating, but compared to the lives some people have, I was privileged. I never worried about money or where my next meal was coming from. Everything I needed, they gave me. They didn't deserve their fate."

"People seldom do, my dear. They might not have been the perfect parents emotionally, but they were the parents you needed. Religiously we might have differed violently, but when it came to you, we were in wholehearted agreement."

"Why do you say that?" Amelia asked.

Sybil poured out the tea and asked Amelia to carry it over to the table. When they sat down, Sybil said, "We needed you away from this paranormal world, away from those who would wish you harm."

"Who would wish me harm? I'm just an ordinary woman," Amelia said.

"Sometimes the most ordinary people do extraordinary things, my dear. The Honey family has a long history with the witches here."

"I know they used to take a group from the church to witch hunt and break up any meetings of new women here in the forest. They made me terrified of what they called the evil occult," Amelia said.

Sybil laughed softly. "David Honey and his father before him were certainly pains in the neck. They tried to break up our meetings, our ceremonies, worshipping the devil as they thought we were, but in the end David and Joy Honey were our saviours."

Amelia was trying hard to keep a clear head and take all this information in, but after a day like today, it was hard.

"Tell me everything."

"First thing you have to know is the history. There was a time long ago when spirits and gods of nature were revered by the human race, and creatures, magic folk, and all manner of paranormals lived alongside them. We were part of their tribes, their ancient rites, births, marriages, deaths, and we sent them to the underworld."

"Like the Celtic tribes?" Amelia asked.

"Exactly. As mystics, we witches helped the humans navigate their lives, helped them honour nature and the gods. Don't get me wrong, there were those in our community who wished to use our advantages over the human world and did. Two groups formed, one that sought disorder and chaos and power over the earth, and one— including ours and Byron's great-great-grandmother's coven—who tried to protect humankind.

"As human society and achievement moved on, the old natural religions began to be forgotten. Gods and spirits who were worshipped were demonized, as all paranormals were. We weren't trusted any more, even those who were trying to help. We were persecuted by humans and driven into the shadows. Some of us believed that the shadows gave us safety, while some longed for a return to controlling and influencing the world to their ends. Power, it's all about power."

"So where do I come into this?"

"We were given a vision that a darkness would come, a darkness brought by a witch who had once been human, that would devastate the land. A witch named Anka."

"Anka?" Byron replied.

Amelia turned to Byron. "You've heard of her?"

"Only in legends over the years. People tell stories of an ancient human woman who coveted the power of the witches and sold her soul to gain power."

Sybil nodded. "You are right. A long, long time ago our ancestors managed to trap her, but somehow she got free again. As each decade passes, she gets stronger. Left unchecked, the darkest of paranormals will rule, with war and hate feeding her, until the day comes when she is unstoppable."

"What did the vision say about me?" Amelia asked.

"That two descendants of those of us on the side of good would bring together the paranormal world. One witch, and one from a family of vampire slayers. Both would bring together witches and vampires and humans to defeat the darkness, because only with everyone pulling together can we even hope to beat her. She has some evil backers, *ancient* evil."

Amelia was silent for a few seconds then said, "Who is the other descendant?"

"I don't know, but you will find them."

"But wait, witches and vampires attacked you tonight. Aren't they already united?"

"Not all covens fought for good, my dear. Some witches have an incredible lust for power."

"What happened to my birth mother, and why did you give me to David and Joy Honey?" Amelia asked.

Sybil got up and went to a drawer. She brought out a photo album and walked back over. Sybil opened the first page, and Amelia saw a picture of a dark-haired woman, who looked very like her, cradling a new baby in her arms.

"That's your mother, Bronte. She came to us when she was nineteen. On the run from something, she wouldn't talk about it. I became a sort of grandmother figure for her."

Byron watched Amelia flick through the photo album with tears starting to run down her face. She sat closer and put her arm around Amelia.

"Who was Amelia's father, Sybil?" Byron asked.

"I don't know. Bronte realized she was pregnant not long after she joined us, and she wouldn't talk about the father. She was so happy when she had you, Amelia. Bronte said you gave her life meaning."

Byron gave Amelia her handkerchief as she began to cry more.

"What happened to her?" Amelia asked.

"I and a few of the elder witches had a vison the night you were born, that you were one of the descendants. We prepared ourselves for a special birthing ceremony, and the night of it, David and Joy Honey and their friends were protesting and singing hymns nearby." Sybil put her head down. "Anka and her people attacked us. They wanted to kill you."

Byron pulled Amelia into a hug to give her support.

"What happened?" Amelia asked.

Byron guessed this truth was going to upset Amelia even more.

"They were targeting Bronte, so she gave you to me and told me to get out of the ceremonial circle in the forest. I ran, dodging dark witches along the way, until I ran right into David and Joy's group. I made a snap decision—I asked them to take you, protect you, and keep you away from anything in our paranormal world, and they did."

Byron remembered what Joy had said when she lay dying. "Sybil, Joy said she was told one day a vampire would come along. Was that me?"

Sybil smiled. "Yes, you were always part of the vision, part of our plans."

She watched Amelia trace her fingers over her face in the picture, then say, "Hello, Bronte, hello, Mum."

CHAPTER FOURTEEN

Alexis walked back inside the cabin and found Katie talking on her phone. Trying not to disturb her, Alexis walked to the fridge to get some water. She heard Katie whisper, "You have to be careful, Daisy...Yes, I know I said I would, but...okay, we'll talk when I get back."

Katie turned around and jumped when she saw Alexis there. "God, you'll give me a heart attack."

"Sorry, would you like a drink?"

Alexis was sure something was going on. The phone call coupled with Katie's increased heart rate suggested that.

Katie rubbed her bandaged wound and snapped, "No—sorry, I'm just sick of this. I want to be better."

Before Alexis had time to think about what she was saying, she blurted out, "I could make that injury better, you know."

Katie's eyes widened and she walked closer. "What? By drinking your blood?"

Alexis wished she'd never opened her mouth. Her heart was pounding. Katie looked shocked at the suggestion of drinking her blood, and she'd nearly done that to her. Now was she offering to break another Debrek rule? She'd lived by them strictly, and now because of Katie she was willing to break them.

"No, not that. This only works for minor wounds, and we're

not supposed to, but my blood dripped onto your wound can heal it. The Debrek clan banned the practice because we are not supposed to interfere with humans in that way."

"I wouldn't want you to break a rule for me," Katie said.

Alexis took Katie's hand. "We could keep it our secret."

Katie shook her head. "Secrets take a heavy toll on you, Alexis."

Alexis put her head down. "I know that, believe me, but it's not a cardinal rule, like consent. Let me heal it?"

"I'm not sure," Katie said.

"Okay, well, I'll change your bandage. Come on," Alexis said.

Katie followed Alexis to the kitchen table and sat down while Alexis got the first aid case out. There was such a tension between them. It had been building since Alexis's kiss earlier before the attack on Sybil. She didn't know how she would handle Alexis touching her. Just being this close was giving her goosebumps.

Alexis got the new bandage ready then started to unwrap the old one. At the touch of Alexis's fingertips, Katie had an intake of breath.

Alexis stopped. "Sorry, did I hurt you?"

"No." Katie's lips parted, and she moistened them with the tip of her tongue. She saw Alexis's eyes focus on her lips and the blood-red colour of hunger wash across her eyes. Katie had the urge to push her fingers into Alexis's hair and bring Alexis's lips to hers. Instead she looked down, away from temptation. "No, you didn't hurt me."

Alexis pulled off the bandage, and then she did feel pain. "It feels worse. Hot and painful."

Alexis threw down the bandage, and growled, "It looks like it's infected. Fucking Josie."

Katie tried to see as much of the wound as she could. It looked fiery red. "It's not your fault—it's mine for not listening to you and going to the club. I realize now you've always been trying to look after me, and I just saw it as you bossing me around."

Alexis cupped her cheek, and Katie saw tears forming in her eyes. "I didn't protect you." Katie watched Alexis pinch the bridge of her nose. "I can't do this any more. I'm no better than Josie, no better than Victorija Dred," Alexis said angrily.

Katie had no idea what was going on now. Alexis looked tortured by something. "What are you talking about? You're nothing like them. You're the Debrek Duca. You take care of us all and uphold the high ideals that the Grand Duchess gave this clan."

"No, I don't. I'm a fraud. I have no nobility."

Katie reached out to touch Alexis but she pulled away.

"Tell me what's wrong, Alexis?"

Alexis closed her eyes momentarily and took a breath. "When I lost Anna to the Dreds, my heart was smashed into so many pieces I was certain it would never recover, and that's what I wanted. I didn't ever want to feel again. I had a single purpose to my life from then on—do my duty and uphold the beliefs of our clan."

"And you have," Katie said.

Alexis shook her head vigorously. "No, I haven't. I've been on this path heading to this destination for five years now."

Katie was utterly confused. "What path? What destination?"

"The path to my own downfall and betraying everything I believe in. Do you remember when you left to go to college in America?"

Katie didn't expect the conversation to go in this direction. "Um...yes."

"Byron, her family, the clan, and your family had a leaving party for you in Monaco," Alexis said.

"Yes, it was an exciting day. Byron organized the Debrek plane to take me to America. What about it?"

"I watched you that day, so full of excitement, hope, a bright future ahead of you, everything that I couldn't be, everything that was lost to me so long ago, and looking back now that was the day that the first piece of my shattered heart came back to me."

"It did?" Katie was lost for words.

Alexis nodded. "And each holiday from college, every time you came home to us, I found another piece of that shattered heart."

"Oh God. Alexis, but I thought—you took my first blood, and then you ran."

"When I tasted you, the final piece of the jigsaw of my heart slotted in place, and I ran in terror, because I know what it means to feel that for a human. What happened to Anna...I couldn't do that again."

Katie stepped right beside Alexis and slipped her hand around her waist.

Alexis allowed her fingertips to caress Katie's cheek. "There's something no one has told you about your attack."

Katie stepped back. "What? Why?"

"The Principe and Principessa wanted to give me a chance to confess."

Katie was starting to panic now. Why had she been kept in the dark? What could Alexis possibly have done?

"What?"

"When I found you, you were nearly dead. I felt panic and pain like I had never felt before. Then Byron and Amelia came, and Amelia saw your spirit rising out of your body. I didn't think twice. I ripped open my wrist to feed you blood. Byron told me not to do it, told me not to break our rule of consent, but I didn't care about your consent. I carried on and was about to drip blood into your mouth when Bhal arrived and stopped me. She then saved you."

Katie was silent. She didn't know what to say or think or do. Her mind was struggling to take it all in.

"The next morning you could have woken up to the decision of living your life as an undead vampire or facing an agonizing death. I've always hated Victorija for doing that to me, and all I can say is that I would have done it, and I would do it again. I would do it again because..." Alexis took Katie's hand. "I'm a soldier, and I was brought up not to show my feelings. I don't know how to. All I can say is this."

Katie watched as Alexis placed the palm of her hand on her heart, as she had earlier today when they were in hiding outside Sybil's cottage. The simple gesture conveyed more than words to Katie, and she teared up.

Alexis shot out of the cabin in an instant.

❖

Katie rubbed her forehead, trying to make sense of what Alexis had told her. Despite what Alexis thought, what was more shocking than the fact that she could have woken up to the biggest decision of her life after the attack, was the fact that Alexis was willing to break the Debreks' most sacred tenet.

She knew what rules meant to Alexis and her wish to put duty above all. For her to be not just willing, but eager to break it must mean that Alexis truly loved her. Now Alexis's determination to look after her made sense.

Katie had to do something. Alexis was torturing herself. Katie never thought she'd need to be the strong one between them, but here it was. Hoping Alexis hadn't ran off into the forest, she walked to the front door and opened it.

Luckily she found Alexis leaning against the wooden porch post, just looking out into the night.

"Alexis, I need to talk to you."

Alexis didn't turn around. "You don't have to say anything. We're going back to London tomorrow, so I'll keep out of your way. I want you to know that I offered to leave my post as Duca, but the Principe refused."

Katie walked up to Alexis and said, "Turn around."

Alexis sighed and turned. Katie put her palm on her heart as Alexis had done. She felt it conveyed more than words would at that moment.

"You forgive me?" Alexis looked taken aback.

"There's nothing to forgive, Alexis. True, I believe in consent, and I'm not saying that it would have been easy to wake up knowing I had to turn or die, but that is not what Victorija did to you. She did it for her own twisted purposes, but you did it because—" Katie didn't want to put words in Alexis's mouth. "Well, for very different reasons."

Alexis touched her fingers to Katie's hand. "Tell me you forgive me?"

"If you need to hear it, then yes, I forgive you. Come inside and heal my neck," Katie said.

Alexis was overwhelmed with emotions right now, and her brain was trying to catch up. "Are you sure?"

"Yes, this was inflicted on me, and I know how much seeing it disturbs you, so let's take away Josie's power and what she did to me."

Alexis allowed herself to be pulled inside the cabin and over to the couch. Katie sat down and Alexis kneeled in front of her.

"Are you sure?" Alexis asked.

"Are you?"

Alexis nodded. She wanted to make Katie better more than anything. "Yes. If you could move your jumper past your shoulder...?" Alexis asked.

Instead of doing that, Katie took her thin cashmere jumper off completely.

Alexis gulped and her eyes went straight to Katie's black-lace covered breasts.

Oh God, she's beautiful.

"Alexis? My wound?" Katie said.

Alexis shook herself. "Yes, sorry."

She bit into the palm of her hand with her fangs, allowing the blood to flow. "Are you ready?"

Katie nodded, so Alexis lowered her palm to Katie's infected neck wound. Katie hissed when Alexis's blood touched her.

"Okay, relax and look in my eyes," Alexis said.

Katie did that, and Alexis asked, "How does that feel?"

"It burned like acid at first, but now it feels nice, warm."

"Good, it'll not take too long."

Katie's lips parted slightly, and Alexis could see the tip of her wet tongue. She had the urge to suck on it, to taste Katie anywhere she allowed her. Her teeth had fully erupted, and days of no fresh blood made all this stimulation much worse. But she had to stay in control for Katie's sake.

"Your eyes are red," Katie said.

Alexis had no doubt they were. Katie had forgiven her, and she was touching her skin, at the same time trying not to let her eyes wander down to Katie's breasts. Instead of explaining, she asked Katie, "Why do you think they're red?"

Katie reached for Alexis and lightly grasped her hair. "Because you want me, because you're hungry."

Katie took the initiative and pressed her lips to Alexis's. Alexis moaned. She felt like she had been waiting for this kiss her whole life. Katie pushed her tongue into Alexis's mouth and ran her tongue around her fangs.

Alexis responded by sucking it deeper into her mouth. Her own mouth was watering and aching for blood. Not any blood, Katie's blood.

Katie pulled back for air, and Alexis took her hand off Katie's wound. All that was left was the stain of Alexis's blood.

"It's gone," Katie said with amazement.

❖

"Josie has gone." Alexis felt like Josie had been between them as long as her bite had been on Katie's neck, a reminder to Alexis of her failure.

Katie took Alexis's hand and placed it between her breasts. "Touch me."

Alexis trailed the back of her hand down between Katie's breasts. Katie gasped and pushed Alexis's hand onto her breast. Her sex clenched when Alexis squeezed. She pulled Alexis closer by her hair.

Katie didn't know if it was having some of Alexis's blood in her system, but she was feeling so much more like herself, grounded, and with more energy than she'd had since the attack.

She grabbed for Alexis's T-shirt and pulled it off. Alexis didn't wear a bra, her breasts were small, and Katie could see how it was possible for her to pass as a male soldier without much trouble.

Katie scratched her fingernails down Alexis's back. She shivered but then pulled back from their kiss.

"We have to stop. You're not strong enough," Alexis said.

"I am strong enough. Your blood has made every part of me stronger already, and I need you to touch me," Katie said.

"I don't—"

Katie took off her bra and dropped it at her side. Alexis's eyes went an even darker red. She then said, "You remember when we kissed in my bedroom and I did this?"

Katie pierced her finger against Alexis's fang and let the blood flow into her mouth. She hoped it made Alexis unable to resist her.

Alexis sucked on her finger and moaned, then lifted her off the couch and onto her back in front of the fire. She sucked on Katie's finger for another few seconds then broke away.

"God, you taste so good," Alexis said.

Katie smiled then unbuttoned her jeans. "I hope I taste good everywhere."

Alexis groaned and put her mouth on Katie's breast, kissing everywhere except her nipple, teasing Katie, making her want Alexis's mouth all the more.

"Oh God." Katie, now buoyed by her newfound energy, wanted Alexis as close as possible. She shuffled out of her jeans and encouraged Alexis to do the same, and finally the heat of their sexes came together.

Katie wanted to bring Alexis as close to her as possible and wrapped her legs around Alexis's hips.

Alexis finally put her lips back on Katie's breast. She sucked and swirled her tongue around her hard nipple. Katie felt an electrical jolt of pleasure every time Alexis's fang grazed her. The energy building between them was powerful, and Katie couldn't help but start to rock her hips, trying to find some relief.

Alexis followed suit and let her nipple go with a pop. "You're so wet—I can feel it."

Katie smiled and pushed Alexis onto her back and started kissing her jaw and neck. "Youre too," Katie said.

Alexis looked in awe at Katie. She couldn't believe she was able to touch her. The taste of her blood was like nothing else, and it ignited a spark of hope in her heart. Hope that she hadn't felt for a long time.

Alexis turned Katie onto her back again and said, "Let me taste you and make you come."

"Yes," Katie breathed.

Alexis grasped Katie's sex and squeezed while she kissed her breastbone and down onto her stomach. Her mouth watered at the thought of tasting Katie. She moved down between her legs and kissed all around her wet sex. It made her feel so good that she could make Katie feel like this.

She opened Katie up and was about to start making Katie feel good when her attention was caught by the pounding artery on Katie's thigh. Her mouth watered at the thought of her fangs piercing Katie there and drinking. There was no other feeling like feeding there, from a lover. It was so intimate, so personal, but she didn't want to scare Katie their first time.

Although Alexis was sure Katie must have had sexual partners before her while at university, she suspected she was not too experienced and didn't want to make her uncomfortable.

She felt Katie's hand in her hair trying to push her lips and tongue back to her sex. Alexis forced herself to ignore the heavy beat of the artery there and started by licking around her clit but not touching it.

Alexis groaned. "God, you taste so good."

"Alex, I need you. Please make me come?"

Alexis took her two fingers and slowly and gently circled the entrance to Katie's sex. She wanted to fuck, suck, and taste Katie's blood, all at once, but she wasn't going to scare her off by being too rough the first time.

"Alex, I'm going to explode," Katie said.

She smiled and then sucked Katie's clit into her mouth. Katie moaned and thrust her hips in rhythm with Alexis. While she sucked and kissed, Alexis pushed two fingers inside Katie, and she gave a low groan.

"Yes, just like that, Alex, faster," Katie said.

She sped up, and very soon she felt Katie's walls start to flutter against her fingers. Katie grasped frantically at her hair and thrust her hips, her moans getting louder, until she went still and nearly crushed Alexis's skull with her thighs then cried out.

"Oh God, oh God. *Alex*," Katie said breathily.

Alexis carefully pulled out her fingers and climbed back up to Katie, who was still trying to get her breath.

"That was...amazing."

Alexis brushed Katie's hair from her face. "Do you feel okay?"

"Okay?" Katie said with surprise. "You blew my head off."

Alexis laughed and then felt Katie's hips rock again. Katie put her legs around Alexis, squeezing her close.

"I need to—" Katie moaned. "I need to come again. Come with me, Alex. Come on me."

Alexis nearly came on the spot at that request. She pushed her sex as close as she could to Katie and began to thrust.

"I can feel you, Alex." Katie moaned into her neck as she pulled her close. Alexis's orgasm was soaring closer and closer to the edge with every thrust of her hips.

"Fuck." Alexis moaned. It had been so long since she'd indulged in a casual sexual encounter, so her need for an orgasm was great, but with Katie it was like being allowed to touch bliss.

Just like when she was making Katie come with her mouth, all she could think about was sinking her fangs into Katie, this time into her neck, but she didn't. Alexis used all her resolve and kissed Katie instead of biting her.

Katie pushed her head back and said, "Bite me, drink from me when you come?"

"I don't think—"

"I'm strong enough. I want this, Alex. I consent, okay?" Katie said firmly.

Alexis's mouth watered, and her eyes darted to the pulse point on Katie's neck. Should she do this?

Katie, apparently sick of waiting, pulled Alexis's face into the crook of her neck. "Please, Alex?"

Alexis couldn't say no. She licked the area where she would bite, once, twice, then sank her teeth into Katie's neck.

The rush of that first taste of blood was like flooding her body with a drug. With her hips thrusting into Katie and feeding from her neck, Alexis doubted there was anything that could ever have felt better.

She drank greedily and then thrust until all the pain, frustration, and love for Katie came out in a long orgasm. Her body rocked with an electricity that sparked all over her.

"Jesus," Alexis said as she tried to get her breath back. "Are you okay?"

Katie caught her breath. "More than okay. I've dreamed about being in your arms since I understood that I liked women."

Alexis felt such a surge of pure love for Katie. She cupped her cheek and looked deeply into her eyes. "Katie, I…"

Katie stroked her hair. "What?"

Alexis couldn't say it. An immortal vampire, and she didn't have the courage to tell her lover that she loved her.

"You're the most beautiful woman I've ever seen."

CHAPTER FIFTEEN

B yron entered the bedroom to find Amelia sitting on the side of the bed in her nightdress. She seemed to be concentrating deeply and trying with all her might to lift one of her shoes off the floor with her untapped power. She raised it a few inches, and then it wobbled and crashed down.

"Pathetic," Amelia said. "I'm supposed to be a descendant, someone who has to fight against a darkness that's coming, and I have no idea how to use magic."

Byron walked over to the bed and got in. "You will learn. We go back to London tomorrow, and we'll contact our friends at The Portal—then you'll be more confident. Besides, do you think I'd let anyone get through me?"

Amelia gave up with her magic and slipped under the covers beside Byron. "That's the thing that puzzles me. Why would a relatively weak grade-one beginner witch be the one prophesied to fight the darkness that this Anka woman brings? You are the most powerful vampire alive. Why not you?"

Byron pulled Amelia into her arms. "We must trust your ancestors. They can see the whole picture. Can you still hear the voices?"

"Yes, in the background, when I concentrate, but I can't hear them very clearly again."

"Maybe that's a good thing. Or they might drive you insane," Byron said.

"Sybil said that Bronte, my mum, will be one of those voices, and that I will find a way to hear her one day."

"I'm sure the strength of a mother's love will make that happen," Byron said.

"I wish I could have known her and what she was running from."

"We'll keep looking for information, I promise," Byron said.

Amelia was quiet for a while and then started to pull off her nightdress.

"What are you doing?" Byron asked.

"You need to feed," Amelia said flatly.

Byron pulled the nightdress back. "Oh no. Not after today. I fed on a blood bag before I came through."

It was jarring, every time she thought of today. The parents she thought she hated had actually protected her all her life. Their actions towards her and their intentions were so conflicting.

"I phoned Uncle Jaunty to tell him about Mother and Father."

"What did he say?" Byron asked.

"The same as me, really. He hadn't seen Mother in twenty years, but it still hit him hard. Do you think everything will be all right with the police?"

"I assume so. What can they say? *We know you're a vampire and probably you or someone you know killed them?*" Byron shrugged. "I'm sure they'll release the bodies soon for burial, and if they don't, I'll have a word with the police commissioner. The Debrek name carries some weight."

Amelia leaned up on her elbow. "I really want to honour their lives, what they did for me." As Amelia said that, the tears that she wished earlier she could cry for her parents started to fall.

"It's all right. Let it all out." Byron pulled her into a hug. "We will give them respect and all my gratitude for keeping you safe. I promise you."

"Do you think Victorija is involved in this? In killing my parents?" Amelia asked.

"It would have been my first thought. Alexis was sure the vampires she dispatched today were Dreds, and the intelligence we are getting is that the Dreds are becoming more active, turning humans left, right, and centre, and bringing dark witches to their cause, but Victorija has vanished from public view. No one has seen her, and I'm concerned."

"Why?" Amelia asked.

"Because my cousin likes the world to know what havoc and destruction she is causing. She thrives on others being afraid of her power. Her sudden introverted behaviour makes me suspicious that she has something else going on, or that someone else is using her vampires. Sometimes it's better the devil you know."

"Hmm. Maybe killing Lucia had a greater effect than we realized," Amelia said.

"Lucia never gave up hope on her, even after her death. She was sure there was a way back for Victorija, despite everything."

They both listened to the noises of the forest outside the bedroom window for a while, and then out of the darkness, Amelia said, "Who was my father, and how will we ever find out if Sybil doesn't know?"

"I'm sure all the answers you need will come to you."

❖

Katie tried to catch her breath, then rolled on top of Alexis. She smiled down at her and stroked a dark lock away from her eyes. They had moved to the bedroom and been making love for some time now. It was better than Katie could ever have imagined.

"What are you thinking?" Alexis asked.

"The first time you drank blood from me. I wanted you so much. You made me feel like a sexual being for the first time. I'd never felt like that before. I used to fantasize about you touching me."

Alexis grinned. "Even when we fought with each other?"

Katie lightly scratched her nails down Alexis's face. "Even more so. You made me frustrated, horny, like I wanted to fight with you and tear your clothes off at the same time. At night in bed when I'd be lying in the dark, you kept coming into my mind, and you didn't take no for an answer."

"I wish I'd known." Alexis smiled. "I would have been happy to fight and tear each other's clothes off. How is your neck now?"

"You mean the bite that I've always wanted from you?" Katie grinned.

She touched her fingertips to the fresh wound, covering them in blood, then painted them across Alexis's lips. Alexis's tongue snaked out to taste it, and her eyes glowed red. She flipped Katie onto her back.

"You know how to tease a vampire, don't you?" Alexis said.

"Teasing you comes natural to me. You were my first crush and…" Katie hesitated. "My first love."

Katie could see the tension in Alexis's eyes, but instead of saying anything back, Alexis kissed her deep and hard, as if trying to let her actions tell Katie what she felt. Like touching her heart.

Katie hoped she'd be able to say it soon. She understood Alexis's difficulties, but she did need to hear the words.

Alexis lifted Katie's hand and put it between her breasts, over her heart, and silently looked into her eyes. Katie's eyes were full of love and trust, which Alexis felt she didn't deserve.

"Don't let go," Alexis said. She slipped her fingers into Katie's sex and, splitting her fingers around her clit, softly, slowly stroked her while never taking her eyes off her. She hoped this would show Katie what was truly in her heart.

Katie kept her palm on Alexis's heart and never looked away, even as her orgasm was building towards the edge.

"Come for me," Alexis said.

She smiled as Katie went taut and struggled to keep her eyes and their hearts' connection open. Katie cried out and pulled Alexis down to kiss her.

"Oh God, that was so…I mean, it felt like you were inside my heart."

Alexis smiled. "Good, I only want to make you feel good."

She went to Katie's lips for another deep kiss, but Katie pushed her back. "Oh no, no more. You've killed me already."

Alexis laughed and lay back on the bed, and Katie took her place under her arm. "You humans have no stamina."

"How am I supposed to keep up with an immortal vampire for stamina? It's lucky I'm so much younger than you, at least," Katie joked.

They lay in the quiet for a minute or so, enjoying the afterglow, but there was one thing that was niggling at Alexis, and she knew it was maybe too much to ask, but she had to get it out of her head.

"Katie, when we go back to London…I feel stupid asking this."

"Don't feel stupid, ask me anything, Alex."

Alexis smiled at her new nickname. "I like that you've started to call me Alex. My best friend in the army, Angus, used to call me that."

Katie took their clasped hands and kissed Alexis's knuckles. "I want something that nobody else would ever call the tough, scary Debrek Duca. Ask me what you want."

Alexis felt like a jealous fool, but the thought that another vampire—one under her, one of her foot soldiers—would sink their fangs into the woman she loved tortured her. But she had no say in that. It was Katie's body and only she had a say in what she did with it. Consent meant everything, even if she had tested that tenet's limits recently.

"I wondered if you would be going back on the blood rota. It's up to you of course, and I don't—"

Katie silenced her with a kiss. "Of course I won't. I'm yours for as long as you want me."

"Thank you. I really don't want to share you." But Katie's words reminded her of Katie's mortality, and her heart sank. This was the terror that kept her love buried for so long. She turned over on her side to face Katie. "Will you promise me something?"

"What is it?" Katie replied.

"I'm not trying to be controlling or to boss you around, but will you promise me you'll be really careful? Don't take any silly risks. You're mortal, and everything is in flux just now—vampires distrusting each other, some European covens working with vampires, whatever fight is coming with the Principessa—don't let me lose you. Please?" Alexis begged.

Katie stroked her face. "I will do my best and not take any silly risks. I promise you, and if death comes to me, I will have done my best to avoid it."

"Thank you." Alexis kissed her forehead.

Katie went quiet as if she was thinking hard.

"Is something wrong?" Alexis asked.

"With everything going on with the Dreds, there's something you need to know."

Alexis was suddenly on alert. "What?"

"It's about Daisy."

CHAPTER SIXTEEN

I'm trying to find out, Madam Anka." Drasas paced up and down at the back entrance to the Dred castle. Madam Anka had called seeking an update on Victorija's situation.

"I need Victorija better. She is a born vampire, and I need her power, and if you hope to have any at all, you will find out who she was blood bonded to."

Drasas looked around for anyone listening in to her conversation. "I'm trying, but I wasn't with her every second when she fed in Britain. It could be anyone."

"If you ever hope to lead the army I'm building or become the most powerful vampire alive, then you will hurry up and find out, so we can get them to your Principe. To give you what you want, I shall have to harness her power."

"I will find out, I promise you, Madam Anka."

"Make sure you do, and make it a better attempt than your vampires did trying to kill Sybil. I want her dead."

"We got her mother and father," Drasas pointed out.

"I needed Sybil too, before Amelia Debrek finds out who she is. Make things right, or I will find another worthy vampire, understand?" Anka said.

"Yes, Madam Anka." She hung up the phone.

"Busy, Drasas?"

Drasas nearly jumped out of her skin at Victorija's voice. "Principe? Just giving out the orders. Are you feeling better?"

If Victorija knew what she was doing, she'd rip her limb from limb. It wasn't that she didn't admire her Principe still, she did, but the events in Britain had made her soft. It was time for new, strong leadership.

Victorija looked at her silently. Her eyes were edged with red permanently now that she hungered for the blood of her bonded. Drasas held her breath. Had Victorija heard her?

Victorija looked over at the stables and said, "I'm going riding."

Drasas couldn't believe it. "You're going riding? You haven't ridden in a century."

Victorija's eyes went even redder in anger. "Well, today I feel like it, okay?"

"Forgive me, Principe. Have you thought of who your blood bond is yet?" Drasas asked.

"No," Victorija said firmly. "I'm going riding." She strode off.

She knows something, Drasas thought, but why would she try to keep the identity of that person a secret? Victorija was a woman who saw humans as simply there to feed her. Why was she not telling the whole truth?

As she watched Victorija ride off, she realized she could look around her private apartments freely. Drasas sped back into the castle.

❖

Alexis was worried. They had been back in London for a week, and the reality of being in a relationship with a human was hitting home.

She glanced at the time on her phone and paced up and down, her worry never letting her calm down. Byron was having lunch with a government official in a private dining room of a top London hotel. It had been a long lunch. Two hours now, and the longer she waited the more her mind drifted back to Katie.

This morning when they woke, Katie told her she was going shopping in the afternoon. Despite being out on duty with Byron, Katie was all she could think about.

Alexis was so on edge just now. There hadn't been a more dangerous time for them in a hundred years. The whole paranormal world was shaken from its slumber and it seemed there was danger everywhere.

When Katie told her about Daisy MacDougall and the fact that her bite from Victorija hadn't healed, she knew sooner or later the Dred clan would descend upon them, looking for her. She had never kept something from Byron before, but Katie persuaded her to let Daisy be the one to tell.

She only agreed if Daisy told Byron in the next few days. Her love for Katie was making her fearful.

"Duca? Is everything all right?" Bhal said.

Alexis pushed her phone back in her pocket quickly. "What? Yes."

Bhal nodded and returned to her post on the side of the dining room door. If one of her vampires was caught looking at their phone, they'd be peeling potatoes in the kitchen for two months straight. Alexis looked up to see if her vampires posted at the end of the corridor noticed. Luckily, they were all concentrating elsewhere.

The constant worry she had felt over the past week was paralyzing. Every morning she left Katie to work, she had the gut-wrenching worry that she might not see her again. This was why she never wanted to be in love with a human again.

She resumed pacing. It was so hard not to be at Katie's side all the time.

"Duca?"

Alexis was instantly pulled from her tortured thoughts by Byron's voice. She turned around and saw Byron had exited the dining room and was looking at her quizzically. So were Bhal and all her vampires.

She couldn't believe she hadn't been aware of Byron leaving the room—with her enhanced hearing she was always ready and waiting when Byron was leaving an engagement. Instead she'd been lost in her mind.

Alexis decided to carry on as normal and simply apologize. "My apologies, Principe. Are we leaving now?"

Byron looked at her through narrowed eyes. "Yes, I want to go to the office now, Duca."

"Of course, Principe."

Alexis took point and led them out to the waiting cars outside. Once Byron was safely inside her car, Alexis looked at the time again. Was Katie back home safely by now?

Being distracted was unforgivable. Her worry for Katie was compromising her duty. She had to get a handle on this paralyzing fear of losing her lover.

Amelia loved her new design room. In the basement of her shop, she had an office design room that looked out onto the workshop. There were two design tables, one for her and one for Daisy when she was working downstairs with her.

She looked up from her desk and through the glass windows, watched her all-female cutting and sewing team busily working hard. Amelia knew how it felt to be the only woman working in a tailoring workshop. It was still a man's world, except in this little corner of Savile Row.

Giving all these women the chance to work in a safe, uplifting environment was special, and as the demand for women's tailoring grew, so would the opportunities for the women leaving design school.

It was a big undertaking running her own business for the first time, but Amelia also had the comfort of knowing that she had her Uncle Jaunty for support in the shop next door, if she needed him.

Amelia pulled her attention back to her design and smiled as she realized she'd drawn Byron as her model. She touched her finger to Byron's face, represented in the drawing, and as she did the voices of the ancestors got louder. The background noise had been quiet since they returned from the New Forest, so this was a surprise. She tried to discern and differentiate the words, but they were too muffled.

The sound of the room door opening made Amelia look up. It was Daisy.

"Hey, how are things upstairs?' Amelia asked.

"Fine. I just finished an appointment. Can I have a word with you?"

"Is there something wrong?"

In the week since they had been back, Amelia had noticed that Daisy had been quieter than normal. She was a larger-than-life character and generally lived loud, and so it was apparent something must be on her mind.

"I wondered if I could come and see you and Byron, talk to you about something."

This was strange.

"Of course. It's Saturday tomorrow. How about you come over in the afternoon. I can show you the work we've done to the house and have a cup of tea and a chat."

"I'd like that."

Daisy closed her eyes quickly and swayed, grabbing the edge of the desk for support.

Amelia got up quickly and put her arm around Daisy. As she did the voices of her ancestors got exponentially louder, but more garbled. "Are you okay?"

"Yeah, I'm just tired. I'll be okay," Daisy said.

"You've been working too hard recently. You looked after this place all by yourself when I was away. Why don't you take the afternoon off? Go home and rest. I'll take care of everything here."

"Are you sure?" Daisy said.

"Yes. On you go and relax. I'll see you tomorrow."

"Thanks, Amelia."

Once Daisy had gone, she sat down at her desk and rubbed her forehead. The noise of the ancestors was driving her crazy. Why had they gotten louder when she touched Daisy?

She picked up her pencil and tried to get back to the design she was working on. As time passed, the voices quietened down a lot, until they were hardly audible.

What would Daisy want to see them about? It was all very strange.

When she looked back to her design pad she had doodled the head of a woman and a circle with a geometric daisy wheel symbol underneath.

Strange.

❖

Katie walked down the stairs just as Byron and her entourage came through the front door. Her heart skipped when she saw Alexis. Alexis looked up, and Katie smiled at her, but Alexis didn't smile back. She looked worried.

Uh-oh.

She waited at the bottom of the stairs until Byron walked away to her office, and Alexis and Bhal had given their orders to the assembled vampires and warriors. As they dispersed, she skipped over to Alexis.

"Hi, Alex. I missed you." She grasped at her hand and felt Alexis stiff as a board.

"Did you go shopping?"

"Yes, I was back ages ago," Katie said.

Alexis nodded and gulped hard. "Can we talk later?"

Katie heard tension in Alexis's voice. Okay, something was going on.

Alexis looked around her, presumably checking if they had privacy. "I need to talk about today, about every day. I'm struggling—"

Katie cupped her cheek. "Hey, what's wrong? Did something happen?" Katie expected Alexis's annoyance to subside, but it didn't.

"I need to talk to you," Alexis said softly.

Katie felt Alexis was retreating into her stoic self again. She thought they had gotten past this. "What's wrong? Something's changed," Katie said.

Alexis had spent every night with her this week, but as each day passed, the open Alexis from their time away from London had started to slowly fade, each day becoming a little more distant. She had thought it was just because Alexis's mind was back on her clan duties rather than spending all her time helping her feel better. But there was more to this.

"Later," Alexis said.

"No, talk to me now. I'm worried, Alex."

"I have duties I need to attend to. Later this evening."

Then she walked off, leaving Katie wondering what was going on. Katie started to get a bad feeling in the pit of her stomach.

Was Alexis pulling away from her again?

❖

Amelia's car pulled up outside The Portal bookshop. Amelia was to have her first lesson with Magda after closing time.

Wilder opened the car door, and Amelia got out. She walked through the shop door and only saw Piper.

"Hi, Piper. Is Magda ready for me?"

Piper smiled. She seemed a lot warmer now that Byron wasn't with her.

"She's waiting for you downstairs, Amelia." Piper pointed to a door in the corner, beside the till.

"Thanks."

When Wilder tried to follow, Piper said, "No, not you."

"I go where Amelia goes," Wilder said firmly.

"Only witches are welcome in our most private space," Piper replied.

Amelia noticed Piper didn't seem to care much for anyone who wasn't a witch. She said to Wilder, "I'll be fine. You stay up here with Piper."

Wilder looked torn. "If Byron finds out I—"

"I will take the blame. Don't worry," Amelia said.

"Just shout if you need me."

Amelia smiled and went through the door and down the stairs. She arrived in a large open room. It was plain with little furniture, apart from what looked like a ritual table with incense and sacred statues and other items, where Magda was currently kneeling.

Symbols were carved into the stone on the otherwise bare walls, and in the middle of the floor was a large circle. Symbols similar to the ones on the wall were all around the circle.

"Welcome, Amelia," Magda said without turning around.

"Hi, I'm not late, am I?"

Magda bowed her head and stood. She walked over to Amelia with her hands outstretched. "Not at all. Welcome, sister."

Amelia took the offered hug and felt a warmth from her new teacher. Magda took her jacket and hung it on the back of the door.

"Did you find out about yourself in the New Forest?"

"Yes," Amelia said, "it was hard to hear, but I'm glad I know something about my mother and what happened the night she had to give me up."

"I knew Sybil would help you. Apart from Sybil, after the attack, the cunning folk that were left fled to London and joined my coven. Did you find anything else?" Magda asked.

Amelia wasn't sure what she meant at first, but then it came to her. "Oh, the voices?"

"The voices of our ancestors, yes. What did you hear?" Magda guided her over to just outside the circle.

"Voices all at once, loud and confusing, then…" How to explain the very private lovemaking that opened her heart and mind to the powers beyond?

"Your vampire helped you let go?" Magda smiled and Amelia felt heat in her cheeks.

"Um…"

"Don't be embarrassed," Magda said.

"After that, the voices started to become less clear."

"Come in the circle and let me explain."

Amelia followed her and sat on the ground. The circle had the same burr or buzz on her nerves and skin as the one in the forest. "This feels like the circle the cunning folk made in the forest."

"Yes, and I will teach you the basics of our craft and how to cast a circle, but for now I want you to concentrate on hearing our ancestors. Get comfortable," Magda said.

Amelia shifted around until she was in a meditative pose and tried to relax as best she could.

"Our ancestors, their spirits, their voices are where our power comes from. Every witch who has lived is a part of how and why we can use magic and manipulate reality. For now we are on this side, but one day we will be on the other."

"The Grand Duchess and my mother?" Amelia asked.

"Yes, both powerful witches, and they are with us always."

"Why did my mind open when I was, you know, with Byron?" Amelia felt heat building in her cheeks.

"That celebration of love, of passion, leaves you as open and vulnerable as you can possibly be. You let go of worldly concerns, worries, problems, and the voices of our ancestors are tuned in and turned up, like a radio. Every witch has a different method of tuning in, whatever they most identify with or find important. So how do you think you can get in tune with that experience?"

Amelia knew immediately. "I didn't know who I truly was until I met Byron. She gave me the freedom and security to become the Amelia I always wanted to be."

Magda smiled. "Then you focus on Byron and your love. Take my hands and close your eyes."

Amelia held Magda's hands and closed her eyes as directed. She heard Magda gasp at her touch, and she opened her eyes quickly. "What's wrong?"

Magda stared at her silently. "Do you feel quite well?"

"Yes, why? In fact I've been full of more energy since we came home," Amelia said.

"Good, good. Now close your eyes."

Amelia did as she was asked. There was something Magda was keeping from her, she knew it. It was a strange question to ask out of nowhere.

Magda continued, "Now think about Byron, picture her, and feel the love filling up your body."

She started to feel the love and warmth spread around her body, then envelop it.

"Take deep breaths and concentrate on the garbled voices," Magda said.

The voices were loud, shouting over each other, but with each breath they quietened, slowed, and started to become an individual voice.

We will help you, Amelia. You are the descendent, the voice said.

"I can hear it." Amelia was amazed. She'd done it.

"Good, now thank the ancestors."

"Thank you." Amelia did feel a bit strange thanking something she couldn't see.

"Now open your eyes, but keep that channel open. Breathe and stay calm."

Amelia did that and stayed focused. "It's hard work."

"Magic is hard—that's why not everyone is capable of it. You must practise every morning in quiet meditation," Magda said.

"Will I be able to call for the Grand Duchess or my mother?" Amelia asked.

"If you practise, you have the capacity to do anything, Amelia."

Katie finally finished for the day. She made her way upstairs and made a beeline to Alexis's room. They needed to talk after earlier today—plus Alexis hadn't fed from her since this morning. Before they left the New Forest they'd agreed that Alexis would only feed from her, so Katie assumed Alexis had drunk bottled, and she'd be hungry.

Bottled Debrek Special Reserve and blood bags did the job in a pinch but were never as satisfying. Katie always got a little thrill at the thought of feeding Alexis. It was something that meant so much to her. To be the one providing what Alexis needed fulfilled a need she didn't know she had, plus it turned her on.

She approached Alexis's door and shivered at the thought of

Alexis's teeth in her. Katie knocked at the door and Alexis soon opened it.

Katie smiled. "Hi."

Alexis was tense. "Come in."

At the beginning of the week, they were jumping on each other after being apart for the day, but now the old stiff Alexis was creeping back in. Whatever was causing this, Katie had to fix it.

She walked in and looked around Alexis's old-fashioned room. They had been staying in Katie's room, so this was her first time seeing Alexis's space. It hadn't been refurbished in years and was cold and unwelcoming with no family pictures or artwork.

"Okay, what's wrong? You've gone from sweet, loving, and hot Alexis to worrisome and tense in days. What's going on?"

Alexis sat on her bed and clasped her hands tensely. "I don't know how to cope with this."

Katie was starting to worry now. Alexis appeared overwhelmed with emotion. She wasn't going to run away from their love, was she?

She kneeled in front of Alexis. "What can't you cope with?"

"You, loving you and worrying about you is paralyzing me. I was distracted today when I should have been guarding Byron, and she noticed."

Katie sighed and took Alexis's hands. This again. How was she supposed to get Alexis over this fear of losing her, like she had done the first time love had claimed her heart?

"I was only going shopping, not going for a night out at The Sanctuary," Katie said.

"But I need to know you're safe all the time. The stress is overwhelming. For all I knew you could have been dead, lying in a ditch somewhere."

"Oh, don't be silly, Alex," Katie said. "I went to a few shops, then back home."

"I'm not silly," Alexis said with frustration. She pointed out the bedroom door. "Not long ago I found you nearly dead on the landing out there. I was so frightened today that my team and the Principe noticed how distracted I was, worrying about you."

"I'm sorry, but love is frightening in any circumstance. I promise to always take care and not take chances. You have to be brave to take the love that I'm offering you," Katie said softly.

She was scared about what Alexis's answer might be.

Alexis shook her head. "I told myself never to get involved with a human again because of this. I'm immortal, you're mortal. Byron is lucky—her blood bond and the Grand Duchess's ring make Amelia immortal." Alexis's voice cracked. "I'm going to have to watch you die, and I can't deal with that."

Katie put her head on Alexis's lap. What could she say? It felt like this could break them, and Katie loved Alexis too much to let her go. But Alexis was right—Amelia was lucky. She was now as immortal as Byron was.

Byron wouldn't have to watch Amelia grow old and die, and Katie didn't want Alexis to live with this fear. She would do anything to give Alexis that security. She thought of Alexis holding her first lover Anna as she died, and tears sprang to her eyes. Katie couldn't let Alexis feel that pain again.

Katie looked up at Alexis and said, "I don't want you to go through what you did with Anna. I want to transition, Alex."

"What?" Alexis said with surprise.

"I want to become a vampire. I want to live by your side as long as you do."

Alexis stood up immediately. "No way."

"What do you mean no way?" Katie said.

"I mean no way are you giving up your mortality for me."

Katie stood up and approached her. "Alex, it's not just for you. I don't want to live with the fact that I'm going to cause you so much pain," Katie said.

"No," Alexis said angrily.

"I consent. You have my consent. I mean, you were going to change me when Josie nearly killed me."

"That was different," Alexis said. "You were in immediate danger. I'm not doing it, Katie. You have no idea what you have to give up. It's not a decision you should take lightly, on a whim."

"But, Alex—"

"No."

Katie was frustrated. "I'm not taking it lightly. You forget that I was torn back from the hands of death already. I know how it would feel."

Alexis started to pace up and down. "You don't know—you had a glimpse at best. Your parents would be horrified, and they'd blame me for influencing you."

"Stop treating me like a child." Katie stopped Alexis and put her hand on her chest. "I can make the decision for myself."

Alexis looked her in the eye. "No, okay? No."

Katie had enough. She grasped Alexis's wrist and bit into it hard. Alexis pulled her wrist away, but Katie already swallowed her first gulp.

"What do you think you're doing?" Alexis said angrily.

"Making the decision for you."

"No, you're not. You can't complete the transition unless you die with my blood in your system, and I'm not going to kill you, and I doubt you'll do it yourself."

Katie said nothing. She knew she couldn't take her own life.

Alexis looked furious. "I can't believe you did that. Do my feelings mean nothing to you? Do you know how much guilt I would feel to turn you? There would be no going back, and you and everyone who cares for you would blame me. I can't deal with this any more."

"What do you mean deal with *this*?" Katie asked.

"This, us. I knew a relationship was a bad idea. It's too much."

Katie was getting angrier by the second. "If loving me is too much for you, then go! Go back to being the stoic, emotionless Duca, who has no joy in her life. Go." Katie's anger fuelled her words, and she immediately regretted them when she saw the look of hurt on Alexis's face.

Alexis sped off out of the room in a flash and left Katie standing there regretting her angry words.

"Why did I say that?" Tears filled Katie's eyes.

She should have chosen her words more carefully. Everyone thought Alexis was this tough, stoic soldier, but only Katie knew that she was in fact a sensitive soul underneath it all, especially in love.

She should have been talking Alexis through her fear and her confusion over their new relationship, and instead she'd been rash and hurtful. She wanted to go back to her bedroom quickly so no one would see her tears, but just as she was about to leave the room, something caught her eye sitting on Alexis's desk. She walked over and found a small hand-painted picture of a beautiful dark-haired young woman. Below it was signed *Anna*.

Katie wiped away her tears on the back of her hand. "So, this is Anna."

Next to it was a lock of brown hair encased in glass.

This was why Alexis was terrified and scared she was going to lose her. Despite Alexis being much older in age, Katie felt she was more in tune with love, its consequences, and how they could make it work between them.

"I need to think."

Katie put down the picture and said, "I'll take care of her, Anna."

❖

Byron and Amelia were sitting on the couch, in front of the fire. Byron had her arms around Amelia.

"Do you need me to do anything for the funeral?" Byron asked.

Early that day, Byron had a phone call from the police commissioner to say Amelia's parents' bodies were being released from the authorities.

"No, Uncle Jaunty and Uncle Simon are going to help me. It's funny—I mean strange. Nothing will change my upbringing and how repressive and loveless I thought it was, but I can now see they were showing me love in the only way they knew how."

"Yes?"

Amelia nodded. "They rescued me from a world they thought was in league with the devil, and they combated that with the only weapons they knew to protect me. Their own brand of fundamentalist

Christianity. It won't change anything, but in their way, I think they loved me."

"I think you're right. So why do you think Daisy wanted a meeting tomorrow?"

"I've no idea. It's strange. She wasn't herself."

"Someone else wasn't themselves today," Byron said.

"Who?"

"Alexis. She was distracted all day, and that's not like her. I think being in love is a learning process for her."

Amelia smiled. "I'm sure it is. It was for you."

"True, but I'm still learning, believe me. How did witch school go today?" Byron asked.

Amelia chuckled. "Witch school? I suppose it is. Great. We were meditating. She was trying to train me to control the voices of my ancestors. Only when I harness them can I use magic. I think it's going to take a lot of practice."

Byron kissed her head. "Yes, I'm sure. You'll be fantastic—I know it."

Amelia lifted her head from Byron's chest and kissed her chin. "It turns out my love and passion for you open me up to my ancestors."

"Oh yes?"

"Yes, so Magda told me," Amelia said.

"So that means it's better for your development as a witch if you keep acting passionate with me?"

"Yes, are the staff still around?" Amelia grinned.

"I dismissed them for the evening. We won't be disturbed, and besides I can hear anyone coming for a mile away."

Amelia placed little kisses on Byron's mouth, then licked all around her lips with the tip of her tongue. Byron groaned and Amelia laughed.

"You might have super hearing but I think you might be distracted when I've finished with you."

"Someone's feeling frisky," Byron said.

"I'm just feeling full of energy just now, and you are the only one I want to use it with."

Amelia slid onto the floor and kneeled in front of Byron. She then unbuttoned her blouse slowly, never taking her eyes off Byron, and threw it to the side.

She was pleased to see Byron's eyes glowed red and kept transfixed on her. Next she unclipped her bra and discarded it. Byron made almost a growling noise, and she noticed Byron's teeth had erupted.

Amelia crawled forward and leaned over Byron's lap. She squeezed Byron's strap-on through her trousers, and Byron groaned.

"Would you like me to suck your cock, Principe?"

Byron grasped Amelia's hand and placed it on her buckle. Amelia grinned. She loved this. She loved being this for Byron, was more to the point. Before she met Byron, Amelia didn't consider herself a confident sexual being, but Byron taught her and gave her the confidence to unleash the raw sexuality inside her.

Now she could proudly be everything Byron needed and satisfy her in so many ways. She unfastened Byron's belt and zip, then pulled out her hard strap-on.

Amelia looked to the door and then back to Byron. "You better let me know if anyone's coming."

Byron's gaze didn't waver. "Put it in your mouth."

Amelia decided to tease Byron and place kisses up and down the shaft. Although it wasn't real, in Byron's headspace it was, and that's all she needed to enjoy this act. And unlike a real cock, neither Byron nor her lovers were ever let down.

Byron put her hand in Amelia's hair and encouraged her to put her mouth on her. Amelia took the tip into her mouth and Byron groaned. She looked up and saw Byron's red eyes focused firmly on her.

It was all about the act, the performance, to keep Byron in the right headspace, and so she had learned over time just what Byron needed. She sucked as much of the strap-on in her mouth as she could and then slowly lifted her head and let it pop out of her mouth.

"Jesus," Byron said with a mixture of pleasure and frustration.

Amelia grasped the base tightly and pumped her hand up and down while she teased the head with the tip of her tongue.

"You're so good at that," Byron groaned. "Suck me."

This time Amelia sucked it all in and started a regular rhythm, up and down. She felt both of Byron's hands on the back of her head.

"Yes, just like that. Take it all in," Byron said.

Amelia began to suck faster, and Byron's hips rocked with her. She didn't want to make Byron come this way, just take her to the brink. Once Byron's hips went too fast, hurtling to the edge of orgasm, she let the strap-on pop out of her mouth.

"Don't stop now, mia cara." Byron groaned.

"I want more," Amelia said.

She got as close as she could and placed her breasts around Byron's cock, which was still wet from Amelia's mouth. She knew Byron was crazy for this, but if she did it for too long, it would be over too soon.

"Fuck. Yes." Byron placed her hands on top of Amelia's, which were holding on to her breasts, and tried to control the pace of her wet cock, which was rubbing between Amelia's breasts.

"Good girl," Byron said, as she pumped, "I'm going to come on you."

"Not yet." Amelia pulled away from her.

Byron growled in frustration. "Stop teasing."

Amelia stood and took off her tights and underwear but left her skirt on, then climbed on top of Byron's lap. She kissed her, then whispered, "I want you to blow inside me."

Byron immediately grasped the base of her cock and eased the tip inside Amelia. She then allowed Amelia to control how quickly she lowered herself onto it. They both moaned when it was finally deep inside her.

"You are so beautiful." Byron pushed her face into Amelia's chest and began to suck on one of her breasts while her hand squeezed the other.

They started to rock together, "I feel so full. It's really deep."

Byron moved back against the couch and put her hands on Amelia's hips, while she braced herself against Byron's shoulders.

"So good," Amelia said.

She closed her eyes and started to rise and fall on Byron's cock faster and faster. Her mind was clearing, and all she could think about was the intense pleasure that was building up inside her.

Again, the voices in her head got louder and more clear. It really did work. Byron's love was her connection to her ancestors.

Byron grasped her buttocks and pressed even deeper. "Jesus, I love you."

Amelia was so close, so close to bliss, and Byron did something she loved, that made her almost fall over the edge—she slapped her buttock, once, twice, three times.

"Oh yes," Amelia said. "Again, I'm nearly there."

Byron smacked her twice more. "I'm going to come inside you."

Then all she could feel was the intense white heat of pleasure, and then the sensation of Byron's teeth in her neck. Just as Amelia was coming down from her orgasm, Byron was going over the edge. She thrust fast, gripped her buttocks tightly, and moaned as she fed.

This set off a second orgasm in Amelia, much deeper and more overwhelming this time. She pumped her hips erratically on Byron's cock until they both fell backward onto the back of the couch.

"Jesus Christ, that was good. I'll help you commune with your ancestors anytime."

Amelia's mind was clear. There were no garbled voices or words competing with each other. It was silent, but Amelia felt in her bones that the ancestors were waiting to help her whenever she needed it.

Amelia smiled when she looked at Byron and saw her blood around her lips. She wiped some off onto her finger and offered it into Byron's mouth.

Byron sucked it off and smiled. "Thank you. I love you."

"I love you, vampire."

CHAPTER SEVENTEEN

Drasas startled as Victorija burst into the throne room. The Principe was breathing hard and looked desperate to feed. She grabbed the nearest female vampire and started to feed on her. This was the first time Victorija had kept something from her. It hurt, but at the same time made Drasas realize she was right to take action.

Victorija had been weakened.

After searching Victorija's computer, she'd found a name. Daisy MacDougall. The Debrek Principessa's friend. Drasas remembered now how that Daisy female had bitten her Principe and been bitten in return. That was where the infection happened. Other vampires liked to be romantic about it, but to Drasas, that's all the blood bond was.

Now all she needed was to bring the female here, and her blood would save Victorija from madness and loss of her faculties. Just enough time for Madam Anka to harness Victorija's power.

She saw Victorija pull away from the vampire she was feeding on and shout, "It's not enough!"

Drasas hurried down to her. "Principe, can I—"

Victorija pushed her. "Get out of my way." She then sped off down the castle stairs.

Sometime later, Leo came into the room, and Drasas waved him over.

"Where did she go?"

"An old disused graveyard. She paced up and down muttering something, and then came back here. I'm worried about the Principe, Duca," Leo said.

Drasas patted him on the shoulder. "Don't worry. I'll take care of her."

He nodded and walked off. Drasas took out her phone and dialled Madam Anka's number.

"Yes?"

"You will give me the power you promised me? Then I have the name," Drasas said.

❖

Alexis didn't know where she was headed—she just knew she wanted to get away from the Debrek house and Katie. She ran and ran, hoping for the exhaustion that she could hardly remember as a mortal.

The exercise being futile, she slowed after a few miles and found herself outside the gates of a small local park. She wandered in, and the gathering evening darkness made the park look eerie.

There was only one other person in the park, a man with his dog at the other gate, just about to leave. Alexis walked over to the children's playground and sat on a bench. She let her head fall back and stared up at the evening sky. The moon hung in the sky, dazzling and bright. Now that she had some distance from Katie and their argument, guilt was starting to gnaw away at her stomach.

She looked down at her rapidly healing wrist. It had totally shocked her that Katie bit her, tried to initiate the transition. Alexis went through decades of pain trying to come to terms with losing her humanity, and she couldn't let Katie go through that.

"Why did I let this happen again?" Alexis asked the sky.

The first time she had fallen in love, with Anna, she was a green vampire, not fully grasping the problems of falling in love with a human. Now she knew the full horror of watching your lover die, yet her heart still fell in love again. Why?

Why had she done this to herself? Alexis remembered Byron telling her the advice the Grand Duchess had given her. *Love doesn't give you a choice.* Maybe that was the penalty, the cost of immortality.

Humans always hungrily tried to find ways to live forever, but would they if they knew the full cost? The realization then hit her— whether she was in a relationship with Katie or not, she would still have to watch her grow old and die, unless her love faded, which she knew it wouldn't.

Katie was a loving, warm woman. She needed love, and Alexis was sure she would eventually find someone who would give her everything Alexis couldn't, and that would be horrendous.

She fell forward and covered her face in her hands. Love was meant to be joyful, and yet she was in torment.

Through her messy thoughts and painful feelings, Alexis became aware of the scent of fresh blood, then the noise of something in the trees on the other side of the park. As she got closer, she heard a noise—something breathing and feeding.

Alexis ran at super speed into the trees. She arrived at the park wall just as something had left the scene and dropped on the other side of the wall. When she climbed the wall to follow, there was no one there.

Alexis dropped back down to where the blood scent was coming from and found a collection of dead birds and a few squirrels. All had been killed viciously, their flesh torn and ripped apart, as if in a frenzy.

It could have been another animal, but the creature she'd heard, which had jumped over the wall and slammed down on the pavement, sounded like a human, and that gave her an uneasy feeling.

Alexis made her way out of the trees and took out her mobile. She called her lieutenant. "Peter? Get a team to patrol a two-mile perimeter from the house. I found something in the park, and I have a bad feeling we have another vampire in the area."

"Yes, Duca."

When Alexis hung up the phone she went into her photos and

gazed at the picture of Katie. There would be pain if she was with her, and if she wasn't. Which was worse, loving her every day and losing her to age, slowly, or to danger out there in the world, or watching someone else love her?

Chapter Eighteen

The next day Byron and Amelia were due to meet Daisy. Byron waited in the drawing room, where Amelia said she would bring Daisy, and wondered what on earth she needed to talk about. Whatever it was, Byron had a bad feeling.

Byron looked at her watch—it was two o'clock in the afternoon. "Time for a quick drink."

She walked over to the drinks table and poured out Wulver Whisky, given to her by Kenrick Wulver at her wedding. It was a one of a kind tipple, and Byron had promised herself to ration it. She didn't have that many cases, and rationing was not going well so far.

Byron took a sip and closed her eyes to appreciate the flavour. "Hmm." She picked up the more than half empty bottle. Maybe Kenrick could be persuaded to keep this whisky on continuous order for her. Byron would pay anything for this blend.

The door to the drawing room opened, and Amelia led Daisy into the room.

"Ah, good afternoon, Daisy."

"Hi."

"Sit down here, Daisy," Amelia said. "Tea won't be long."

"How are you, Daisy?" Byron asked as she sat down next to Amelia.

"Okay, thanks."

Daisy usually had a cheeky or punchy reply, but not today. She sounded down, worried, and that made Byron worried.

Amelia put her hand on Byron's knee then said, "What did you want to talk about?"

Instead of answering, Daisy took off the scarf around her neck. Amelia gasped, and Byron felt like gasping herself when she saw that the vampire bite Victorija had given Daisy at The Sanctuary had not healed. The full implications hit Byron like a ton of bricks.

Amelia got up quickly and went to Daisy. She sat down next to her and touched the wound on Daisy's neck.

"Tell me this is not—"

"Victorija's bite? Yeah, it is," Daisy said.

Amelia looked back to Byron quickly before saying, "Why didn't you tell us?"

"I didn't believe it at first, and then I was too scared to face it. I told Katie, and she told me I should tell you, but I begged her for time to get my head around it."

Amelia couldn't believe this was true. Daisy was bonded by blood and fate to Victorija Dred just like she was to Byron.

She turned to Byron. "Byron…"

Byron got up and said, "You should have told us straight away, Daisy. You could have been captured by Victorija by now. You probably would have been if she wasn't missing in action."

"Byron, I have a lot of experience chasing the paranormal and occult. I won't accept there isn't a way to stop this. But I tried to research and find something that could break this, and I found nothing."

"Do you think she knows?" Amelia asked.

Byron let out a breath. "She's got to be having some serious problems by now. It explains why Victorija has been quiet, but her clan is attacking at will and not being careful. I'm now sure someone else is giving the orders at the moment."

Amelia rubbed her forehead. She remembered that confusing time of being newly bonded and trying to push Byron away, but at the same time fighting an unquenchable need to be close and feed her.

"Nothing will stop Victorija coming for you, Daisy. She'll use you for blood and never stop, just like Victorija's father did with her mother."

"There must be some way to break the bond. There's always a way. I'm not going to be some vamp's everlasting meal."

"Maybe Magda might know of something buried deep in the magic literature?" Amelia said to Byron. "Or maybe Sybil?"

"We will look into it, but be assured, Daisy, we will protect you."

"Thank you. I should probably mention, when Victorija tasted my blood, she said it was strange," Daisy said.

"What was strange?" Amelia asked.

"After she tasted my blood, she recoiled and looked deeply into my eyes as if she was remembering something."

What could it all mean? What Amelia did know was that suddenly their lives had gotten even more complicated.

❖

Alexis stood in the entrance hallway with the two-person team she had put together—Owen, one of Bhal's warriors, and Trista, a turned vampire with a lot of experience.

"Okay, stick close to Daisy. Byron has assured her that we will keep her safe, and I intend to keep that promise."

"Yes, Duca," they both replied.

"Now keep on your toes because Daisy has no fear and mistakenly thinks she can take on the world. Another thing is that she can't be compelled. We don't know why, but it helps us. It means that a Dred can't lure her away. If you need backup, call immediately."

They both nodded and went to the drawing room doors to wait on Daisy.

Just then the front door opened, and Katie came through it. Alexis had to physically stop herself from running to her. Katie had been out for a jog after lunch before she started her afternoon tasks. Alexis was comfortable enough with that because after the other night at the park, she'd put a guard on Katie with orders to keep off Katie's radar.

They hadn't talked since their argument. Alexis hadn't wanted to face the decision she had to make—love Katie completely and live with the fear of her mortality, or walk away.

It was so hard to keep away from Katie. Alexis ached for her deep in her soul, and the ache was made worse by not feeding. She didn't want to hurt Katie's feelings by feeding on another, so she'd been surviving on bottled. One thing was for sure, if she fed on Katie, there would be no going back. She loved her too much.

Katie had on a little pair of shorts and a tight bra top. Vampires were blessed with enhanced hearing, taste, and smell, and she was using all three while lusting after Katie. Sweat was dripping down Katie's chest and into her cleavage, her breathing heavy from the exertion. Alexis imagined that this was what she would hear and taste if she made love to Katie again.

Then she smelled blood, and panic filled her. She hurried over to Katie and saw she had a cut hand.

"Katie? Are you all right?"

"Oh, you're talking to me, are you?" Katie said with her hands on her hips.

"Yes, of course. What happened?" Alexis asked.

Katie looked puzzled for a second and then looked down to her cut palm. "Oh, this? An aggressive thorny bush on my run. Nothing to worry about."

Katie dipped her finger onto the fresh looking wound. The tip of her finger was now bathed in red blood. Alexis couldn't take her eyes from it. She was salivating both for blood and to touch Katie. Alexis didn't know what she'd like to run her tongue over first, the blood or Katie's breasts, kept tightly in that teasing crop top.

Then Katie teased her even more by putting the tip of her finger, with the blood on it, into her mouth and sucking her finger seductively. Alexis was gone. In that moment Katie owned her, and if Katie had taken her hand, Alexis would have let her lead anywhere.

But instead Katie popped the finger from her mouth and said, "I better get showered and back to work. See you later, Alex."

Alexis found herself standing alone. Hungry, ravenous, and no way to sate it.

❖

Later that day, Byron called Alexis and Bhal for their usual evening meeting. After Daisy's revelations, it was even more important.

"Things have gotten ever more complicated," Byron said. "Duca, is your information still that Victorija remains conspicuous by her absence?"

There was a long pause. Alexis looked as if her mind was somewhere else. Byron looked at Bhal and Bhal raised her eyebrows.

"Duca?" Byron said a little louder.

Alexis jumped. "Sorry, Principe. You were saying?"

"Is Victorija still keeping a low profile?"

Alexis sat up straighter in her seat. "Yes, my informant in France says that she hasn't been seen. Drasas, her Duca, has been taking care of clan matters."

"If she knows about Daisy," Bhal said, "she will move heaven and earth to get her."

Byron sighed. "I know, and once she does, she will never let her go. The Grand Duchess wanted me to attempt to bring Victorija back into the fold, but that seems even more remote now that she is bonded by blood to Daisy. She will be going slowly insane. I know how that feels."

"We can't afford any olive branch to Victorija now, Principe." Alexis slammed her hand down on the desk. "Forgive me, Principe."

Byron saw how red Alexis's eyes were. She was hungry for blood. "Have you fed recently, Duca?"

"I'll be fine."

"I need every one of my people in readiness for whatever is coming our way. Our resources will be stretched. We have the Principessa's parents' funeral at the end of the week, Daisy needs to be protected, and Sera arrives back tomorrow."

Bhal said, "I'll go myself and pick up Sera from the airport."

"I'd be grateful, Bhal. I need more people surrounding her, and make sure Wilder understands how important her job is, protecting the Principessa. I feel there's a war brewing, but whether it's with Victorija or someone else, I'm not sure."

❖

Alexis felt like a thousand fires were erupting under her skin. They had been lit by Katie this afternoon. When she left Byron's office, she didn't know how she could stomach any more bottled blood or not touch Katie.

How could she think about living without her? But if she gave in to her lust for her blood, her body, her heart, then she would be setting herself up for more heartbreak in her long existence.

She put her foot on the first step of the staircase and closed her eyes. Alexis tried to breathe calm into her soul.

Just get up to your room and lock the door.

She ran up the stairs but stopped on the top landing. Alexis looked to her left, towards the corridor that Katie's room was on, and then right, in the direction of her room. It was physically painful trying to make herself go right.

Alexis was fighting a greater foe than she had ever faced—her own self. Her grip weakened for a second, and then she sped off to the left and found herself in front of Katie's door.

You don't have to do this. Don't do it.

Alexis could almost taste Katie. She put her hands and head on the door.

If you do this, losing her will destroy you.

❖

Katie was lying on her bed scrolling through her iPad. She was a little bit disappointed that her teasing of Alexis earlier hadn't worked. She had planned it all. The other night after thinking about what Alexis had been through, losing Anna, she'd decided that she had to take charge of the situation.

Alexis was stubborn, though, and so she made plans to tease the vampire out of her. Katie planned her run during the busiest part of the afternoon to hopefully catch Alexis going about her business in the house.

Katie had seen Alexis's eyes on her before when she went out running, so she wore her skimpiest outfit and, while out running, thought up the brilliant idea of drawing blood from her hand, with the help of a bramble bush.

Katie looked down at her bandaged hand and remembered the reaction she had gotten from Alexis when they talked in the hallway. Alexis's eyes were blood red, and her fangs had erupted. She looked as if she was about to give in to their passion right there and then.

But then Katie had walked away, hoping that would nudge Alexis to come to her later. She'd waited and waited this evening, but nothing.

Katie sighed. Maybe Alexis wasn't as desperate as she was to make this work.

Then she heard a soft thud on her bedroom door. Not a knock, a thud as if something was thrown against the door. She got up and tiptoed over.

From underneath the door she could see the shadow of feet standing just outside. She put her hand on the doorknob, her heart thudding in her chest, and opened the door quickly.

Alexis was standing there, breathing hard, her eyes dark blood red.

"Alex? Are you okay?"

Alexis took a step inside the door and, without saying a word, simply put her hand on her chest. Their sign of love and honesty. Katie responded by returning the gesture. Alexis shut the door and said, "I can't fight it any more, Katie. I don't have the strength or courage to live without you or your love. I love you."

Tears came to Katie's eyes. Those were the words she had been waiting to hear since they'd first gotten together. Alexis cupped her cheek and used her thumb to wipe a tear away then rested her forehead against Katie's.

"I'm sorry if I upset you," Alexis said.

"I should be sorry. I'm sorry for what I said and did the other night. I love you, Alex. We can make this work if you trust me," Katie said. "When did you last feed?"

"The other day. I didn't want to feed on anyone else," Alexis said.

Katie was blown away by Alexis's devotion. She stepped back, pulled off her nightie, and dropped it on the floor. She watched Alexis's eyes turn an even darker red and her tongue snake around her teeth, but yet she didn't move.

"Alexis? I consent, and I'm yours."

At the sound of those words, Alexis shot over to her. Still, she didn't dive in. Alexis trailed her fingers from Katie's cheek, down her chest, and circled her nipples.

Katie moaned and pushed one of Alexis's hands onto her breast, but Alexis pulled it away and turned Katie around, so she was facing away from her.

"No, I want to feed from you the way I wish I could have, the way I wanted to the first time around."

A ripple of pleasure ran through her at the memory. "Yes, Alex, just like that."

Alexis ran her lips over the area she was going to bite and Katie shivered. "Do you consent?"

Katie looked over her shoulder. "I always consent to you."

Alexis immediately sank her teeth into Katie's neck. Katie gasped but then let her body relax. Katie took Alexis's hands from her waist and moved them to her breasts.

Alexis squeezed them, and Katie felt the jolt of electricity shoot down to her clit. She wanted to come with Alexis's teeth in her.

"Alex, show me what you would have done our first time, if you could have," Katie said.

Alexis moved one hand from Katie's breast and pushed past her underwear. She pushed into Katie's wetness and moaned against her neck. Katie pushed back against Alexis's groin, and she thrust her hips back.

She could hear how overcome Alexis was becoming and

reached her hands back into Alexis's hair as she had done the first
time they had done this. Only that time, Alexis had run.

Alexis needed to come, needed to make Katie come. All the
fears, the confusion, the love she had for Katie had to find an outlet.
She quickly looked around the room and saw the chest of drawers.

She walked Katie over to it and heard Katie moan, "Yes."

Alexis stopped her feeding and pushed Katie over the chest
of drawers. She needed to thrust, needed to come so desperately,
that her hand shook as she pulled down Katie's underwear then
unbuckled her combat trousers and dispensed with her own jockey
shorts.

She opened herself up and pushed her clit against Katie's
buttock, then slipped two fingers into Katie easily. Katie gasped and
then moved her hips with Alexis.

"Is this what you wanted to do to me the first time?" Katie
asked in a breathy voice.

"Oh yes, I wanted to fuck you."

Alexis felt the burning pressure build up inside her sex as she
thrust into Katie. Her eyes drifted to the fresh bloody bite mark on
Katie's neck. Her mark. It turned Alexis on even more. She thrust
faster as her need demanded and heard Katie beg, "Faster, Alex. I'm
so close."

"Fuck." Alexis did as requested and put her other hand on the
back of Katie's neck, holding her in exactly the right place.

She felt Katie's walls start to clench her fingers, and then Alexis
was gone. Her hips pounded against Katie's buttock as her torrent of
an orgasm rushed out of her, feeling like it was rushing into Katie.

"Fuck, fuck," Alexis cried, and then all the energy left her legs
and she leaned over Katie. Katie's orgasm had passed, but she still
felt the fluttering of her walls on her fingers.

"I love you," Katie said.

Alexis got her breath back and pulled Katie up and into her
arms. She hugged her tightly. "I love you, Katie, and I always will."

❖

Katie lay with her head on Alexis's chest and her leg wrapped around her. They had been lying in quiet contemplation for a while now. Alexis was calm now that she had fed on her. Katie was so happy to have her lover back and trusting her. She had to find a way to bring up the question of transition without upsetting Alexis.

"Alex?"

"Mmm?"

"I've been thinking about something since we argued in your room." Katie pushed herself up on her elbow. "I just want you to know I understand how hard it is for you to be in a relationship like this, with a human."

Alexis sighed. "I tried to stay away from you, but it was too late for my heart."

"I know it upsets you, but I do think we should talk about me transitioning."

Alexis sighed again. "Katie, let's not ruin the moment."

"I'm not, and don't get upset. I just want to talk about it in a calm and adult way," Katie said.

"If you must."

Katie had gotten past the first hurdle. "Okay, well, you thought I didn't take the change seriously enough, and I probably didn't. I'm sorry for hurting your wrist, by the way." Katie lifted Alexis's hand and kissed the now healed wrist.

"Don't worry about it," Alexis said.

"What if I thought it through and showed you I was serious about this?"

Alexis took her hand. "I know your heart is in the right place, but if this is something you want to do, I'd need to be sure. Otherwise I'd always feel selfish for allowing you to do it."

"Okay, fine, but I want you to promise we'll talk about this in a few months' time. I'm going to prove to you I'm serious. I love you, and I don't want us both to be in such pain leaving each other. Promise we'll talk about it in a few months' time?" Katie said.

"Six months. I promise, if you think about what you'd be losing very carefully," Alexis said.

"Okay, deal," Katie said quickly.

That was as good a deal as she was going to get. She rolled on top of Alexis and grinned. "Now I'm going to show you how much I want to spend forever with you."

CHAPTER NINETEEN

Byron wrapped her arm around Amelia's waist as they were gathered around her parents' grave. She saw the other attendees from the church look at her in disdain. It had been quite an experience for the church members to have Byron, dressed in a man's suit, and Jaunty and Simon in their church. She could only imagine what they would think if they knew she was not only gender nonconforming but a vampire.

At the service the pastor had given the assembled mourners a lecture about hell and had looked at their small group and shouted, "Where will you be when the Lord comes? Where will you be? You'll be in hell if you don't change your ways!"

It was not the kind of church service she was expecting. The church was an old community centre outside the village where Amelia's parents lived. Amelia explained that the locals went to the more traditional—more normal—Church of England church in the village. But this small congregation was quite different. The church members were not local—they travelled here from all over. And Byron realized how oppressive this extreme church would have been for Amelia growing up.

Amelia stepped forward, took some earth from the pastor, and threw it down into the grave. As she did, she said, "Thank you for protecting me."

The graveside service was now at an end, and everyone started to file back to their cars. Byron tried to take her hand, but Amelia said, "I'll just go and thank the pastor. I'll see you in the car."

"If you're sure," Byron said.

Byron went back to the car and settled inside. Five minutes later a stony-faced Amelia joined her.

"Is everything all right? If he's upset you—" Byron asked.

"Let's just go."

Byron nodded to Alexis in the front, and she told the driver to drive. She took Amelia's hand. "What did he say?"

Amelia sighed. "Oh, just that I'm going to hell to burn forever, and how ashamed my parents were of me."

Anger simmered inside Byron. If she had been there, she would have scared the living daylights out of him for upsetting her wife.

"Nonsense. He doesn't know that your mum and dad showed love to you the only way they knew how, by protecting you. Don't even listen to that fire and brimstone stuff."

"I know. It's still hard to be reminded that my childhood was spent listening to this." Amelia got out her phone and started texting.

"Who are you texting?"

"Magda, to see if she can give me a lesson when we arrive back in London," Amelia said.

"You can't go right after your parents' funeral. I know you're sad, frustrated, and angry. But I thought we could have supper and go to bed early. You said you felt queasy earlier—you need a rest."

"Byron, I want to be distracted. Learning how to control my powers will do that. Please?"

She wasn't so sure it was the best idea, but if that was what Amelia wanted... "Okay, if Magda can see you, we'll drop you there, and I'll do some paperwork." Byron said to Alexis, "We're taking the Principessa to The Portal bookshop."

"Yes, Principe."

Byron watched Amelia rub her stomach and screw up her face. "Why don't we stop and get a sandwich first. That should settle your stomach."

Amelia nodded. "Okay."

❖

It was now early evening, and after dropping Amelia off, Alexis, Byron, and the rest of the guards went back to the house. The cars pulled up in front of the Debrek mansion, and Alexis was anxious to go talk to Katie as soon as Byron was safely inside. The funeral had brought her thoughts and feelings about Katie into sharp focus.

One day she would be attending Katie's funeral. She'd already realized that she couldn't just *not* be in a relationship with Katie. Loving Katie wasn't a choice. Her heart would simply always be Katie's. So if Katie was sure, Alexis had decided to help her turn, and then she could spend eternity worshipping her.

Alexis jumped out of the car and opened the door for Byron. Byron got out and straightened her black tie.

"I'm glad that day's over, Duca," Byron said.

Alexis was just about to reply when the guard she had put on Katie came running down the front steps.

"She's gone, Duca. Katie slipped out while I was in the blood room."

"Fuck. Principe, may I go and look for her?" Alexis asked.

"Of course. I'm sure she's fine, Alexis. Take Bhal with you."

Alexis sped off down the road towards the park. She knew that was Katie's regular route, although she had told her not to cut through the park any more since she had discovered the suspicious dead animals there.

As she got nearer the park, Alexis picked up the telltale scent of blood, and her chest felt like it was under the weight of an elephant.

"No, no. Please, no."

As she zipped into the park, she came across two dog walkers. She grabbed the first one she came across, looked deeply into his eyes, and said, "Leave the park now and go home."

The dog barked incessantly, and the man repeated her words, "I'll leave the park now and go home."

She did the same with the other human and followed the scent of the blood, all the time her heart pounding with true fear. The scent took Alexis into the cover of trees surrounding the park.

The branches smacked against her body as she pushed through the trees at speed. She slowed down as the blood scent got stronger. She pushed past the last tree and came upon a scene from her worst nightmare—Josie hunched over Katie's body, feeding from her neck.

The next few minutes were a blur. She grabbed Josie and threw her against a tree. She threw her so hard that the tree trunk cracked. Then she dropped to her knees beside Katie.

"Katie? Katie? No, no, no, please be okay," Alexis pleaded.

Katie's throat was worse than the last time Josie had attacked her. She reached out a shaking hand to feel for a pulse. There was nothing there.

"Please don't be gone. Please, Katie. I love you." Alexis felt tears running down her face.

Bhal dropped down beside her and felt for Katie's pulse. She sighed and then placed her hand on Katie's forehead.

"Bhal? Can you save her? There's a fountain in the park. I can get you water."

Bhal shook her head. "I'm sorry, Alexis. She's too far gone. She's dead."

From behind them, Alexis heard the sound of laughter. She turned her head slowly and saw Josie slumped against the tree where she had thrown her, her face caked in Katie's blood.

Josie grinned and said, "I told you she was mine."

The words had barely left Josie's mouth when Alexis was on her. She grabbed her then threw her against another tree. Josie cried out, and Alexis did the same again. Josie was moaning in pain. She might be immortal, but she could feel the full force of the pain until her bones knitted back together again.

Alexis was caught in a storm of red hot rage, like nothing she had ever experienced. This time when she grabbed Josie, Alexis began pounding her fists on her face and body, unleashing both fury and grief.

"No, no, stop!" Josie cried.

Alexis didn't stop until Bhal pulled her off. "Duca, that's enough. End this, and let's take care of Katie's body."

Alexis stood on wobbly legs and held her hand out. Bhal took her sword from the scabbard on her back and handed it to Alexis.

Bhal then pulled Josie onto her knees. Josie's face was a mess, her nose badly broken. Alexis walked forward and pulled her closer by the hair.

"You've just killed the kindest, most gentle woman, and for that I'm going to take your head." She pushed Josie back and held up the sword.

"I'm sorry, please don't kill me," Josie said.

Alexis didn't even consider her pleas. She swiped the sword through the air and cleanly took Josie's head from her shoulders. Alexis's breathing was heavy. She was so lost in her rage, her pain, she was unaware of anything around her until Bhal grabbed her and said, "Alexis, come here."

She turned around and saw Katie gasping for air. She rushed over. "What happened? What's going on?"

"She started gasping and coughing when you took Josie's head."

Alexis cupped Katie's cheek. "Katie, Katie, I'm here."

At those words Katie opened her eyes, and the whites were edged with red.

"She's turned, Bhal. I don't know—" Alexis then remembered the other night when Katie bit her arm. "I *do* know. She bit my arm the other night."

Katie lifted her hand to Alexis. "Alex? What's happening?"

"Her pulse is strong now," Bhal said.

Alex pulled Katie into her arms and kissed her head. "You're alive. I love you, I love you."

Katie grasped into her tightly. "I feel strange, Alex."

"Don't worry. I'll get you through this, okay?"

Bhal patted Alexis on the shoulder. "I'll call and get a clean-up crew here. Let's get her back home."

CHAPTER TWENTY

A melia sighed in frustration as she again failed to tune in to her ancestors. She had been sitting in the witches' circle with Magda for thirty minutes, and nothing.

"I can't do this. It's not working," Amelia said.

Magda squeezed her hand. "Take deep breaths and try to focus."

Another minute passed. "This is pointless. It's like there's a block in my head." Amelia slammed her hand down on the floor, and a bolt of power came from her hand and scorched the floor within the circle.

Magda opened her eyes and said, "You see what happens when you don't have control? There *is* a block. You were at your parents' funeral today. Your grief and anger are getting in the way."

Amelia got up and walked out of the circle. "What's the point anyway? I've had four lessons with you, and all we've done is sit in this circle and try to listen to voices. I'm supposed to be fighting and defeating a great darkness that this Madam Anka is bringing. How am I meant to do that listening to voices?"

Without saying anything, Magda raised her arm. An object on the ritual table rose and then flew past Amelia's head and was impaled into the wall behind her.

Amelia jumped in fear and looked behind her at the knife and contemplated how close it got to her.

Magda got up and walked over to the knife. She pulled it out of the wall and rested it in her hand.

"We are not tuning in to listen, Amelia. We are tuning in to our ancestors to harness their collective power. That's why this basic level of understanding is key. Once your mind becomes more disciplined, you can use it to dangerous effect, I think you'll agree."

Amelia rubbed her forehead. "You're right. I'm sorry for my outburst. It's been really difficult. I shouldn't have come."

Magda put the knife down on the table again and came back to give Amelia a hug.

"I understand, and I promise you, I will teach you so you are well equipped for what lies ahead. I promise you."

"Thank you, Magda. I'll be more patient." Amelia clasped her hand to her mouth and took deep breaths. "I'm sorry, I haven't felt well today."

Magda smiled. "No, you wouldn't, but it'll soon pass."

"Why? Is it a magic thing?" Amelia asked.

Magda chuckled and stood up. "No, it's a baby thing."

Amelia's stomach dropped, and she stood up quickly. So quickly that she felt a wave of dizziness and grabbed onto Magda. "What—what are talking about?"

"Can you not feel it? I did as soon as I touched you," Magda said.

Amelia's mouth went dry. The Debreks were the only vampire clan who could reproduce and the others coveted that skill, as every new generation became stronger than the last.

"I knew that the Debreks could have children but…I mean, we never discussed or planned when it would happen."

Magda took her hand and rubbed the back of it. "Lucia was the Debrek life force until she died, and now it is you. Byron's blood already flows within you from your blood bond, and from what I understand Debrek conceptions happen when you are the closest to each other's love and touch the beyond. I would suggest you think back to your visit to the New Forest."

When she and Byron had made love that night in the cabin, Amelia opened up her very soul to the beyond, the other side. It had been unlike anything she'd ever experienced, past or since. It must have been then if what Magda said was true, but deep down she knew it was.

"After all, it was a deal that the Grand Duchess made with her coven, with the ancestors, to allow her and her husband Cosimo to conceive all those long years ago. That night you were in direct contact with the ancestors."

Amelia put her hand on her stomach protectively. "Magda, I'm supposed to be fighting a great evil. How can I—"

Magda must have seen the trepidation in her face. She gave her a hug and said, "Don't worry, everyone on the side of good— werewolf, witch, fae, and vampire—will stand behind you."

"But it won't be safe."

"When is the paranormal world ever safe?"

Amelia went over to her bag and got out her phone. She dialled a number and said, "Doctor? It's Amelia Debrek. Could you see me at short notice?"

❖

Katie felt cold and had the sensation of ants crawling under her skin. The worst thing was the deep hunger, worse than any need she'd ever had for food or water, but she felt safe in Alexis's arms. She'd carried her like a baby all the way back to the Debrek house.

When they walked into the hallway, there was a crowd of vampires, warriors, and human staff waiting to see how she was. Byron rushed to their side and stroked her hair.

"Are you all right, Katie?"

Katie could only answer truthfully. "I don't know. I'm so hungry."

Byron looked at Alexis pointedly.

"She's in transition, Principe. It wasn't my doing, but it was my blood. I'll take her upstairs and help her with what comes next."

"Very well. Let me know if you or Katie need anything," Byron said.

"I will."

Alexis carried her up to her room and opened the door with one hand. Once they got into the bedroom, Alexis let her down onto her feet.

"How do you feel?" Alexis asked her.

"Empty, like I have no energy, like there is nothing holding me up, and it hurts in here." Katie pointed to just under her breasts. "It's painful, and I'm so hungry."

Alexis cupped her face and leaned her forehead on Katie's. "I'm going to make you feel better, I promise." Alexis pulled back and Katie saw tears rolling down her face. "Thank God you didn't listen to me. If you hadn't drunk my blood, you'd be dead now, and I would want to die."

Katie wiped Alexis's tears away with her thumb. "I'm here and I love you."

Alexis composed herself. "I have to ask you if you're certain you want to complete the transition. You do have a choice, remember?"

Katie took a breath and said, "I'm never leaving you, Alex."

Alexis smiled and led her over to the bed. Alexis sat down on the end and pulled off her T-shirt, leaving herself naked from the waist up. She then patted her lap.

"Sit here."

Katie walked closer and touched the wound on her neck.

"Don't worry—it'll get better once you feed."

Alexis held out her hand. Katie took it but didn't move. "I'm scared, Alex."

Alexis looked at her with eyes full of love and devotion. "I'm here, and I'll always keep you safe. Do you trust me?"

Katie had no hesitation in saying, "Yes."

She walked forward and sat on Alexis's lap. Alexis put her arm around her and pulled her into a deep kiss. When they broke apart, Alexis said, "I love you."

"I love you too, but I'm frightened of hurting you," Katie said.

"You can't hurt me—I promise you."

"You were my first," Katie said. "I'd never fed a vampire before. And now you're going to be the first one I feed on."

"And the only one, I hope. You're my first as well."

"What do you mean?"

Alexis tenderly stroked the hair from Katie's face. "I've never let another vampire feed from me."

"Really?" Katie was shocked. "In all the years you've been alive, you've never—"

Alexis shook her head. "No, it all seemed too personal. It was a part of me I didn't want to give anyone, until you."

Katie felt tears come to her eyes. Alexis furrowed her eyebrows and smiled.

"Don't cry, darling."

"But that's so sweet," Katie said.

"It's just the way I felt."

Katie kissed Alexis. "Then thank you for sharing it with me."

Alexis lifted and kissed each of Katie's hands, then guided Katie's head to her neck.

"I can't do it, I can't," Katie cried.

"You'll be fine. Once you taste it, you'll start to feel a million times better than you do on a good day. Here, let me help." Alexis's fangs erupted from her gums, and she bit her own lip making the blood flow from it. Alexis then kissed Katie, and the blood flowed into her mouth.

As soon as the blood hit her tongue, Katie felt a pressure in her gums and then a sharp pain as her fangs burst through. She sucked on Alexis's blood like it was the last water on earth.

"It's not enough," Katie moaned.

"Bite my neck."

Before she had time to think about it too deeply, every fibre in her being made her body act and bite Alexis's neck. Her initial shock at the act of biting through Alexis's skin was soon banished when the rush of blood entered her mouth.

Katie gulped and gulped it down, and as she did, the hunger inside her started to calm. The taste of Alexis's blood was better than any indulgent food treat she had eaten to sate a physical hunger. It tasted like it was made for her. Despite the fact that Katie had no experience feeding from anyone else, somehow she just knew nothing would taste like Alexis.

Then something else happened. The weakness, the tiredness she had felt since waking from death was disappearing. Every cell in her body was being renewed, and it felt amazing. Katie had never taken drugs, but she imagined that high didn't even come close to what she was starting to feel.

"Are you all right, Katie?"

Katie took her teeth from Alexis's neck and gasped some calming air into her lungs.

"I feel like..." Katie stood and took stock of how her body felt. It was shocking. Every small ache and pain she'd ever had was gone. "I feel like every cell in my body is filled with bright, intense energy."

Alexis smiled. "It'll feel overwhelming for a while, but you'll get used to it. You're safe now. That's all that matters."

Katie's nerves were jangling like she had taken an amphetamine. She had to do something with this energy or she might burst. She sped from one side of the room to the other, at top vampire speed. She laughed. "I can sneak up on you now."

"You can. There's so much to learn about your new abilities, but I'll be with you at every stage," Alexis said.

Katie touched her fingers to her mouth and saw the evidence of the blood Alexis gave her, and she experienced an unbelievable aching need in her sex. She leapt onto Alexis and pushed her back on the bed.

Alexis then used her strength to flip her on her back, but then Katie did the same. After a tussle Katie finally lay underneath Alexis, and they both laughed.

"I want you so much, Alex. I feel like I'm going to explode."

Alexis stroked her head. "Feeding from someone you love does that to you."

"I love you, Alex."

"I love you. Thank God you didn't listen to me about drinking some of my blood. Tonight would be very different otherwise."

"Don't think about that. I'm here, and I need you to make me come."

Alexis kissed her, and the kisses soon became frantic as they tore at each other's clothes. Without preamble Alexis pushed her fingers inside Katie, who was wet and ready for her.

Katie gasped and said, "Yes, Alex."

Alexis thrust on Katie's leg while she thrust two fingers inside her. It got fast and near the pinnacle very quickly.

Katie wanted more of everything. "Alex, I need more. Faster, harder."

Alexis obliged and brought them both to the brink. Katie dug her nails into Alexis's shoulder, and Alexis groaned. "Fuck, I'm going to come. Bite me, Katie."

Katie bit deep into Alexis's neck, and Alexis did the same to her. Katie didn't think anything could make sex with Alexis better, but sharing blood did. As both their orgasms overtook them, Katie felt she was drowning in bliss.

"I love you, Alex."

❖

"Are you sure she's okay?" Amelia paced around the bedroom.

After returning from seeing the doctor, Amelia got the news about Katie and was beside herself with worry.

"She's okay, or she will be. Alexis will look after her. Come and sit. You've had a hard day."

One of the maids had brought up some simple soup and bread, since Amelia wasn't feeling great, and left the tray on the breakfasting table. She walked over and sat down with Byron at the table.

"Everything's changing," Amelia said.

Byron covered her hand with hers. "I know it's not ideal, but at least Katie is still with us. We could have been mourning Katie's death tonight, and I would never have forgiven myself."

Amelia had come to see that Byron saw herself as a big sister figure to Katie and understood how hard it would be to lose her.

"I know, and I'm thankful she's okay, but it's not just that. My parents are gone, I'm learning to control a power that I never knew I had, and…"

"And what?" Byron asked.

How could Amelia say this when she couldn't even process it herself?

"I..." Amelia hesitated. "I found out something today. Something that's going to change things."

Byron frowned. "You're starting to worry me now."

"I suppose there's no other way than to just come out with it. I'm pregnant," Amelia said in a low voice.

She had never seen Byron look so shocked in her life. "What?"

"Magda told me she could sense it, so then I stopped by Dr. McKenzie's office on the way home, and she confirmed it," Amelia said.

"But...but we hadn't even discussed having children yet. My mother said that, as a vampire and you a witch, we both had to make a conscious decision to have a baby."

"Magda said it was probably that night we spent in the New Forest, when I opened myself up to the other side. It must have been an unconscious need or desire," Amelia said.

Byron stood silently. Amelia had no idea what her reaction was going to be, but she soon found out. Byron fell to her knees in front of Amelia, and she saw something she hadn't seen before—tears running down Byron's face.

"My God, I can't believe it. A baby for us?" Byron asked.

The joy Amelia felt under the surface came out. "Yes, a little baby." She took Byron's hand and placed it on her stomach. Byron touched her stomach with reverence, almost like she thought she could hurt it.

Byron was overwhelmed with emotion. "This is the most joyful moment of my life, mia cara. Thank you, thank you."

She put her head on Amelia's lap and Amelia stroked her hair.

"I couldn't believe it myself, but Dr. McKenzie thinks the baby is making its presence known earlier than usual because it's a born vampire."

Byron lifted her head and took her hand. "It's our child. A part of us."

"I'm scared, Byron," Amelia said.

"What could you be scared of?"

"I'm supposed to be learning about my magical powers, in order to defeat evil. How can I do that pregnant?" Amelia said with panic in her voice.

"You listen to me. I won't let anyone or anything near you. Saving the world will have to come another day, or I'll defeat this Madam Anka. You and our baby's safety are more important than anything. Whatever lies ahead, we'll face it together."

Amelia had calmed and she smiled. "I did always want a baby one day. It's just come sooner than expected."

"Quite right. Wait till Sera finds out she's going to be an aunty." Byron laughed. "That'll make her feel older than she already is."

Amelia laughed. "Then there's Uncle Jaunty and Uncle Simon."

"Uh-oh. Your Uncle Simon is going to be angry that I got you into trouble," Byron joked.

"Shut up." Amelia laughed. "He secretly likes you."

Byron raised her eyebrows. "It must be very secretly then."

Amelia gave Byron a serious look again. "I hope Katie is all right."

"She will be. Alexis will take the best care of her," Byron said.

CHAPTER TWENTY-ONE

Anka kneeled before an altar set deep in a dark cave system known only to her and her most trusted witches. As she whispered her prayers to the darkness she worshipped and drew her power from, you could hear the drip, drip of water falling from the rocks, and the smell of incense permeated the air.

She heard footsteps approach behind her. "Asha? How can I help you?"

"Forgive me disturbing your devotion, Madam, but we have found the location of the second descendent, but she is now guarded."

Anka bowed her head to the alter and stood. "The Debreks know Ms. MacDougall is bonded to Victorija then?"

"Shall we send a team to bring her to feed Victorija?" Asha asked.

Anka held up her hand. "Slow down, Asha. We take this slowly. I have been building my power and my resources for a very long time, and I will take my time on the next phase of my plans."

"I'll keep someone watching her then."

"Yes. When the time comes to bring her here, it won't be easy. Daisy MacDougall comes from a long line of agitators and general pains in the neck—trust me, I've met a few. I need to seal my position with the Dred clan, and then we will hand her over to Victorija. Only then can I absorb her power."

"And then what?" Asha asked.

Anka laughed and started to walk through the cave, Asha by her side. "Then we will put our puppet Principe in charge of the Dreds, and Drasas would make a lovely puppet, don't you agree?"

She laughed again and the echo reverberated through the cave system.

❖

Alexis couldn't believe she was standing here, under a floral archway in the Debrek mansion gardens, pledging her immortal life to someone. Not just someone, but Katie. Beautiful Katie who had started to mend her broken heart, fiery Katie whom she had squabbled with incessantly, sweet Katie with whom she woke each morning to a loving smile that brightened her day.

They stood under the archway, each with a cut on her palm, and clasping each other's hand for the bonding ceremony.

Katie hadn't wanted a big bonding ceremony, so she, her mum, Amelia, Sera, and Daisy planned this smaller—but still special—ceremony in the garden. The guests were seated in rows behind the happy couple, and luckily it was a warm, dry day.

Katie looked beautiful in the white dress that Amelia and Daisy designed for her, and she held a deep blood-red bouquet of roses. After swearing she'd never fall in love again, here Alexis was getting married in her dress uniform.

Byron's father Michel, the Grand Principe, was conducting the ceremony as the elder statesmen of the clan. Byron was standing beside Alexis as her best friend, with Daisy as Katie's bridesmaid.

"Alexis, do you consent to pledge your life and your blood to Katie Brekman?" Michel asked.

She smiled at Katie and said, "I consent to pledge my life and my blood to Katie Brekman."

"And Katie, do you consent to pledge your life and your blood to Alexis Villiers?"

Katie winked at Alexis. "I consent to pledge my life and my blood to Alexis Villiers."

They then exchanged matching gold rings set with blood-red rubies.

Michel smiled and said, "That only leaves me one thing to say. Alexis, if you don't look after young Katie, we will have your head."

The congregation chuckled, and Michel held up his hands, "No, seriously. I now give you Alexis and Katie, blood bonds for eternity."

Everyone clapped, and Alexis finally got to kiss her bride. "I love you."

"I love you."

It was a perfect day, and all their friends would be joining them for a party later at The Sanctuary. Slaine had promised them a special night, and as much as Alexis was looking forward to it, she was more looking forward to getting Katie alone later. Now that Katie was a vampire, she had so much energy, and she was so enjoying it.

They walked into the crowd and hugged and kissed their guests.

❖

Victorija was consumed with maddening hunger. It was getting overwhelming. She gasped and braced herself against the desk. Her hands shook, and the pain in her stomach was making her double over in pain. She reached for a small drawer on the desk and took out a picture of a young woman. She tried to steady her shaking hands so she could gaze properly at the picture.

"Angel, I can't do this."

Victorija closed her eyes and heard Angele's voice in her head. *Promise me, you will never hurt or drink the blood of my descendants without consent.*

She remembered the words she said in return. *I swear on my life. It'll be the only vow I ever keep. I swear, Angel.*

Victorija felt the stabbing pain in her stomach and neck flare up, and her knees buckled beneath her. She collapsed to the stone floor and shouted, "Daisy!"

❖

The happy couple finally made it to The Sanctuary. Katie was dancing with Alexis on the dance floor, the music was pumping, and the open bar that Byron was paying for was making the guests—and Slaine—very happy.

Sera and Daisy were up dancing with a couple of vampires, and Katie had never been happier, nor felt so incredible. Alexis had told her that being a vampire felt like your best day as a human, only a million times better, and she was right.

It was strange getting used to not having aches and pains or injuring herself. Sometimes she did think about living the long stretch of immortality in front of her and felt overwhelmed, but she just tried to concentrate on her love, Alexis.

"I knew you could do it," Katie said.

"Do what?" Alexis asked.

She moved her arms around Alexis's neck. "Smile, Duca."

"You're the only one who can make me," Alexis said.

Katie sighed in contentment. "I remember the last time we were all here, and I was dancing with someone else wishing they were you."

Alexis pulled her in tighter. "And I was watching you, wanting to kill your dance partner."

Katie pecked her on the lips. "You'll always be my dance partner now."

The music faded out, and servers walked around with glasses of champagne. Katie looked over to Daisy and saw her sway a little. She made eye contact with her and mouthed, "Are you all right?"

Daisy smiled and nodded. She had been dealing with difficult side effects from Victorija's blood bond, Katie knew, and Byron was doing everything she could to support her and protect her.

Slaine stood on the small stage with the microphone and said, "Let's have quiet for Principe Debrek, everyone."

Bhal stood at one side of the stage and Wilder at the other beside Amelia. A hush came over the crowd when Byron took the microphone and said, "I just wanted to say a few words. I've known Alex for a long, long time, and she has been the most dedicated Duca anyone could hope to have, but I'm so happy that love is taking some of her attention away from her job. You deserve it, Alexis."

Alexis moved behind Katie and put her arms around her waist.

Byron continued, "Katie, you know what I think of you. I've watched you grow up from a little girl to a beautiful young woman. You've always been like a little sister to me, so if Alexis does anything you don't like, send her to me."

"As if I'd dare," Alexis whispered in Katie's ear. "You'd kill me."

Katie chuckled.

Byron put her arm around Amelia's waist. "There's another reason for celebration today. Only our closest friends and family know about this, but we thought it about time we shared it with the world."

Amelia's uncles looked on proudly from below the stage.

Byron leaned into Amelia and gave her a kiss. "The Principessa and I are going to have a baby."

Katie whooped and clapped along with the crowd. She shouted over the noise to Alexis, "About time they told everyone. It's the best news ever."

"It was a shock to them both. I think they just needed time to get used to the idea. I've never seen Byron so nervous," Alexis said.

"A little baby for you to protect."

Alexis squeezed Katie. "I have a lot to protect, and I will, I promise you."

Katie grasped Alexis's hair lightly to pull her in for a kiss. "I know you will. You are the Debrek Duca and the woman I love and trust with all my heart."

Byron's voice took on a more serious tone when she said, "This may be the last time we are able to celebrate like this together for a while. As you know, our world is in flux, and there are dangers to us growing in number, so let us enjoy this happy time while we have it. A toast to Alexis and Katie, our new baby, and the clan we are a part of. *Et sanguinem familiae*—blood and family."

Those in the Debrek clan repeated her words. Then a cry of pain interrupted them. Katie turned quickly and saw Daisy grasping her neck and doubling over in pain. She rushed over to her and was met by Amelia.

"What's wrong, Daisy?" Katie asked.

"I'm dizzy, it hurts. It hurts!"

Alexis shouted, "Get back, give her room to breathe."

In an instant Byron, Amelia, and Sera were around Daisy.

"Is she all right?" Amelia kneeled down and took Daisy's hand.

Byron shouted, "Where is Dr. McKenzie?"

Dr. Tyler McKenzie came pushing through the crowd. "I'm here. Let me take a look." Tyler took Daisy's wrist in her hand. "Her pulse is too fast."

Then Daisy grasped her neck and said in a pleading voice, "Victorija."

About the Author

Jenny Frame is from the small town of Motherwell in Scotland, where she lives with her partner, Lou, and their well-loved and very spoiled dog.

She has a diverse range of qualifications, including a BA in public management and a diploma in acting and performance. Nowadays, she likes to put her creative energies into writing rather than treading the boards.

When not writing or reading, Jenny loves cheering on her local football team, cooking, and spending time with her family.

Jenny can be contacted at www.jennyframe.com.

Books Available From Bold Strokes Books

Bet Against Me by Fiona Riley. In the high-stakes luxury real estate market, everything has a price, and as rival Realtors Trina Lee and Kendall Yates find out, that means their hearts and souls, too. (978-1-63555-729-9)

Broken Reign by Sam Ledel. Together on an epic journey in search of a mysterious cure, a princess and a village outcast must overcome life-threatening challenges and their own prejudice if they want to survive. (978-1-63555-739-8)

Just One Taste by CJ Birch. For Lauren, it only took one taste to start trusting in love again. (978-1-63555-772-5)

Lady of Stone by Barbara Ann Wright. Sparks fly as a magical emergency forces a noble embarrassed by her ability to submit to a low-born teacher who resents everything about her. (978-1-63555-607-0)

Last Resort by Angie Williams. Katie and Rhys are about to find out what happens when you meet the girl of your dreams but you aren't looking for a happily ever after. (978-1-63555-774-9)

Longing for You by Jenny Frame. When Debrek housekeeper Katie Brekman is attacked amid a burgeoning vampire-witch war, Alexis Villiers must go against everything her clan believes in to save her. (978-1-63555-658-2)

Money Creek by Anne Laughlin. Clare Lehane is a troubled lawyer from Chicago who tries to make her way in a rural town full of secrets and deceptions. (978-1-63555-795-4)

Passion's Sweet Surrender by Ronica Black. Cam and Blake are unable to deny their passion for each other, but surrendering to love is a whole different matter. (978-1-63555-703-9)

The Holiday Detour by Jane Kolven. It will take everything going wrong to make Dana and Charlie see how right they are for each other. (978-1-63555-720-6)

Too Hot to Ride by Andrews & Austin. World-famous cutting horse champion and industry legend Jane Barrow is knockdown sexy in the way she moves, talks, and rides, and Rae Starr is determined not to get involved with this womanizing gambler. (978-1-63555-776-3)

A Love that Leads to Home by Ronica Black. For Carla Sims and Janice Carpenter, home isn't about location, it's where your heart is. (978-1-63555-675-9)

Blades of Bluegrass by D. Jackson Leigh. A US Army occupational therapist must rehab a bitter veteran who is a ticking political time bomb the military is desperate to disarm. (978-1-63555-637-7)

Hopeless Romantic by Georgia Beers. Can a jaded wedding planner and an optimistic divorce attorney possibly find a future together? (978-1-63555-650-6)

Hopes and Dreams by PJ Trebelhorn. Movie theater manager Riley Warren is forced to face her high school crush and tormentor, wealthy socialite Victoria Thayer, at their twentieth reunion. (978-1-63555-670-4)

In the Cards by Kimberly Cooper Griffin. Daria and Phaedra are about to discover that love finds a way, especially when powers outside their control are at play. (978-1-63555-717-6)

Moon Fever by Ileandra Young. SPEAR agent Danika Karson must clear her werewolf friend of multiple false charges while teaching her vampire girlfriend to resist the blood mania brought on by a full moon. (978-1-63555-603-2)

Serenity by Jesse J. Thoma. For Kit Marsden, there are many things in life she cannot change. Serenity is in the acceptance. (978-1-63555-713-8)

Sylver and Gold by Michelle Larkin. Working feverishly to find a killer before he strikes again, Boston homicide detective Reid Sylver and rookie cop London Gold are blindsided by their chemistry and developing attraction. (978-1-63555-611-7)